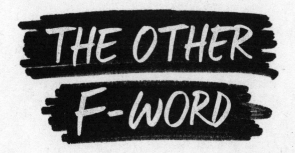

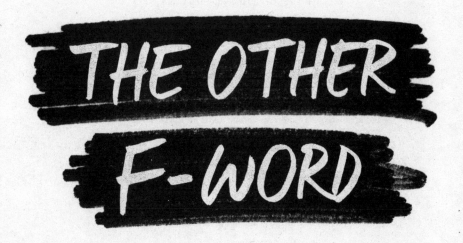

THE OTHER F-WORD

A NOVEL BY

NATASHA FRIEND

SQUARE
FISH

FARRAR STRAUS GIROUX
NEW YORK

SQUARE
FISH

An imprint of Macmillan Publishing Group, LLC
175 Fifth Avenue, New York, NY 10010
fiercereads.com

Square Fish and the Square Fish logo are trademarks of Macmillan
and are used by Farrar Straus Giroux under license from Macmillan.

Our books may be purchased in bulk for promotional, educational,
or business use. Please contact your local bookseller or the Macmillan Corporate
and Premium Sales Department at (800) 221-7945 ext. 5442 or by e-mail at
MacmillanSpecialMarkets@macmillan.com.

Library of Congress Cataloging-in-Publication Data

Names: Friend, Natasha, 1972–, author.
Title: The other F-word / Natasha Friend.
Description New York : Farrar, Straus and Giroux, 2017. | Summary: "A teen girl who
    was conceived via in vitro fertilization goes off in search of answers about her
    past"—Provided by publisher.
Identifiers: LCCN 2016009256 (print) | LCCN 2016036127 (ebook) |
    ISBN 978-1-250-14415-7 (paperback)   ISBN 978-0-374-30235-1 (ebook)
Subjects: | CYAC: Test tube babies—Fiction. | Identity—Fiction.
Classification: LCC PZ7.F91535 Ot 2017 (print) | LCC PZ7.F91535 (ebook) |
    DDC [Fic]—dc23
LC record available at https://lccn.loc.gov/2016009256

Originally published in the United States by Farrar Straus Giroux
First Square Fish edition, 2018
Book designed by Elizabeth H. Clark
Square Fish logo designed by Filomena Tuosto

1   3   5   7   9   10   8   6   4   2

For my McGiffert cousins.
I am proud to call you my other f-word.

Twin Cities Cryolab ...

where families are made!

An industry leader in reproductive
services since 1991

✔ FDA regulated
✔ Caring
✔ Experienced
✔ Quality controlled

*TCC proudly offers the largest selection of
willing-to-be-known donors in the country*

THE OTHER
F-WORD

HOLLIS

THE PICTURE OF PAM HANGING OVER THE FIREPLACE WAS like the portrait of Phineas Nigellus hanging over the headmaster's desk at Hogwarts. Watching. Judging. Pam was a perpetual presence, a denim-clad specter presiding over the suckfest that was Hollis Darby-Barnes's life.

Pam's eyes: the golden brown of a Siberian tiger.

Hollis's eyes: the brown of a dung beetle.

Pam's hair: the neat, feathered cap of an Olympic skater from the 1980s.

Hollis's hair: a blender experiment. Bon Jovi, the perm years.

Hollis wanted to rip Pam off the wall and throw her into the fireplace. Also, she wanted to throw Pam's cat into the fireplace. Pam's cat was named Yvette. She was fifteen—exactly a year older than Hollis—but unlike

Hollis, she had white, fluffy hair, a smashed-in face, and a problem with fur balls.

Hollis hardly remembered Pam. She wasn't biologically related to Pam. She felt no emotional connection to Pam whatsoever. And yet Hollis's mother continued to insist that Hollis share Pam's last name, Barnes. This, among a million other things, pissed Hollis off.

It pissed Hollis off that her mother still wore Pam's bathrobe. It pissed Hollis off that her mother referred to Pam as Hollis's "mom." It pissed Hollis off that even though Pam died seven years ago, her mother had yet to go on a single date. Worse than anything, it pissed Hollis off that her mother maintained Pam's Hotmail account. Because A) Pam was dead, and B) who the hell had a Hotmail account?

"Why?" Hollis would ask her mother every time she placed an order on Amazon as PjBarnesie_373@hotmail .com.

Her mother always gave the same answer: "Pam was the love of my life. It makes me feel better to know she's still here."

"But she's *not* still here," Hollis would say.

"When a package arrives with Pam's name on it, I feel like she is."

It was a freaking losing battle. Did Hollis want Pam's memory hanging around their house like a bad smell? No, she did not. But what could she do? Her mother was all she had. Leigh Darby wasn't a bad mom as mothers went. She didn't do drugs. She didn't bring perverts home from bars. She didn't dress like a stripper. She made good money as a real estate agent. Every morning, Hollis's mother got up, took a shower, blew her hair straight, and put on a pantsuit. She poured cereal for Hollis. She went out into the world, smiled, and said things like "cozy three-bedroom" and "granite countertops."

Then she came home, put on Pam's bathrobe, and talked to the picture above the fireplace. "My feet are killing me, babe." Or, "Guess what, babe? I made a sale today!" Would Hollis's mother ever take Pam down and move on with her life? No, Hollis was certain she wouldn't. Even four years from now, when Hollis left for college, her mother would still be here, festering. So would Yvette, no doubt. That cat refused to die.

God, it was pathetic. Even more pathetic than the fact that today was December thirty-first and Hollis had no plans whatsoever for New Year's Eve.

"Honey?"

Hollis looked up from her cereal bowl. She gave her mother a blank stare.

"Pam just got an email."

This depressed Hollis even more. And pissed her off. "You know dead people can't get email, right?"

"It's from Milo Robinson-Clark."

Okay, wait. "What?"

Hollis's mother smiled. "Milo Robinson-Clark is trying to get in touch with you."

Milo Robinson-Clark. Milo Robinson-Clark. Why does that name sound— Oh God. Lodged in Hollis's mind was the image of a little dark-haired boy on the other end of a seesaw. Train conductor overalls. A red juice mustache.

"That kid we met when Pam—"

Hollis's mother nodded vigorously. "That's right."

"What were his moms'—?"

"Suzanne and Frankie."

"Right," Hollis muttered. Then, "Jesus."

Milo Robinson-Clark emailed a dead woman. He emailed a dead woman to contact the girl he met once, a million years ago, on the other end of a seesaw. This made no sense. It only made sense if he didn't know Pam was dead, and even then—

"How does that make you feel?" her mother asked. She sounded like the stupid grief counselor Hollis had been forced to see after Pam died. *Draw a picture of your feelings, Hollis. Use this puppet to have a conversation, Hollis. How does that make you feel, Hollis?*

How did Hollis feel about her sperm donor's son suddenly popping up in Pam's Hotmail inbox? She felt weird, that's how she felt. She felt weird all over. Hollis barely remembered meeting Milo Robinson-Clark. She'd been, what, six years old? There was a photo somewhere.

The whole thing had been Pam's idea. Right after her ovarian cancer diagnosis, Pam had tracked down Milo's moms through some lesbian life partner/sperm donor website. Hollis wasn't exactly sure how it worked, except that sperm donors had ID numbers, and her donor's ID number and Milo's donor's ID number matched, so that's how Pam and Leigh and Suzanne and Frankie found each other. The four moms had conducted a reunion of sorts. There was a playground. A picnic. Hollis vaguely remembered brownies.

And then Pam got sick, like really fast, and that was the end of that. Because Hollis's mother was swept up in caring for Pam and then she was swept up in grieving for Pam, and Hollis never saw her half brother again.

Half brother. God.

Hollis was struck, once more, by the bizarre nature of her existence. Most of the time she just futzed along through life—going to school, doing her homework, eating and sleeping and reading—and then, out of nowhere, a lightning bolt would strike.

I was conceived in a petri dish.
My father is out there.
I have a half brother.

"Jesus," Hollis muttered again. "Why does he want to get in touch with me?"

Her mother shook her head. "He doesn't say."

"He *doesn't say?*"

"I have it right here."

"What?"

Her mother held up a piece of paper. "The email. I printed it out."

Hollis felt her stomach tense.

"'Dear Pam,'" her mother began reading, with no regard. "'My name is Milo Robinson-Clark.'"

No forethought.

"'I got your email from my mom Suzanne.'"

Still no indication whatsoever from Hollis that she wanted to hear this.

"'You may not remember me, but we met seven and a half years ago in Brooklyn, where I still live. Your daughter, Hollis, and I have the same sperm donor. Which is actually why I'm writing. I'm hoping you'll pass this message along to Hollis and tell her that I'd like to hear from her. She can email or text or call me, whatever works. Or I can email or text or call her, if you send me her info. Thanks. Hope you and Leigh are both well. Milo.'" Hollis's mother looked up. "So?"

Hollis stared at her.

"What do you think?"

"What do I *think*?"

"Do you . . ." Her mother hesitated. "Would you like me to give him your email address or your cell phone number so he can contact you?"

Hollis picked up her spoon and shoved a massive bite of Froot Loops into her mouth. Chewed, swallowed, shoved in another bite. "Whatever," she said finally, spraying cereal chunks onto the table.

Hollis's mother hated the word *whatever*. She called it a passive-aggressive conversation-blocking tool, but this time she didn't comment. This time, for some crazy reason, she took it to mean, *Do whatever you want*. Which is why, ten hours later—when Hollis's mother went to pick up Chinese food and Hollis was lying in her bed, staring at the ceiling—Hollis's phone pinged from the pocket of her hoodie.

She checked: area code 917. She read: **Hey. It's Milo.**

Hollis almost laughed. It was such a casual text, like they weren't on a hyphenated-last-name basis. Like it wasn't completely absurd and random for her sperm donor's other kid to suddenly be contacting her when they only met once, a million years ago, on a seesaw in Brooklyn.

Hey, Hollis texted back anyway.

Happy almost new year.

To u too.

How r u?

Ok.

How r your moms?

Um Leighs good. Pams dead tho.

O shit. I didn't know.

No biggie. It was 7 years ago.

It occurred to Hollis that it was rude of her mother not to let Suzanne and Frankie know that Pam had died. Because, well, wasn't there some protocol for informing your biological daughter's half brother's lesbian moms that your own lesbian partner was dead?

Hollis stifled a snort. This was so *weird*.

I know this is weird, Milo Robinson-Clark texted.

Hollis was so spooked she sat up. It was like he had read her mind or something, which clearly he hadn't, because how could he read her mind? It's not weird.

No?

No.

Well it's about to get weird cuz I have something to tell u.

Ok.

R u ready?

Yes.

I've decided to find r sperm donor.

Breath caught in Hollis's throat. She stared at her phone. She read the text again just to make sure she'd read it right. Then she exhaled. Y?

Medical reasons.

R u ok?

Yes.

Do u need a kidney?

No.

Bone marrow?

No.

???

It's complicated.

Hollis waited. If Milo Robinson-Clark wanted to tell her about his mysterious medical condition, he would. And apparently he did not, because his next text read,

R u in?

In?

For finding r donor?

Okay, wait. WTF. Hollis's heart was suddenly pounding so fast she needed to lie back down. She tried not to think about this. She tried not to let these thoughts infiltrate her mind. *I am a freak of nature. I am a lab experiment. I am only half a person.* Most of the time she succeeded. But sometimes, just sometimes, she fantasized about tracking down her donor, setting up a time and a place to meet, and then—right after she said "Hi, I'm Hollis"—slapping him across the face.

Because Hollis was pissed at the guy. She didn't even know him and she was pissed. Even if he did donate out of the goodness of his heart to help lesbians make babies. The way Hollis was "made" was fast, cold, and impersonal. Her existence had nothing to do with love. And if you're not going to make a baby out of love, at least have a one-night stand with some hot stranger you met at the Laundromat. At least then there's human contact. A connection between two people. It isn't fair to just go and squirt your jiz in a cup, take your cash, and then not even *think* about where your DNA is going and who might be affected.

Hollis's phone pinged. **Pls? I don't want to do this alone.**

Milo Robinson-Clark did not want to find their sperm donor alone. He wanted Hollis to join him. He was offering her a chance—a once-in-a-lifetime opportunity to meet her genetic father, to have all of her unanswered questions answered. Hollis would be crazy not to take it, wouldn't she?

But no, hell no, sorry, no. The anger that was usually just simmering beneath the surface of Hollis's skin now rose like a tidal wave, taking all good things with it.

I'm out.

Hollis texted the words. Then, for good measure, she chucked her phone across the room and cracked a picture frame. Which made her feel a little better. But not much.

MILO

HOW TO EXPLAIN?

1) His immune system was a paranoid schizophrenic.

2) A peanut was not just a peanut; it was an enemy combatant to which there was only one response: Attack! Attack!

3) He was fifteen years old and he was a prisoner of war.

Okay, maybe that was too dramatic. Milo wasn't literally imprisoned. He was just allergic to dairy, eggs, wheat, gluten, all melons, citrus, tomatoes, potatoes, peanuts, tree nuts, coconut, fish and shellfish, soy, and casein. He occasionally—but only occasionally—had to be hospitalized for an allergic reaction. There was that time in sixth grade when he'd eaten a coconut bar on his class camping trip. He had asked the head teacher, who had asked the mom who made the bars, if they were okay for him to eat. Lists were checked and double-checked. Milo had been *assured* that the bars were safe. No one knew about the coconut. He had never eaten coconut before, and he had never been tested for it. He had no idea he was allergic until he took a bite of coconut bar and his throat closed up.

That visit to the hospital had been crazy. Random details still floated around Milo's brain: the starfish ring on the nurse's finger, the antiseptic taste of the tube they jammed down his throat, the crushing pain in his chest as he gasped for air and found none. Had there been a light, or a tunnel of some sort? If there had, he didn't remember it. But in the moment when he woke up and Suzanne and Frankie were hugging him, crying and laughing, he knew that he had dodged a bullet. According to the attending physician, Milo had been clinically dead for three minutes.

There had been lesser reactions. Times he had needed to use an inhaler because his chest was tight, or an EpiPen because his mouth was suddenly tingling and his lips were swelling up like balloons. Milo was used to it. Used to wearing a medical alert bracelet. Used to checking ingredients. Used to carrying Benadryl and epinephrine at all times. If he ate the wrong thing, he could die.

Milo knew this and, for the most part, acknowledged

that being alive was preferable to being dead. But sometimes he just wanted to eat pizza and french fries like a normal teenager. He wanted not to be the skinniest kid in the locker room. He had been called Twiggy since he was ten years old. Or Skeletor. Or Skindiana Bones. There were so many good nicknames. It was hard to pick a favorite.

Milo knew he wasn't alone. His moms—growing up gay in the Midwest—had endured their share of name-calling. They'd told him all about it. *Dykes! Carpet munchers!* They had suffered, Milo was sure, more than he ever had. Still, could they blame him for wanting his life to be easier?

The TGFB1 gene. That's what Milo's allergist had mentioned at his last appointment. Dr. Daignault was referring to a new study reported in *Science Now,* suggesting that a single genetic aberration of the "transforming growth factor beta 1" could explain everything from hay fever to food allergies to asthma. One mutated gene could be responsible for Milo's whacked immune system—one mutated gene that he didn't get from Frankie because they shared no DNA, and he didn't get from Suzanne because she wasn't allergic to anything. "What about Milo's biological father?" Dr. Daignault had asked as Milo and his moms sat on the hard orange chairs in his office. "Any known allergies?"

"Lactose," Suzanne had answered. "And ragweed pollen."

"Anything else?"

"Not as far as we know."

"Have you considered asking Milo's biological father for some genetic testing? Could be instructive."

Ask his father for genetic testing? It was one of those crazy moments when Milo heard the word "father" and remembered that he actually had one. Not just a sperm donor: a *father*.

Suzanne and Frankie had been open about his conception since Milo was a little kid. "A good and generous guy gave us some seeds so we could grow you!" The story sounded a lot like "Jack and the Beanstalk": mysterious man, magic seeds. A fairy tale. For a long time, whenever Milo thought of his donor, he pictured a giant in the sky, strumming his golden harp. It was stupid, he knew. Juvenile. Just like it was juvenile to walk through Park Slope looking at all the dads and wondering if one of them could be his. There was no logic to it. For one thing, the sperm that made Milo came from a cryobank in Minnesota— where Frankie had gone to graduate school and where, presumably, Milo's donor still lived—so the odds of him walking around Brooklyn were slim. Also, Milo had never seen a picture. Did the guy have a beard? Glasses?

They could pass each other on the street and not even know they were related.

There was a baby album. Pictures of Suzanne pregnant with Milo, lounging on a beach chair, a glass of lemonade perched on her high, swollen belly. Suzanne looked different then. Softer. Her hair hadn't gone gray yet. It was long and chestnut colored, and she wore it in a thick braid down her back. Her face, normally sharp and angular, looked round. There were pictures from the actual birth, Milo covered in slime—which he could do without—and about a million pictures of both his moms holding him, kissing him, feeding him, burping him. Frankie looked the same. Short and stocky, with flaming red hair cut close to her scalp and spiked up in front. There was a series of shots of Frankie holding Milo against her chest, tucking his little bald head under her chin. Milo liked looking at those pictures, but they weren't the big draw. In the back of the album there was a pocket. And in that pocket was the personal profile for Donor #9677.

Race: Caucasian.

Ethnicity: Scottish-Italian.

Religion: Open-minded.

Milo must have read that piece of paper a thousand times. This man was his *father*. He was, according to the profile, six feet tall. He had hazel eyes. His hair, like Milo's, was dark, thick, and curly. Did he have to get it cut every four weeks to avoid looking like a mushroom? Did he also have dark, thick eyebrows? What about body hair? These were the little things Milo wondered about. The big things—the TGFB1 gene, whether his father had been skinny, or nerdy, or a failure with girls, whether he ever wondered where his sperm went—stacked up in Milo's brain like blocks, threatening to topple. There were so many questions.

Suzanne and Frankie were an open book; they always had been. Everything they knew about Milo's donor, they'd shared with Milo. Nothing was hidden. Nothing was shameful. If anything, his moms were proud of the choice they'd made. Every Father's Day, they sent a card to the Twin Cities Cryolab and flowers to Dr. Caroll, the obstetrician who had performed Suzanne's insemination. They showed up for Family Day at Milo's elementary school with a poster board collage about sperm donation. They even included a photo of Hollis Darby-Barnes, Milo's half sister. Hollis Darby-Barnes, whom—for reasons Milo wasn't entirely sure of—he had just texted.

The idea sprang out of nowhere. Not, in truth, because of his appointment with Dr. Daignault, but because Milo was mad at Frankie for telling him he couldn't go to JJ Rabinowitz's New Year's Eve party. Frankie was a certified helicopter mom and JJ was a professional screw-up, who yesterday had left a baggie of pot in his open backpack right there on Milo's bed where Frankie could find it.

Frankie had tried to call JJ's parents, but they were in Europe. So she flushed the pot down the toilet, which was tantamount to flushing Milo's friendship with JJ down the toilet.

"I'm sorry, kiddo," Frankie told Milo after JJ left. "I'm just doing my job as a responsible mother." She had tried to give Milo a hug, to show that she was on his side, but the damage was already done. There would be no New Year's Eve party at JJ's—or rather, there *would* be a New Year's Eve party at JJ's, but Milo would not be going.

"Why are you punishing *me* for JJ's weed?" he demanded.

"I'm not punishing you," Frankie said. "I'm protecting you. JJ doesn't make good choices."

Frankie wasn't wrong. How many times had JJ come to school baked this year? But that was beside the point.

"You don't trust me," Milo said. "You don't believe I can make my own decisions."

"I do trust you, but my job as a parent isn't to be your friend. My job is to keep you safe."

Frankie really believed what she was spouting, but that didn't make Milo any less mad. He wanted to say it—the one thing that he knew would hurt her: *You're not my real mother, and I don't need to listen to you.* If he were to be very honest with himself, sometimes he actually felt this way. Suzanne was his real mother. It was her egg. She grew him. Her vote should count for more. If Suzanne weren't married to Frankie, she would let Milo go to JJ's party. Heck, she would join him.

Because of Frankie, Suzanne was stuck at home playing Scrabble on New Year's Eve. Right now, Milo could hear her shouting from the kitchen. "'Za' is not a word!"

"Yes, it is," Frankie said calmly, "and it's worth thirty-two points."

"You're full of it!"

"You're welcome to challenge me."

"Milo!" Suzanne shouted.

Milo heard his mother but didn't answer. If he ignored her, maybe she would move on to the dictionary and leave him alone. He had enough to think about right now. Like how Hollis would respond to his text. **Pls? I don't want to do this alone.** Did he sound pathetic? He sounded a little pathetic.

"Milo!" Suzanne hollered.

Milo sighed and slid his phone into his pocket.

Suzanne was in a mood. She wanted to go dancing at the Cubbyhole, to "ring in the New Year right," just as Milo wanted to "ring in the New Year right" at JJ's party. Suzanne was ticked, Milo knew, not about the word *za*, but because she could be break-dancing on the bar right now. But no. Now that Frankie knew about JJ's party, she suddenly wanted a "quiet night at home," and Suzanne rarely said no to Frankie. When Frankie said go to bed earlier, Suzanne went to bed earlier. When Frankie said eat more kale, Suzanne ate more kale. Frankie wasn't just Suzanne's wife or Milo's mom; she was their jailer.

Even when you presented a logical argument, like the one Milo had presented yesterday—*If you let me go to JJ's party, I won't drink beer. You know I won't; I'm allergic to gluten*—Frankie wouldn't listen. She had been this way for as long as Milo could remember. Overprotective. Smothering. "A buzz kill," as JJ would say.

"You'll thank me one day," Frankie said.

I'll thank you one day? Ha! It was one of those times when Milo wished he had a brother or sister, it didn't matter which, just someone to turn to and say, "Can you believe this crap?" He had said it to his English springer spaniel. "Can you believe this crap, Pete?" But Pete had just looked at Milo with his usual befuddled expression.

That was when the idea came to him. That moment, right there.

Milo had gone to Suzanne's desk, and he had turned on her computer, and he had found the email address for Pamela Barnes. *You may not remember me, but we met seven and a half years ago . . .* He had typed the message, and he had sent it. As big life decisions went, this one hadn't been particularly well thought-out, but Milo didn't care. He just did it. He set the wheels in motion.

Now, while Milo was on his way to the kitchen to tell Suzanne that *za* was short for *pizza*—and it was, in fact, a legal Scrabble word—he heard a ping. He grabbed his phone from the pocket of his jeans.

I'm out. That's what the text said.

Milo didn't know what he'd been expecting, really. *I'm in*? Or a bunch of thumbs-up emoticons? Hollis Darby-Barnes wasn't exactly a known entity. They'd only met once, when Milo was in second grade. But still, this was their sperm donor they were talking about. Their *father*. Milo would be lying if he said he wasn't disappointed. Because . . . come on. Wasn't she even curious?

"Milooo!" Suzanne hollered again.

She would never shut up. Suzanne was like the lion at the Bronx Zoo, roaring and roaring from boredom. She couldn't stand being penned in. She needed to be on the African plains with the other lions.

This is bullshit, Milo thought. *It's New Year's Eve.*

Forget his moms.

Forget Hollis Darby-Barnes.

He was going out.

HOLLIS

HER PHONE BUZZED IN THE MIDDLE OF THE NIGHT. SHE glanced at the clock on her bedside table. 12:07. Only seven minutes into the New Year and they were already at it.

Buzz, buzz.

Hollis didn't need to look at her phone. She knew who it was. There were these girls from school—not Shay and Gianna, who Hollis sat with at lunch and sometimes hung out with on weekends. These girls weren't her friends, not even close. They were known to call in the middle of the night. Hollis usually powered down her cell before bed so she wouldn't have to deal. Whatever they had to say to her—*Happy New Year, Slut!* or *Skank it up in '16!*—it would sound worse in the dark than it would in the daylight. Lately, Hollis had been erasing the voice mails without even listening. There would be plenty more where those came from. Texts. Tweets. Instagrams. The hits just kept on coming.

Buzz, buzz.

She'd let it go. It wasn't like her mother could hear the phone vibrate. Leigh was downstairs, conked out on the couch in front of the fireplace, where she slept every New Year's Eve so she could ring in the New Year with Pam and her stupid cat.

Buzz, buzz, buzz.

Jesus. Didn't they have anything better to do tonight?

Hollis grabbed her cell off the bedside table and, without even glancing at the screen, pressed it to her ear. "What do you want?" *Slut. Skank. Ho.* It would be one of the three. They weren't very original, these girls. Hollis would respect them a lot more if they called her something with pizzazz. *Floozy. Trollop. Harlot. Strumpet.* There were so many better—

"Hollis?"

A boy's voice. Not Gunnar's. A voice she couldn't place.

"Who is this?" she said.

"What?" There was noise in the background. A lot of noise.

"Who is this?" Hollis said again, louder.

"Milo."

Hollis felt a jolt of—what? Surprise? Relief? She wasn't sure. "Where are you?" she said.

"Party. Big party. Hollis?"

"Are you drunk?"

"A little."

"Should you be drinking, with your medical condition?"

"Probably not. But listen—"

"I'm listening."

"I've been doing some research."

"Yeah?" She was thirsty. She could still taste moo shu shrimp on her tongue, remnants of the Lamest New Year's Eve Ever.

"Hollis?" Milo Robinson-Clark said. "We're not the only ones."

That was the thing about Chinese food. It tasted good while you were eating it, but then, hours later—wait. "What?"

"There's this website," Milo said. He sounded like he'd raised his voice, but the noise in the background still made it hard to pick out, so Hollis pressed the phone closer to her ear. "The Donor Progeny Project."

"What?" Hollis said. Not because she hadn't heard him. She heard, but *what was he telling her?*

"He has five kids. There are five of us."

MILO

HE WOKE UP IN HIS OWN BED, STILL WEARING HIS CLOTHES from last night. Fully functional except for his tongue, which felt like it was wearing a sweater. *The vodka*. He'd brought a bottle of vodka to the party as a peace offering, to make up for Frankie flushing JJ's weed down the toilet. How much had he drunk . . . three shots? Four? The taste had been awful at first, like battery acid, but when the heat hit Milo's chest, then his belly, suddenly it was like his whole body—every cell, every follicle—was filled with warmth, and he realized, standing on JJ's coffee table, surrounded by dancing bodies, that *this is why people drink*.

Someone was knocking on the door. Milo felt a moment of panic. He'd left the apartment after his moms were asleep, but when had he come home? *How* had he come home? His memory was hazy. Maybe Suzanne and Frankie had slept through it, but Milo was still in his clothes. This would raise suspicion. And if it didn't, the missing bottle certainly would. He'd taken it from the cabinet above the refrigerator—a full liter of Grey Goose—and he hadn't even thought about how he would replace it. He'd *stolen* Suzanne's vodka.

Pete, who had been asleep at the foot of the bed, now looked at Milo with woeful eyes. Pete knew.

Milo had never stolen anything in his life. He'd never snuck out. He'd never drunk alcohol. JJ had. JJ was a master delinquent, but not Milo. How to explain? The fact was that until this week Milo had never been invited to a party. Okay, this wasn't strictly true: he had been invited to parties when he was younger—birthday parties, the ones thrown by parents, where the whole class got invited and everyone went home with a balloon. But all that stopped in seventh grade. Groups formed. Sports teams. Kids Milo had hung out with in elementary school started drifting away with other kids. It didn't happen overnight, but that's how it seemed. One day he had friends and the next he was . . . well . . . the weird, skinny kid eating beets in the cafeteria when everyone else was eating pizza bagels.

JJ was new this year—a transplant from the Buckley School. JJ was tall, good-looking, and loaded. The fact that he'd chosen Milo as a lab partner was as much a mystery to Milo as to anyone. But he had. And he'd invited Milo to his New Year's Eve party—the first high-school party Milo had ever been invited to—and Milo wasn't about to let something as trivial as an overprotective mother stop him from going to his first high-school party.

"Milo?" Frankie's voice. Door opening. Pete, lifting his furry head in anticipation. *Treat? Walk?*

Crap, Milo thought. *Crap, crap, crap.*

It wasn't just Frankie walking into his room; it was Suzanne, too. Both his moms in their pajamas. Frankie in her brown fleece robe, Suzanne in some multicolored silk number, bare feet pointed out like she was about to teach a ballet class. Frankie pulled the swivel chair over from Milo's desk and sat. Suzanne perched on the bed beside Pete, pelican legs folded beneath her.

"Hello, Pete," Suzanne said, giving his nose a pat. Then, "Hey, kiddo."

Milo nodded. He didn't trust his voice.

Frankie slid her hand into the pocket of her robe, and when she pulled it out, she was holding Milo's phone.

"You want to tell us what's going on with you?" she said.

Where to begin?

The truth was, Milo hadn't had a real conversation with either of his moms since before seventh grade. Not about anything that mattered. And he wasn't about to start now.

What good would it do? Suzanne and Frankie didn't want to hear about him changing for gym in the bathroom stall to avoid comments about his chicken chest. They didn't want to hear that he got a boner every time he saw Hayley Christenson walk down the hall. And anyway, did Milo want another "open dialogue" about puberty from his mothers? Did he want another "masturbation is healthy" proclamation at the dinner table? Hell no. What Milo needed was a man to talk to. Not Dr. Daignault. Not his moms' gay friend Charles, who once took Milo out for ice cream in an attempt to jump-start—at Suzanne and Frankie's request—a painfully awkward conversation about male anatomy. Milo needed a father. He felt guilty for thinking this, because even though they drove him crazy, he loved his moms and didn't want them to think that they weren't enough.

Milo tried to shrug his shoulders under the blanket, without revealing his clothes. "Nothing's going on with me."

"Let's talk about these texts," Frankie said, cupping Milo's phone in her hand.

Milo closed his eyes. This was the deal he'd made when they first bought him a phone: full parental access. They had his password. They had his consent to monitor all activity. He'd signed a *contract*.

"Texts?" he said, playing for time. His stomach was

flipping around like crazy. Had he done something stupid last night? Had he inadvertently forwarded a naked photo to the whole school? Or, worse, had someone at the party taken his phone and done something to mess with him? This was entirely possible.

"The 612 number," Frankie said.

The 612 number? Milo opened his eyes. His mouth was so dry. He would kill for a glass of water.

"Honey." Suzanne squeezed Milo's leg through the blanket. "Why didn't you tell us you were in touch with Hollis Darby-Barnes?"

Milo almost laughed. Here he was, afraid that his moms had found out about the party—the sneaking out, the vodka, some idiot thing he'd done with his phone while he was drunk—and all they were talking about was Hollis Darby-Barnes. They'd seen his text asking Hollis to help find their sperm donor, and her text back to him saying—wait a minute . . . a memory was forming in the back of Milo's mind. JJ's bedroom . . . JJ's laptop . . . the Donor Progeny Project. Had he really gone onto that website last night and plugged in his information?

To his mothers, Milo croaked, "He has five kids."

Frankie gave him a funny look. "Who does?"

"My sperm donor."

Suzanne let go of his leg. "You started looking?"

"Yeah," Milo said. "I started looking."

*　　*　　*

They'd talked about it, the three of them. Right after the appointment with Dr. Daignault they'd gone out to lunch at Taco Pacifico—one of the few restaurants in Brooklyn where Milo could eat safely—and discussed the possibility of finding his donor. Suzanne had been pretty cool about it, but Frankie was another story.

"*Instructive?* He thinks it would be *instructive* to ask this man we've never met to undergo genetic testing?"

"Information gathering, Frankie," Suzanne said calmly. "That's all Dr. Daignault is suggesting."

"Opening a can of worms is what he's suggesting."

"It's a noninvasive procedure. It's a Q-tip swab on the inside of the cheek."

"That's not the point."

"Ma," Milo said to Frankie. "Didn't you hear what he said? There was a whole article written about this gene. My donor might carry the mutation."

"And?"

"And that could explain why I'm allergic to everything."

"And?" Frankie persisted.

"And . . . I don't know . . . it might help me."

"How?"

"What?" Milo said.

"How would it *help you* to know that he carries this aberrant gene? *If* he actually does."

Milo didn't have an answer for that. And even if he did, Frankie wasn't in a listening place. Frankie was off and running.

"Here's what I don't get . . . I'm unclear on how finding your sperm donor is actually going to *benefit* you. If I knew that it would . . . oh, honey, of course I would say let's track this guy down. I would pin him to the floor and swab his mouth with a Q-tip myself. But it's not like finding him is going to make an anti-allergy pill appear out of the blue."

"I know that," Milo said.

"It takes *years* to develop drugs."

"I know."

"You're not going to find him and suddenly be able to eat a peanut butter sandwich."

Suzanne had stopped her right there. She said Frankie needed some air. She said Frankie needed a margarita. But later that night, when Milo was in bed, he could hear his moms arguing again.

FRANKIE: He's too young!
SUZANNE: He's not a little kid anymore, babe. It's his
               decision.
FRANKIE: It can be his decision when he's eighteen.

SUZANNE: It's not about age, Frank. It's about medical history. It's his birthright to know where he came from.

FRANKIE: Easy for you to say. You're his biological mother.

SUZANNE: Did you seriously just go there?

FRANKIE: Yeah. I did.

SUZANNE: You're as much his mother as I am. You know that.

FRANKIE: Am I?

SUZANNE: (Silence)

FRANKIE: Am I really?

SUZANNE: Come on, Frankie. This isn't about your ego. It's *his choice*. You agreed to this when we decided to use a donor. You knew this day would come.

FRANKIE: So—what? You're saying we should just go ahead and let our fifteen-year-old get in touch with a complete stranger on the off chance that this guy has some genetic mutation? A mutation that scientists in this one study *theorize* might be connected to food allergies?

SUZANNE: Yes. That's exactly what I'm saying.

* * *

Now, in Milo's room, they were both looking at him. Frankie from the swivel chair, Suzanne from the edge of his bed. Milo looked at the ceiling, avoiding eye contact. Frankie didn't know what Suzanne and Milo knew. Frankie had no idea, but when Milo was thirteen Suzanne had told him about the Donor Progeny Project. She'd explained how the site worked. She'd said that he was officially a member. The login name and password—whenever Milo was ready to use them—would be his and his alone. Suzanne had handed Milo an envelope. She'd asked him to please not tell Frankie until he had actually decided to start searching. In the meanwhile, Suzanne had said, there would be no reason to cause Frankie undue pain. Which was bullshit, Milo thought now. Cause *Frankie* pain? What about *Milo's* pain? What about Milo spending his entire life without a father? Fifteen years without a man to talk to? No one to show him how to tie a tie, or how to shave, or how to ask a girl out?

Milo had kept the envelope in his sock drawer for a while, until he'd realized that Frankie sometimes rearranged things when she put away his laundry. So he'd folded the envelope into thirds. He'd stuck it in his wallet. He'd carried it around with him for over a year, and he never opened it. Until last night, at JJ's party, after he'd drunk an indeterminable amount of vodka.

Milo peeled his eyes away from the ceiling and looked

at his moms. He didn't know what to say. Or rather, he did know what to say, but he couldn't say it out loud. Deep down, Milo knew why he'd gotten on the DPP website last night. Did he really expect to find a cure for his allergies? No. How would it *help him* to know if #9677 carried this aberrant gene? Maybe it wouldn't. Maybe he was just looking for an excuse to start looking.

There. He'd admitted it. He wanted to find his father. Was Frankie capable of hearing this? No chance. Suzanne would be okay, but not Frankie.

Milo's head was starting to ache. His mouth was a desert. All he wanted was water.

"I need a drink," he rasped.

"Don't we all," Frankie said drily.

HOLLIS

FATE. KARMA. DESTINY. IT WAS ALL CRAP, AND YET HOLLIS'S mother was convinced that the email from Milo Robinson-Clark to PjBarnesie_373@hotmail.com was Pam's work. Pam, reaching out from the grave—just as she had once reached out in life—to bring Hollis and her half brother together.

This is what Hollis discovered on New Year's morning, when she shuffled into the kitchen and found her mother waiting for her. "Happy New Year," Leigh said. She was smiling, which was weird enough. She was fully dressed. And, weirder still, she had made some slimy-looking egg dish.

The sight of pans on the stove was so rare it actually spooked Hollis. Her mother never cooked. Pam had been a chef, so when she was alive she did all the cooking. Pam had owned a restaurant in Maple Grove called Figs. That's where she and Leigh had met. After Pam died, Hollis's mother stopped appreciating food. She made sure Hollis was fed, but meals were usually takeout, and breakfast was always cereal.

Hollis stared at the disgusting egg dish. "What the . . ." she muttered.

"Pam loves eggs Benedict."

Hollis shot her mother a look. Did she even realize she'd used the present tense? It pissed Hollis off, but she didn't have the energy to fight. She didn't have the stomach for eggs, either. Between last night's moo shu shrimp and the bombshell from Milo Robinson-Clark, Hollis felt vaguely nauseous. Her mouth still tasted like garlic.

"Sit," Leigh said, sweeping an arm through the air like a game-show host. "Eat."

Hollis sat tentatively on the edge of a chair. There was something wrong with her mother; that much was clear. Maybe she'd been drinking. Hollis looked around for evidence, but found none. Maybe she'd finally started taking her happy pills. The thought of this made Hollis livid. But why? For years she'd been begging her mother to take the depression medication prescribed by her shrink—not the grief counselor Hollis once saw, but some other woman.

"I'm not depressed," Leigh said, every time Hollis's Uncle Drew, a psychiatrist in North Carolina, brought up the subject of medication. "I'm grieving."

Well, she certainly wasn't grieving now. She was digging into her eggs Benedict with gusto. She was smiling across the table.

Hollis scowled.

"Why the face?" her mother said.

"Why are you acting so weird?"

"I'm not acting weird."

"Yes," Hollis said. "You are."

"Look under your plate."

"Why?"

"Just humor me."

Hollis felt her eyes roll upward—the clichéd teenager. Well, forgive her, but she was exhausted, and what was her mother doing, exactly?

"Go on," Leigh said.

Hollis sighed and lifted her plate.

There were three photos. Not just the one Hollis remembered—of her and Milo on the seesaw with their matching juice mustaches—but two others. Group shots with Hollis, Milo, and the four moms. Leigh looked so young and so pretty, Hollis barely recognized her. Her face was tan. Her hair was streaked with blond. She was smiling up at Hollis, who was perched on Pam's shoulders and grinning wildly at Milo, who was held aloft by one of his mothers. Hollis wasn't sure which—Suzanne or Frankie.

"Huh," Hollis said.

"It's your family."

"What?"

"Those people, right there. They're your family. That's what Pam has been trying to tell us."

Here we go, Hollis thought. Her mother was forever looking for signs that Pam was still with them, imbuing even the most random occurrence with meaning.

"The email," her mother said now. "It was a sign."

Of course it was.

"It came to Pam's Hotmail account for a reason."

Right.

"Pam wants you and Milo to find each other again."

"Mom," Hollis said with as much restraint as she could muster, "I don't know how to break this to you, so I'm just going to say it . . . Pam's dead."

"In the physical sense, yes."

"In *every* sense."

"Love never dies."

"And unicorns are real."

There was no point in using sarcasm on Hollis's mother. It rolled right off her.

"Pam arranged that visit, you know." Leigh gestured to the photographs. "She organized the whole thing."

"I know."

"It was important to her."

"I know."

"We wanted to give you a brother or sister. We wanted to use the same donor and have Pam carry the baby. But then she got sick."

"I know, Mom."

If Hollis had a dollar for every time she'd heard this story she could buy a boat and sail away from the kitchen. Find an island somewhere. She wouldn't need much, just some food and her favorite books and—

"He had hazel eyes."

"What?"

"Your donor. We picked him because he had hazel eyes, like Pam. And he was smart. And tall."

Hollis gave her mother a blank stare. "Why are you telling me this?"

"I wanted to give you some information."

"Why?"

"I thought you might like to know something about him."

"Well, I don't," Hollis snapped. "I don't want to know one thing about that mother-effer."

Mother-effer. The irony of the word was not lost on Hollis. She would laugh if she weren't so mad. Her body was pulsing with anger. She would chuck her eggs Benedict across the room if the sight of them quivering on the plate didn't make her stomach churn.

Leigh's eyes widened. Blue eyes, not hazel.

"Sorry," Hollis muttered.

"No. This is good. I want to know how you feel."

"He has five kids, you know." Hollis stabbed a piece of toast with her fork. "That jackass."

"I know."

Hollis looked up. "What?"

"I spoke to Suzanne. She filled me in."

"What?"

"I couldn't stop thinking about that email yesterday. I couldn't stop thinking that if I'd closed Pammy's account Milo would never have found us. Everything happens for a reason, Hollis. It wasn't random. It wasn't an accident. He found us because of Pam."

She sounded excited. Hollis couldn't remember the last time her mother had been so excited. She hated to piss on her mother's parade, but this was the twenty-first century. Milo could have found them any number of ways. Google. Facebook. Whitepages.com. But her mother was on a roll about Pam. And when her mother was on a roll about Pam, nothing Hollis said could stop her.

"So I started thinking, what would Pam want me to do now? And I thought, she'd want me to call Suzanne and Frankie. So I did. First thing this morning. And they invited us to Brooklyn. And then I thought, what would Pam want me to do with this invitation? She'd want me to book us a flight—"

Okay, wait. "What?"

"She'd want me to book us a flight. So I did."

Hollis stared at her mother. "Are you serious?"

"We leave at two o'clock. We fly back Sunday afternoon."

Here her mother was, smiling. Practically clapping her hands. How could she book them a flight when they hadn't been on an airplane since before Pam died? They never went anywhere. Not even to North Carolina to see Uncle Drew and his kids. But now—all of a sudden—they were flying to Brooklyn to see three people they barely knew? *Now* Hollis's mother wanted her to have a family?

"Well?" Leigh was waiting.

WTF? That was Hollis's response. She was tired, nauseous, disgusted by the sight of Pam's cat, who had just leaped onto her mother's lap and was proceeding to lick herself another fur ball.

"What about Yvette?" Hollis said.

"She'll come with us. She'll be my carry-on."

"Mom."

"What?"

"Please don't bring the cat."

"Okay."

Okay? Hollis stared across the table. Her mother loved that cat like the second coming of Pam. "Seriously?"

"This is your trip," her mother said. "You make the call."

MILO

YOU'D HAVE TO BE DONOR-CONCEIVED TO GET IT. OR
adopted, Milo supposed. Or switched at birth or left on the
doorstep of an orphanage. But how many of those people
actually got the chance to drive to the airport and pick up
their half sister? Not many, he would bet. It was surreal.

Hollis and her mother were due to arrive any minute,
but Milo's moms were not exactly rolling out the welcome
mat. They were still arguing. This morning had been fine.
The phone call with Hollis's mom had been fine. But as
soon as Suzanne hung up and broke the news to Frankie
about the Donor Progeny Project, they'd been at each
other. All the way to JFK in the cab, it was Frankie accusing Suzanne of betrayal and Suzanne accusing Frankie of
self-absorption.

FRANKIE: You lied to me, Suzanne.

SUZANNE: I didn't *lie* to you, Frankie. I just didn't tell you.

FRANKIE: That's a lie of omission.

SUZANNE: It wasn't a *lie of omission*. The information was for Milo. It didn't apply to you. Not everything applies to you.

FRANKIE: You think the possibility of our son finding his sperm donor and genetic half siblings doesn't *apply to me*?

SUZANNE: I didn't say that. I said the *information* didn't apply to you *at the time* I gave it to Milo. It was his choice whether or not to use it. And now that he's chosen to use it, I'm telling you.

FRANKIE: Well, thank you for keeping me in the loop like I'm actually a member of this family.

SUZANNE: Are you serious?

Here they were at the baggage claim, still going strong. Milo did his best to mediate. "Drop it," he said. And, "Point made." "What's done is done." "We all have the same information now." "We're in this together." "You're my family." And finally, "Shut up. I think that's them."

Frankie got in one last dig: "Great time for houseguests."

"Leigh lost her partner," Suzanne hissed. "Hollis lost her mom. This is what people *do*."

"I just don't see the urgency. Couldn't we have done this another time?"

"Super idea." Suzanne smiled and waved across the room. "I'll just send them home."

There, coming down the escalator, were a girl and her mother. The girl was uneasy. You could see it in her eyebrows, which were thick and dark and scrunched together, and in the way she clutched her messenger bag to her chest like a security blanket. Her hair, on the other hand, looked thrilled to be here. It sprang out from under her black skullcap in all directions. Thick, dark, wild.

Milo knew that hair. He saw it every morning when he looked in the mirror.

"Suzanne?" the mother said, stepping off the escalator first. She was thin and pale, with a limp ponytail and tired eyes. "Frankie?"

"Leigh!"

Milo watched as his moms, one after the other, hugged Hollis's mom.

"We're so sorry about Pam," Suzanne said.

"So sorry," Frankie said, squeezing Leigh's hand.

"Thank you." Hollis's mom nodded. Milo could see fine

lines around her eyes, grooves on either side of her mouth. "There's no place Pammy would rather be than here."

Milo saw Hollis smirk.

"Mi," Suzanne said gently, "you remember Leigh."

"Of course." Milo stepped forward. He stuck out his hand and they shook. In his peripheral vision, he saw Hollis smirk again. Or maybe it wasn't a new smirk; maybe she'd never stopped.

"Hollis," Suzanne said, holding out both arms like Maria von Trapp. "Welcome, sweetheart."

"Welcome!" Frankie echoed joyously.

His moms were putting on a show, as if they hadn't spent all afternoon fighting. As if this weren't the most loaded family reunion ever.

"Thanks," Hollis said. She didn't move in for a hug. She just stood there at the bottom of the escalator, clutching her messenger bag.

"Hey," Milo said, lifting his chin in greeting.

"Hey." Hollis opened her mouth to yawn, revealing her pierced tongue. One of those silver barbell thingies. It matched the two in her ear.

Hollis's look—the skullcap, the ripped jeans, the piercings—wasn't strange for New York, but Milo wondered how it translated in Saint Paul, Minnesota. Was Hollis a fringe kid? A rebel? A freak?

"They look alike," Hollis's mom murmured to no one in particular, but Suzanne answered, "They certainly do."

"The miracle of DNA," Frankie said heartily. Then, placing a hand on Leigh's arm, "Do you have any baggage?"

Hollis snorted. "We have baggage, all right."

"Hollis." Her mother looked pained, like Hollis was giving her a headache.

"What? It's a double entendre."

"We packed light," Leigh said, patting the black roller suitcase beside her. "We're all set."

"Great." Frankie's smile was so wide and bright Milo almost couldn't look at it.

"I'll get us a cab," Suzanne said. "Okay, hon?"

"Okay, hon."

Milo watched his mothers exchange a look that said, *We are not finished fighting, but as long as we have guests we will pretend, for decorum's sake, that we are on our honeymoon.*

HOLLIS

HOLLIS WALKED INTO HER HALF BROTHER'S ROOM FOR THE first time ever, feeling strange and gawky because A) she'd never been in a high-school guy's room before, and B) this wasn't just any high-school guy; this was her own flesh and blood. Only, it wasn't like she and Milo had grown up together. They were basically strangers, and yet here she was in his most personal space, his inner sanctum, looking at all his stuff. Beanbag chair. Juggling sticks. Lava lamp. Pile of dirty clothes shoved in a corner. Framed photos. Here was Milo in a black robe and mortarboard, sandwiched between his moms. Middle-school graduation, Hollis guessed.

She leaned in closer. The three of them looked nothing alike. Suzanne was so tall and angular, like Professor McGonagall from *Harry Potter* if Professor McGonagall had ever smiled. Suzanne looked more like a benevolent headmistress than a software engineer, although that's what she was, apparently. Milo didn't resemble Suzanne in any obvious way. Maybe they had the same eyes, but Hollis couldn't be sure. They definitely didn't have the same nose. And Frankie was . . . Professor Umbridge, short and thick. No. That wasn't a fair comparison. Frankie had *way* cooler hair than Professor Umbridge. A red buzz cut with these awesome spikes in front. And Hollis could bet she wouldn't be caught dead in an Umbridge dress. Frankie was a jeans girl, like Hollis. Frankie was built like a wrestler. She looked like she could kick some serious ass. Although how ass kicking would come in handy for a social worker, Hollis didn't know. Maybe Frankie drop-kicked deadbeat dads until they paid their alimony.

"Eighth-grade graduation," Milo said, suddenly appearing on Hollis's right. His sorry-looking mutt appeared, too, gazing up at Hollis with watery eyes.

"Oh." She nodded. "Uh-huh."

"Hollis, this is Pete. Pete, Hollis."

Hollis looked at the dog. The dog looked at Hollis.

Hollis looked at her watch. It had been twenty minutes since she'd arrived at Milo's house, or "brownstone" as he called it—which must be Brooklyn code for "small and cramped." First, Frankie had insisted on snapping a photo of Hollis and Leigh and Milo and Suzanne all scrunched together on a couch. Then, Suzanne had insisted that the three moms have tea while Milo showed Hollis his room. Well, she'd seen his room. And now the conversation had run dry, and Milo's dog was staring at her in an unnerving way, and there was nowhere to escape to, so she was just going to have to find something in this room to focus on so she didn't completely freak out.

Why am I freaking out?

Hollis made a beeline for the bookshelves over by the window, because books were her saviors. They had always been her saviors. Whatever crap was happening in her life, whatever was bringing her down, she had books.

Hollis tilted her head. She squatted. She ran her fingers along the books' spines like a blind person.

And then she saw it, wedged between *The Sorcerer's Stone* and *The Phantom Tollbooth*, looking not quite as decrepit as her own treasured copy, but worn enough. And she knew, instinctively, that he had read it at least three times, and not just because it was on the recommended summer reading list, but because, from the opening line of the first page to that perfect last sentence, this book spoke to him the same way it spoke to her. And she was so struck by this thought that she forgot she was in a stranger's room, and she took the book off the shelf and held it in her palm like a revelation.

"My favorite book," Hollis said.

"*Gatsby?*" Milo raised his eyebrows, which in that second Hollis realized looked just like hers.

"Yeah."

" 'It takes two to make an accident,' " he said, and she knew that he was quoting Jordan Baker.

"Do you hate careless people?"

"Of course," he said.

"Me too."

And what followed was the kind of conversation that could only happen between two people who love books. It didn't matter that *The Great Gatsby* wasn't his favorite. Hollis could appreciate *The Catcher in the Rye*. Hollis could appreciate Tolkien. It wasn't that she and Milo had the exact same taste—God knows Hollis hated *Animal Farm* with the heat of a thousand suns—it was that even when they disagreed, she recognized the value in what he was saying.

"It's a cartoon."

"It's political satire."

"It's talking pigs."

"Yes, but pigs as the *ruling class* . . . It's brilliant. It wouldn't have worked if Orwell had chosen any other animal. Think about it."

At some point there was a lull in the conversation and Milo pulled *The Hobbit* off a shelf. "Listen," he said. "I know you're not sold on finding our donor or his other kids. But this is my quest, okay? I know that sounds cheesy, but it's true. And I want you to come with me."

"On your quest."

"On my quest."

"You want me to leave the *Shire* and go face the freaking *dragon* with you?"

"In a manner of speaking." He grinned.

"Because you're dying."

"I am not dying."

"Because of your mysterious medical condition."

"If that's what it takes for you to join me," he said, "yeah."

*　　*　　*

Dinner answered Hollis's question—one of them, anyway. It was chicken breasts on a bed of rice, asparagus spears, plain green salad, and grapes.

"We eat pretty simply around here," Suzanne said when everyone was seated around the butcher-block table and dishes were being passed. "Because of Milo's food allergies."

"What are you allergic to?" Hollis asked.

Milo shrugged. "A lot." His thick, curly hair, the same molasses color as Hollis's, bounced slightly when he lifted the salad bowl. His arms, Hollis noticed now that he'd taken off his sweatshirt, were pale like hers, but skinnier.

"Dairy," Frankie said. "Eggs. Wheat. Gluten."

"Peanuts and tree nuts," Suzanne said, scooping rice onto her plate. "Fish and shellfish. Soy. Casein. All melons."

"Potatoes, tomatoes, coconut . . . what am I forgetting?"

"Citrus."

"Right," Frankie said. "Citrus."

"My goodness," Hollis's mother said, fork hovering in the air. "I remember the nut allergy from when we visited before . . . I didn't realize the list was so extensive."

"It is," Suzanne said. "He has to be very careful."

Hollis turned to Milo. "What happens?"

"If I eat one of those things?"

"Yeah."

"Depends."

"On?"

"How much I eat, how quickly I get treated."

"He had a close call about three years ago," Frankie said. "He was on a camping trip and he ate something with coconut in it. At the time, we didn't know he was allergic . . ."

Frankie told the whole story, and when she finished, Hollis stared at Milo. "You almost died?"

"Yup."

"That's your medical condition? If you eat one of those things it could kill you?"

"Something like that."

He sounded so nonchalant, as chill as his Modest Mouse T-shirt and the ear buds dangling from his neck. As chill as the grapes he was tossing into his mouth the way other kids tossed in Cheetos.

"So—what?" Hollis said. "Our donor can help you?"

Milo finished chewing. "We're not sure yet."

Which is when Suzanne told Hollis and Leigh about the article in *Science Now* and the recommendation from Milo's allergist. "Basically," Suzanne said, "we're looking for anything to explain the severity of Milo's allergies. His donor could provide some explanation."

"What about you?" Hollis's mother asked.

Suzanne shook her head. "I'm not allergic to anything."

"But his donor . . . I remember something from the profile . . . he's allergic to—what? Tree pollen?"

"Ragweed," Suzanne said. "And lactose . . . Obviously, we'd like to find out more. *If* he's willing to be contacted. *If* he's willing to be tested. Ideally, Milo would like to meet with him and talk this through."

Hollis's mother nodded slowly. "Wow."

"I know. It's tricky."

"Nice," Frankie said.

And Suzanne said, "What?"

"Tricky?"

"You don't like my word choice?"

"We're talking about feelings here, Suzanne, not pulling rabbits out of hats. We're talking about real human emotions."

"I know that."

"Do you?"

"Frankie." Suzanne glanced pointedly around the table.

"Can we just eat?" Milo said. "Please?"

Hollis watched as Frankie's face sort of collapsed in on itself. "Excuse me," she said quietly, wiping her mouth with a napkin and dropping it onto the table. "I need some air."

"Are you okay?" Hollis's mother said, but Frankie was already out the door. "Is she okay?"

"She'll be fine." Suzanne poured herself more wine and topped off Leigh's glass. "Frankie is . . . sensitive about the donor situation. She's okay in the abstract, but when it starts to get real . . . Milo taking the initiative to contact you . . . starting the search . . ."

Hollis's mother nodded. "I understand," she said. Then, "Pam was the same way."

"Was she?"

"Early on. Yes."

Hollis watched her mom take a sip of wine, then another. Leigh never drank alcohol anymore, so it was possible, likely even, that if she kept drinking she would lose sense of conversational etiquette and yammer about Pam all night. It was also possible that Milo would eat that entire bowl of grapes. Hollis watched in fascination. He was going to town on those things.

"When Hollis was a baby," her mother said, "Pam used to talk about how invisible she felt, being the non-biological mother. How she loved becoming a mom but she felt left out of the process, you know?"

Suzanne looked at Leigh, flushed and nodding. "Yes."

"She was scared for the day when Hollis might want to find her donor or siblings. Like she would be replaced."

"Exactly."

"But then she got her diagnosis," Leigh said softly, "and her perspective changed completely. She knew she didn't have a lot of time and she wanted to help Hollis connect with the rest of her family . . . she still does." Hollis's mother lifted her wine glass, toasting the ceiling. "We're here, Pammy. It may have taken us a while, but we're here. We're doing it."

If Hollis could jackhammer a hole next to her chair and dive through it, she would. She wished she'd explained it to Milo earlier, when they were in his room. If Hollis had made clear the Pam situation—if she had described not just the billboard-size Pam over the fireplace at home, but also the pocket-size Pam her mother kept in her purse and pulled out on the airplane the way Catholics pull out rosary beads or prayer cards—maybe Milo wouldn't be choking on a grape right now. But he was. Hollis realized this because first, he was pounding on the table, and now, he was holding both hands to his neck: the universal choking sign. Suzanne shrieked and ran around the table to execute the Heimlich maneuver. Hollis's mother dropped her wineglass, which shattered on the floor. The dog sprang out from under the table and started barking. The grape flew out of Milo's mouth, through the air, and onto the platter of chicken and rice.

From the hallway, Hollis heard the sound of horse hooves. Frankie in her big brown clogs came clomping into the kitchen. The dog barked louder.

"Is everything okay?" Frankie's cheeks were pink and she was panting slightly. "What happened?"

"Everything's fine," Suzanne said. "Milo was just choking."

"*Choking?* Is he having a reaction?"

Bark, bark, bark.

"I'm fine, Ma," Milo said.

But Frankie had already sprung into action, bolting across the kitchen to a drawer and whipping out some plastic tube thingy, yanking off the cap then bolting back over to Milo.

"Ma, I don't need the EpiPen. It was a grape."

"A grape?"

The dog barked some more.

"Take it easy, Pete," Milo said. He reached across the table to retrieve the grape from the platter, brushed off a few grains of rice, and held it up for Frankie. "Mom saved my life."

"What?"

"She gave me the Heimlich."

Frankie turned to Suzanne. "You did?"

"See what happens when you go out for air?" Suzanne said. "You miss all the excitement."

"And for my next act," Milo said, "I will dive off the roof with my hands tied behind my back."

Frankie gave him a dark look. "That's not funny."

"It's kind of funny."

"No," Frankie said, shaking her head. "It's not. I am your mother and you are my child, and the thought of you being hurt in any way . . ." Her voice cracked and she said, "Shit," and turned away from the table.

Pete barked.

"Frankie," Suzanne said.

"I'm fine."

"You're not fine."

"Yes I am."

"Clearly, you're not."

Hollis was a fan of well-crafted dramatic scenes, and this—the choking, the Heimlich, the shattered glass, the barking dog, the undercurrent of marital tension—was solid. For a moment, it made her forget that she was a superslut, and that her mother was a ghost whisperer, and that, according to Milo's research, she had three other genetic half siblings with possibly even crazier families. For a moment, she forgot it all and just watched the show.

MILO

IN THE MORNING, THE BUZZER BUZZED. AND BUZZED. AND buzzed again.

When Milo finally opened the front door, there was JJ on the stoop with a king-size package of Twizzlers in one hand and a brown paper bag in the other. He looked like a Swedish lumberjack—all shoulders and flushed cheeks and blond, floppy hair. The sun was barely up, but JJ looked ready to scale a redwood tree. Milo was still in his sweatpants. He was barely conscious.

"Happy New Year, man." JJ grinned.

Milo blinked. "It's January second."

"It's still new. And I come bearing gifts." JJ shoved the bag into Milo's chest. "To replenish your mom's stash."

"What is this?" Milo pulled out a clear glass bottle and then quickly shoved it back in. *"Vodka?"* He was glad he'd made it to the door first. Frankie was in the kitchen making breakfast. She would blow a gasket if she saw this.

"Not just any vodka. High Roller. Some movie producer gave it to my dad." JJ winked. "Top of the line."

"The stuff I took was Grey Goose. This isn't even—"

"Mi?"

"Crap." Milo shoved the bag down the leg of his sweatpants just as Frankie poked her head into the front hall.

JJ raised one arm of his buffalo plaid jacket in greeting. "Happy New Year, Mrs. Robinson-Clark!"

Ms. Clark, Milo thought. But he said nothing.

Frankie's brow furrowed. "Come in if you're coming in. It's twenty degrees out. We're losing heat."

"Sure thing," JJ said, taking one giant step forward and closing the door with a thud.

Frankie frowned from JJ to Milo. "A little early for visitors, isn't it, Mi?" Clearly she thought they were conducting a drug deal. She was scanning the crime scene for evidence.

"I was in the neighborhood," JJ said cheerfully. "I brought you something." He took another two steps forward to deliver the Twizzlers. "A peace offering. Sorry about the weed . . . is that banana bread I smell?"

"Muffins," Milo said, shifting his stance so the vodka bottle wouldn't plummet to the floor. "Frankie makes great muffins."

"I bet she does."

Frankie huffed as JJ ambled past her into the kitchen. Milo could hear her muttering. "By all means, make yourself at home." She turned to Milo. "Really?"

"What? He just showed up."

She frowned. "We have *guests*."

"I know."

"They're asleep in the living room."

"What do you want me to do, throw him out?"

She sighed deeply. "Just take him to your room."

"Okay," Milo said.

"But if that boy has marijuana on him, so help me . . ."

"He doesn't."

"He'd better not."

"Ma," Milo said. He squeezed the vodka between his thighs. He looked at his mother steadily. "He doesn't. Trust me."

"It's not you I don't trust," Frankie said.

"Point taken."

Milo waited until she'd returned to the kitchen. Then he opened the door to the hall closet, shoved the bag into one of Suzanne's rain boots, and buried the boot under a pile of beach towels—like a criminal. It's not as if it was his alcohol. It's not as if he was planning to drink it. This is what he would tell Suzanne if she busted him. But Suzanne would never bust him. Frankie would bust him.

Milo wouldn't be sneaking around like this if Frankie had minded her own business in the first place. Because, come on. What kind of mother takes her son's friend's private property out of his backpack and flushes it down the toilet?

"Dude."

Milo slammed the closet door so quickly, his finger got slammed with it.

"These muffins are the bomb—"

"Ow!" The pain was searing. "Fffffffrick!"

"You okay?" JJ's mouth was full.

Milo couldn't answer. All he could do was bounce up and down, holding his finger and swearing.

"What happened?" Frankie came flying through the doorway. "Who's hurt?"

JJ gestured to Milo. "Slammed his finger in the door."

"I'll go get ice."

"And a muffin!" JJ called after her as she ran back to the kitchen. "He could use a muffin!"

"Fricking ow," Milo said weakly, holding his finger.

"You're gonna lose that nail."

Milo looked up, and there was Hollis, peering through the doorway. "I did the same thing once," she said, stepping into the hall. "Slammed my finger in a drawer. The nail turned black and fell off. It took months to grow back." She leaned against the banister leading to the upstairs apartment, and Milo found himself staring not at her zebra-striped leggings or her *Intellectual Badass* T-shirt, but at her hair, which looked like it had been whipped with an eggbeater.

JJ's eyes widened, probably because Hollis was busting out of that shirt. "Have you been holding out on me?"

"Huh?" Milo stared back at his throbbing finger.

"Who is this vision I see before me? Is this your woman?"

Milo's head snapped up. "No!" he and Hollis said in unison.

"She's my sister," Milo said.

"Since when do you have a sister?"

"*Half* sister," Hollis clarified.

"Since when do you have a *half* sister?"

"We only met once," Milo said by way of explanation.

JJ raised his eyebrows.

Milo tried again. "We have the same sperm donor."

"No shit?" JJ said.

"No shit."

"You never told me you had a sperm donor."

"I told you I had two moms."

JJ grinned. "Cool." He strode toward Hollis, holding out a hand big enough to palm a watermelon. "Rabinowitz. JJ Rabinowitz."

Hollis smirked.

"And you are . . ."

"Hollis Darby."

Milo noted the omission of "Barnes," but before he could comment, Frankie arrived with a bag of frozen peas, which she proceeded to wrap around his finger.

"You gonna shake my hand, Hollis Darby?"

"Sit," Frankie commanded.

Milo sat.

"I don't know," Hollis said. "You gonna tell me what the J's stand for, JJ Rabinowitz?"

Frankie raised Milo's elbow. "Elevate."

Milo elevated.

Glancing over her shoulder, Frankie said, "Good morning, Hollis."

"Good morning."

"You really want to know?" JJ said.

"I wouldn't ask if I didn't," Hollis said.

It occurred to Milo, as the oven timer dinged and Frankie rushed back into the kitchen, that JJ had never volunteered his real name, and that Milo had never thought to ask.

"Jonah Jedediah."

Hollis snorted. *"Jonah Jedediah Rabinowitz?"*

"In the flesh."

"You don't look Jewish."

"How do I look?"

"Like you should be shucking corn on a football field in Nebraska."

JJ chuckled. "Very perceptive, Hollis Darby." Then, after a beat, "I'm adopted."

Hollis nodded. "Well, that explains it."

"Yup," JJ said.

Milo sat there holding his frozen peas and waiting for JJ to elaborate, but JJ appeared to have said all he planned to say on the subject. Hollis leaned against the banister, nodding. Icing, elevating, nodding, standing. The conversation died a slow death.

"Why don't we get some breakfast?" Milo said.

"Now you're talking," JJ said.

"Hollis?"

Hollis shrugged. "I could eat."

*   *   *

"Oh my *God*." Hollis leaned over and spat furiously into Milo's trash can, then swiped at her mouth with the back of her hand. "What *is* that thing?"

"That," Milo said, "is a wheat-free, dairy-free, egg-free, soy-free, nut-free banana muffin."

Hollis stood up, shaking her head. "How do you survive? Seriously, what do you eat?"

66

"A lot of salads," Milo said. "Meat. Rice. Apples and pears. Beets."

"*Beets?*"

"I can vouch for that," JJ said from the comfort of Milo's bed, where he was lounging beside Pete, stuffing his face with muffins.

Hollis turned to JJ. "Do you ever come up for air?"

"I'm a growing boy," JJ said, spewing crumbs onto his shirt. "I need sustenance."

By Milo's count, JJ had plowed his way through at least four muffins. Also a bowl of Frankie's homemade granola with blueberries and a pig's worth of bacon. He ate like a trash compactor.

"Don't your parents feed you?" Hollis said.

JJ shrugged. "They travel a lot."

What he didn't say was that his mom was a movie actress and his dad was a movie director and he lived in a Brooklyn Heights brownstone filled with so much art it could be a museum, and had a Sub-Zero refrigerator so stocked it could feed every person in the five boroughs of New York for a week.

"Only child?" Hollis said.

"Yup."

"Me too."

"Hey," Milo said. "Where's the love?"

Hollis shrugged. "It's not like we grew up together."

"Yeah, but you're not exactly an 'only child' either."

"I am for all practical purposes."

"Okay, but for *impractical* purposes you have me and three other siblings."

"Whoa," JJ said. He sat up straight, sending crumbs flying everywhere. "Hold the phone."

Hollis shook her head. "I don't consider them siblings."

"What do you consider them?" Milo said.

"I don't consider them at all."

"Um," JJ said. "Can we back up, please?"

But Milo wasn't ready to back up. "What do you consider *me*?"

"You're different," Hollis said.

"How?"

"I don't know." She picked up the Rubik's Cube from Milo's desk, turned it a few rotations. "We met a long time ago."

"So if you'd met *them* a long time ago you would consider them siblings?"

"No." Hollis shook her head, put the Rubik's Cube down. "Maybe. I don't know."

This wasn't going very well.

"Yo," JJ said.

"Aren't you even curious?" Milo said.

"*I'm* curious!" JJ leapt off the bed, throwing his arms

out, startling Pete off the bed, too. "Tell me what the frick you're talking about!"

Milo would have thought—after he finished explaining to JJ about the TGFB1 gene and the Donor Progeny Project and the information he'd plugged in to the site from JJ's computer on New Year's Eve—that JJ would think this was all nuts and he'd find some excuse to blow out of there.

But he didn't.

He studied Milo's face intently for a second. Then he nodded. "So, what do we do now?"

"What do we do now?" Milo glanced across the room at Hollis, who had been pacing around the whole time he was talking and had finally landed on his beanbag chair with a book.

"Don't ask me." Hollis held Milo's gaze, almost defiantly. "It's your quest."

"Do we log on?"

"Hell yeah," JJ said. "We log on."

HOLLIS

THE TEXT CAME WHILE HOLLIS WAS SITTING ON A BEAN-bag chair in Milo's room, watching him log on to the Donor Progeny Project.

Your an ugly ho bag slut who dosnt no how to dress. U'l nevr hav a real boyfriend. Hes just using u. He'll use u & then on trash day he'll thro u out w/ the other trash.

Well, someone needed a grammar lesson. Or at least enough sense to turn on autocorrect.

"Who's texting you?" JJ whipped his big golden-retriever head around as soon as he heard the ping. "Boyfriend?"

"Hardly."

Hollis didn't have a boyfriend. What Hollis had was Malory Keener and her size-zero wrecking crew, sending out their daily dose of love.

"No boyfriend?"

"No boyfriend."

Gunnar did not qualify as a boyfriend. Hollis didn't know what he qualified as, but it wasn't that. Given the clearly delineated social strata of high school, it should have been statistically impossible for a girl like Hollis Darby-Barnes to hook up with a guy like Gunnar Mott. It was also quite a feat to steal the limelight away from a girl like Malory Keener. Superslut that Hollis was, she'd managed to accomplish both in a single night. This happened way back on December 4, but the ripple effect was lasting.

Hollis didn't know why Gunnar kept coming back for more. Well, yes she did. Hollis's body was on the Kardashian growth plan and Gunnar was a guy. The real question was why *she* kept going back for more. Sure, Malory deserved it. And sure, Gunnar was gorgeous, in a generic, pass-me-the-football kind of way. But Hollis didn't *love* him or anything. They barely even talked. It was . . . hard to explain. But when Hollis was in the moment—when the two of them were under the bleachers, pressed up against the wrestling mats and it was just lips and tongues and hands and bellies and the smell of Big Red and boy sweat—she forgot about everything else. She forgot about Malory, she forgot about her mother, she forgot how angry and alone she felt. For a moment, she could disappear.

Maybe Gunnar wasn't using her. Maybe she was using him.

"Hey," Milo said. "I'm on."

Hollis deleted the text with her thumb. She stood up and walked over to Milo's desk.

"You want my seat?" JJ said, half rising.

"That's okay."

"Take it," he said. "I insist."

Hollis shook her head. "I like standing."

She didn't, actually. She liked sitting. And she was feeling lightheaded. Part of her wanted to run out of the room, but she wasn't sure why. It's not like her sperm donor was going to pop out of the computer and introduce himself. It wasn't even about him. This was the Donor Progeny Project, after all. This was about the progeny.

Progeny. It was a weird word now that Hollis thought about it. Was it weirder or less weird than *offspring*?

"So here," Milo said, pointing to a form on the screen, "is where I registered. I plugged in my name, my birthday, the city where I was born, the name of the cryobank, the donor number . . . and here . . ." He paused, opening a new tab. "is what I got back. Check it out."

Hollis leaned in.

Welcome to the Donor Progeny Project!

She closed her eyes for a second. Her heart was thumping so hard. She put her hand on the back of Milo's chair to steady herself.

"You okay?" JJ said.

"Why wouldn't I be okay?"

Hollis kept reading.

Our aim at the DPP is to assist you in making mutually desired contact with your genetic half siblings and to facilitate donor family connections. According to our records, sperm donations from **Donor #9677** of the **Twin Cities Cryolab** have resulted in five births to date. What does this mean? This means that you should take a breath.

"Holy crap," Hollis breathed.

"I know, right?" Milo turned to look at her. He was half smiling. There was a muffin crumb stuck to the corner of his mouth.

" 'Whatever you are feeling in this moment is completely normal,' " JJ read aloud. " 'Whatever you decide to do with this information, if anything, is up to you. There is no 'right' "—he paused, scratching quote marks in the air—" 'course of action.' "

Hollis looked at JJ, nodding stupidly. Even though she'd been thinking about it for thirty-six hours now, the magnitude of this moment—of actually being on the Donor Progeny Project website, of possibly finding her other half siblings—was still hard to comprehend.

"So?" Milo said.

"So," Hollis said.

"Do we want to post something?"

"Post something?"

"Everything's anonymous. If we post under Twin Cities Cryolab, our message gets relayed to whatever email accounts they have on record for our match families, but it uses a ghost email address for the sender, like Craigslist."

"Oh." Hollis nodded like she understood. "Uh-huh."

"That way it's up to us whether or not to share our contact information, depending on our comfort level. *Assuming* we get any response at all. Which we may not."

"Right." Hollis nodded.

"It would be so flipping cool if you did, though," JJ said.

"It would," Milo said. He looked at Hollis. "What do you think?"

Hollis hesitated. Her heart was beating hard. The blood that was rushing through her ears was so loud. "Okay."

" 'Okay,' you want to post something?"

"Okay."

"Are you sure?" Milo said.

"Yeah."

"Because . . . no pressure. I don't want to force you into anything."

"You're not," Hollis said. "Let's do it."

*　　*　　*

Dear Donor Siblings
(and/or Donor Siblings' Parents),

We're not sure exactly what to say so we're just going to throw this out there and see what happens. Our names are Milo (age 15) and Hollis (age 14). We met for the first time 7 years ago when our mothers discovered we were half siblings both conceived using donor sperm from the Twin Cities Cryolab in Minneapolis. Our donor was # 9677. We are hoping to make contact with our other half siblings. We welcome anything you would like to share with us. Ummm . . . not sure what else to write . . . Post back if you get this. Thanks!

—Milo and Hollis

With his right hand wrapped in frozen peas, it took Milo a long time to type. When he finally finished, he looked at Hollis. "Your turn."

"What?"

"Click Submit."

So Hollis reached over Milo's shoulder and clicked the mouse.

"'Congratulations!'" JJ read aloud. "'Your message has been added to the DPP database!'"

The three of them stared at the screen in silence. Who knows how long they sat there? Two minutes? Ten? At some point JJ started crunching on a piece of bacon, and Hollis felt her stomach clench. Was it hunger? Nerves? Regret? She didn't know what she was feeling. There was some quote from *The Great Gatsby*, but she couldn't remember the exact words. It was Nick Carraway feeling excited and disgusted at the same time.

"Hey." JJ turned to them, his expression earnest. "We should go bowling."

"Bowling?" Hollis looked at him blankly.

"It'll take your mind off things while you wait."

"There's that place on Thirty-Seventh," Milo offered. "Or there's Strike 10, on Strickland . . ."

"I'm thinking of a different place," JJ said.

"Where?"

"My basement."

*   *   *

"You have a bowling alley in your *house*?" Frankie gaped at JJ.

He shrugged. "My dad likes to bowl."

Hollis, Milo, and JJ were standing in the living room while Hollis's mother and Suzanne lounged on the couch with their coffee mugs and Frankie launched her interrogation.

"Will your father be home?" she asked JJ.

"He's in Budapest."

"What about your mother?"

"She's also in Budapest."

Frankie turned to Milo, shaking her head. "No. No way."

"Ma. Come on."

"Maxime will be there," JJ said.

"And who is Maxime?"

"My au pair. He lives with us."

Hollis nearly choked. "You have a manny?"

"What's a *manny*?" Leigh asked from the couch.

"A male nanny."

"He's not a manny," JJ said. "He's an au pair."

And Suzanne piped in, "I believe the preferred term is *child care provider*."

Milo grinned at JJ. "I prefer *manny*."

"You're just jealous. Maxime teaches me French. He's *trente-trois ans* and *très responsable*."

Hollis was impressed by JJ's French, but Frankie,

77

apparently, was not. Her mouth was set in a grim line. "What is Maxime's phone number?"

Wow, Hollis thought as Frankie proceeded to get on the horn with JJ's Belgian manny to check out his story. *Holy helicopter mom.* Frankie seemed satisfied with whatever answer she got, but as soon as she hung up the phone, she went right back to firing questions. How would they get to JJ's? How long were they planning to stay there? What would they do for lunch? Did Milo have his EpiPen? Did Hollis and JJ know how to use an EpiPen? Frankie opened a drawer in the kitchen, took out an EpiPen, and started giving them a tutorial. "First, you pop the cap. Then you slide it out. And—see this orange tip? It needs to be pointing down . . ." She went through the whole spiel, even grabbing Milo's thigh to show Hollis and JJ how to massage the injection site.

"Ma," Milo groaned. "Come on."

And Suzanne said, "Give the kid a break, Frank. Let him go have some fun."

Frankie turned to Suzanne, her expression inscrutable. Hollis was no relationship expert, so she wasn't exactly qualified to interpret the looks Milo's moms were exchanging, but there was definitely tension.

"Leigh?" Frankie shifted her gaze to Hollis's mother. "Are you comfortable with this?"

"Sure. Hollis has a cell phone."

"Thanks, Mom," Hollis said, although she had no idea

why she was thanking her mother. Leigh ran a loose ship. She treated Hollis like an adult. Last night, when the two of them were lying on the pullout couch in the living room, it struck Hollis that she couldn't remember a time when she and her mother had slept side by side. Not even when she was little. Not even when she had a bad dream. It was Pam whose name Hollis had called out in the middle of the night—Pam who had crawled into Hollis's bed and sung to her until she fell asleep. Not that Hollis mentioned this to her mother. No way. Leigh was in too good a mood last night—relaxed, probably from the wine she'd drunk at dinner. The last thing Hollis wanted was to turn on the waterworks.

Come to think of it, her mother looked pretty relaxed this morning, too, chilling on the couch with Suzanne, wearing jeans and a sweatshirt, hair loose, sipping from her coffee mug. Which begged the question, what was she really drinking from that coffee mug?

"Grab some money from my purse," Leigh said to Hollis. "I think it's on one of the stools in the kitchen."

"Thanks."

"Well then," Frankie said. "I guess you're going bowling." She forced a smile. "Have fun."

"Love you, Ma," Milo said, giving her a quick hug. "I'll call you when we get there."

"I love you, too."

Milo hugged Suzanne.

Hollis, feeling like a bad daughter, hugged her mother.

JJ, inexplicably and somewhat comically, walked around the room, hugging all three moms.

Finally, Milo, JJ, and Hollis stepped out the front door of the apartment building and into the world, where the sky was clear and the air was crisp and the tiny blue ice-melting pellets crunched beneath their feet. From behind them, Hollis could hear Frankie's disembodied voice calling, "Put on your hat! It's cold out there!"

*　*　*

JJ's basement was all shiny floors and vintage bowling signs suspended from the ceiling. Bowl-a-Rama. Lucky Strikes. Hi Roller. The wood-paneled walls were covered in bowling memorabilia: framed satin jackets with names embroidered on the lapels, championship patches, black-and-white photographs of old-time bowlers. Even the air smelled authentic, like popcorn and cigar smoke and feet.

"Wow," Hollis breathed.

JJ flicked a switch and the room filled with disco lights. "Cool, huh?"

"This is more than cool," Milo said, looking around. "This is a nostalgia piece. This is Americana. This"— Milo lowered himself onto a cracked leather bench, shaking his head in amazement—"is a movie set."

"Didn't you see it on New Year's Eve?"

"I was upstairs the whole time. On your computer, remember?"

"Right," JJ said.

Which brought them full circle, back to the Donor Progeny Project, which was the one thing they were trying to distract themselves from by going bowling.

"*Hé là*, JJ."

Maxime, JJ's skinny, scruffy-chinned Belgian manny who had greeted them at the door when they first arrived, suddenly materialized with a tray of food.

"Oh, hey, Max," JJ said.

"*Vous voulez manger ou quoi?*"

Hollis, who had five years of French under her belt, recognized the expression. *You want to eat or what?*

"*Mais oui,*" JJ said, taking the tray. "*Merci, Max.*"

"*Pas de prob, mon homme.*" Maxime gave JJ a fist bump, which didn't seem very Belgian to Hollis.

"*Merci, Max,*" Milo said.

The manny cocked his chin. "Later," he said, and sauntered out of the room in his skinny jeans.

JJ flashed a grin as he slid onto the bench beside Milo. "He'll be playing *Flames of Vengeance* until dinner." Then JJ reached into the chest pocket of his flannel shirt and pulled out a joint.

"Please tell me that's not what I think it is," Milo said.

"Okay, I won't."

"Frankie will *kill* me if I come home smelling like weed."

"She won't kill you," JJ said mildly, rummaging through his jeans for a lighter. "She'll kill *me*."

"Whatever," Milo said, waving a hand through the air. "Just smoke in the corner so I don't reek."

"Relax." JJ got up and walked a few paces to a Formica counter. He reached over the top and came up with an aerosol can. "Spritz yourself with this before you leave."

"Bowling shoe deodorizer?"

"Febreze." JJ spritzed the air a few times. "Long-lasting freshness."

Hollis had been staring in disbelief this whole time, not because she'd never seen a joint before but because JJ didn't seem like the type. "You're a pothead?"

JJ lit up. "I'm not a pothead."

"A stoner then."

He sucked hard on the joint, held his breath, then let it out slowly. "I wouldn't paint myself with that brush." He turned to Milo. "Would you paint me with that brush?"

"You do smoke a lot of weed, man."

JJ shrugged. "I like it."

"Numbing," Hollis said.

JJ cocked an eyebrow at her. "Excuse me?"

"*Numbing*," she repeated. "N-U-M-B-I-N-G."

"I know how to spell."

"Numbing is like armor," Hollis explained. "It keeps you from feeling. Pot, Twinkies, alcohol—they're all the same thing. After Pam died, my mom started drinking wine."

Hollis wasn't sure how much her mother used to drink or whether she was ever technically an alcoholic. All she remembered was Leigh filling a glass every night in front of the fireplace. She remembered how the wine always seemed to make her mother cry. Drink, cry, drink, cry, drink, cry. And then she remembered the morning when her mother suddenly announced at breakfast, "I'm not going to drink anymore."

Hollis was ten. Maybe eleven. It was around the same time when Leigh started attending the Parents Without Partners grief group in the basement of the Congregational church. Every time the group met, Hollis would have to stay with their neighbor, Mrs. Brennigan, whose house smelled like cabbage.

"I've been numbing my feelings with alcohol," Hollis's mother announced that morning. "I need to walk through the pain. I need to let grief in the front door." More feeling, less numbing: this was her mother's new mantra. From that moment forward—until last night, anyway—Hollis hadn't seen her touch a drop of alcohol.

"Who's Pam?" JJ said.

Hollis shook her head. "That's not the point. The point is—"

"Pam was her mom."

Hollis shot Milo a look. "She wasn't my *mom*. She was my mother's *partner*. We weren't even biologically related."

"I'm not biologically related to my parents," JJ said, "but I still refer to them as Mom and Dad."

"That's different."

"How?"

"They adopted you."

"So?"

"Pam couldn't adopt me."

"Why not?"

Hollis felt herself getting agitated. "Because she and my mother weren't married. Because she had no legal rights. Who the hell cares? She wasn't my mom and that wasn't even my point." Hollis waved her arm in JJ's direction. "You're *numbing* was my point, okay? Jesus!"

JJ held out the joint. "Want a toke?"

Hollis stared at him. "No, I do not want a *toke*."

"It'll make you feel better."

Hollis snorted. "Now you sound like a drug dealer."

"That's hurtful," JJ said. "That hurts me right here." He patted his heart.

"No wonder you're numbing," Milo said, "with Hollis saying such hurtful things."

Hollis rolled her eyes. "Shut up. Let's bowl."

MILO

MILO GOT CREAMED IN BOWLING, WHICH TURNED OUT TO be a more enjoyable experience than he would have thought. On the subway home, Hollis sat back in her seat, flushed. "That was fun."

"I'm so glad my gutter balls amused you."

"You were really bad."

"Excuse me—" Milo held up his right ring finger for her to appreciate. There was a dent in the nail where the door had slammed into it, and the blood pooling underneath had started to turn purple. "You try bowling lefty."

"Excuses, excuses." Hollis waved her hand dismissively. "If JJ hadn't kept making me laugh I would have beaten him, too."

"I don't know if he'll be able to walk in the morning

after some of those spin moves. I think he gave himself whiplash."

Hollis smirked. "I thought pot made most people sit in awkward silence or . . . I don't know . . . talk about conspiracy theories and alien life forms."

"JJ Rabinowitz is not most people."

"No, he is not."

"He walks to the beat of his own drummer, as they say."

"Yes." Hollis nodded agreeably. "He sure does."

"He was right about Pam, though."

Hollis narrowed her eyes. "What does that have to do with anything?"

"I'm just saying."

"Well . . . don't."

Milo thought for a minute, trying to decide how to proceed. "Hollis," he said finally. "Here's the thing . . . laws don't make someone a mom. Neither do genetics. Mothering makes someone a mom."

"I know that."

"Good."

Hollis turned and looked out the window. She was telling him the conversation was over. He got that. But she was only here until tomorrow, which didn't give them much time to discuss anything. He tried again. "It's the same for our donor. *Genetically*, he may be our father, but that doesn't mean—"

"Don't," Hollis said to the window. "Please. I'm messed up enough about Pam. I don't need you bringing him into it."

"I hear you," Milo said. "And I respect your feelings. But if we start getting emails from his other kids, and they want—"

"Milo." Hollis turned to him, her expression pained. "Shut up."

"Okay," he said.

"One train wreck at a time."

"Got it."

They sat in silence for a while, buffered by the random sounds of the subway. The squeal of metal. The thump of music coming from someone's headphones. Laughter. When the doors opened at Carroll Street, a family stepped on. Tall blond dad, short blond mom, two small blond boys dressed in puffy vests and snow boots. A matched set. It was the kind of sight that always gave Milo a pang in the stomach—that made him look away.

"Do you regret coming here?" he blurted.

"No," Hollis said. "But if you can't keep your mouth shut for the next fifteen minutes, I will."

"Duly noted."

*   *   *

Most parents would enjoy a break from their children. A chance to relax. A chance to recharge the old batteries. Suzanne could do that no problem. But Frankie? Milo couldn't imagine it. Whenever he went out somewhere, Frankie's mind was all, *What if Milo accidentally eats a pistachio and goes into anaphylactic shock and drops his EpiPen down a sewer drain before he can stab himself in the leg?* It was paranoid thinking, and it drove him crazy. Like now, as he and Hollis walked through the front door and into the kitchen where their moms were sitting. Leigh and Suzanne waved and kept talking, but Frankie stood up immediately. "You're back," she said, crushing Milo in a hug, smelling like soap and hair gel.

"You told us two thirty," he said. "It's two thirty."

How old did she think he was? When Milo was in kindergarten, Frankie used to read him this book about a bunny that kept running away. Wherever the bunny went, his mother always showed up. Hiding among flowers, fishing him out of a river, disguising herself as a cloud so she could look out for him. At the time, Milo had found the story comforting. It made him feel *safe*—but thinking about it now, he felt bad for the bunny. He understood the bunny on a whole new level.

"How was bowling?" Frankie said. Milo could tell she was doing a sniff test, but she must not have smelled JJ's weed because she stepped back and squeezed his shoulder.

We drank grain alcohol with peanut butter chasers, Milo was tempted to say but didn't. "Fun," he said.

"I kicked his butt," Hollis said.

"Woot woot!" Hollis's mother gave a cheer, lifting both hands to the ceiling.

Hollis stared at her. "What are you *doing*?"

"I'm raising the roof."

"Why?"

"Isn't that what you kids do? To celebrate?"

Suzanne nodded. "That's what they do."

"When have I *ever* raised the roof?" Milo said.

"What is this," Hollis said, "1990?"

Suzanne sighed. "Look at them, Leigh, united in their mutual disdain for us. Just like brother and sister."

It was the first time Milo had seen Hollis's mom smile. She had the same crooked eyeteeth as Hollis. Which was weird, because at JJ's house, JJ had pointed out that Milo and Hollis both smiled to the left.

Hollis wasn't smiling now, though. She was rolling her eyes. Watching her expressions change was like watching a real-time weather map on TV. At JJ's: mostly sunny. On the ride home: partly cloudy with a low-pressure system moving in from the south. Sometimes, when Milo looked at Hollis, he felt a flash of recognition. He thought he saw something familiar, but then he would wonder, was it real or was it just because he knew they shared DNA?

"What?" Hollis said to Milo.

"Nothing."

"Do I have something on my face?"

"Yeah," Milo said. "A nose."

"Hardy har har."

"They have the same nose." Suzanne squinted across the table. She lowered her glasses from their perch on top of her head. "Don't they have the same nose?"

"They do," Leigh said. "And the same jawline."

Milo groaned inwardly. No good would come of this conversation. He looked over at Frankie, who had begun to scrub furiously at the counter with a dishrag, seeing spots no one else could see.

"So, Ma," he said. "What's the plan for the rest of the day?"

"Well," Frankie said, looking up from the counter with a smile that was clearly pasted on. "I was thinking about the Museum of Natural History."

"Really?" Milo had been to the Museum of Natural History probably a hundred times. They were members. He could lead the way blindfolded.

"Leigh and Hollis have never been there," Frankie said defensively. "I thought they might enjoy it."

"I'm sure we'll love it," Leigh said.

And Suzanne said, "It really is amazing."

Milo backpedaled. "Sounds good." Then, turning to Hollis, "Sister?"

Hollis smirked, conveying half-sibling telepathy. "I've never met a pterodactyl I didn't like."

*　*　*

Milo, Hollis, Suzanne, Frankie, and Leigh wandered the Hall of Human Origins. They saw the mural of primate evolution and Lucy, the first hominid skeleton. They saw the Peking Man, the Neanderthals, and the Cro-Magnons. They did not discuss the emerging field of genomics. They did not reflect on the origin or evolution of their particular hominid family. They did not address the mastodon in the living room because no one wanted to wake the mastodon. Milo and Hollis kept their mouths shut, but they were edgy and amped and waiting for potentially life-altering emails that might or might not come, and they hadn't even told their mothers about their post.

The sperm donor kids in the Hall of Human Origins. It was an *SNL* skit, a mockumentary, a joke waiting for a punch line. Every so often, Milo slid his phone out of his pocket and casually checked his mail.

"Anything?" Hollis said.

"Not yet."

Taco Pacifico was packed, as it always was on Saturday nights. The general din of conversation was accompanied by the mariachi band playing on the other side of the room.

"I can never decide," Suzanne was saying, "between the chimichangas and the enchiladas . . ."

"You can't go wrong with the chimichangas," Frankie said.

Milo didn't hear the ping of a new email, but since he'd set his phone to vibrate, he felt a buzz against his belly.

"I'm a fajita girl myself," Leigh said.

At least, Milo assumed it was Leigh. He couldn't actually see her lips move because he was pretending to read his menu while simultaneously sliding his phone out of his sweatshirt pocket. *No devices at the table.* This was one of Frankie's cardinal rules. Right up there with *ten o'clock bedtime* and *no TV during the week.*

"What about you, Holl?"

Under the table, Milo opened Mail.

"I don't know. Steak tacos, probably."

49fef37429120a0b3@reply.DonorProgenyProject.org
Re: Post

It was staring right at him, the ghost-mail address, the reply to their post, so . . . undeniable. It was like seeing Hayley Christenson enter a room, a sudden swarm of bees filling his chest. Milo turned to Hollis, who was plunging a tortilla chip into a bowl of salsa. "Look at this," he murmured.

"What?"

He poked her leg with his phone.

Hollis looked down. "Is that—"

"Yup."

"Oh my God."

"I know."

"Open it," she whispered.

Milo tapped the subject line. And bam.

From: 49fef37429120a0b3@reply
.DonorProgenyProject.org

To: MiloRobClark@brooklynIDS.org

Date: Saturday, January 2, at 6:23 PM

Subject: Re: Post

Dear Milo and Hollis,

I think my heart literally stopped beating when my parents showed me your email. They've been members of the Donor Progeny Project since I was born but have never been contacted until today. The irony is that they were going to let me start searching myself on my 16th birthday, which happens to be next month, but when your post got routed to my mom's Gmail, they showed it to me right away. I think I've spent the last three hours trying not to pass out. (In a good way!)

My name is Abby Fenn and I was conceived with donor sperm from the Twin Cities Cryolab. My Donor # was also 9677.

Milo and Hollis were so caught up in reading that they didn't hear the waitress, who had arrived to take their order, or Suzanne, who was practically shouting to be heard from across the table.

"Milo!"

He looked up. "What?"

Suzanne gestured to the waitress, who was looking at him expectantly.

"Oh. Sorry." Milo ordered what he always ordered: vegetable fajitas with rice-flour tortillas, from the gluten-free, nut-free section of the menu.

"Tell Alejandra that this order is for Milo Robinson-Clark," Frankie instructed. "She uses a special pan."

"Got it," the waitress said.

"It is very, *very* important that his food be cooked separately, due to his severe food allergies."

"I understand." The waitress paused, making a note on her pad.

Out of the corner of his eye, Milo could see that Hollis was still hunched over, reading the email.

"And for you?"

Still reading.

"Holl?" Leigh said. "Honey?"

Milo nudged Hollis in the ribs and her head snapped up. "Okay! So apparently Milo and I have a sister and her name is Abby." The moms stared across the table. Hollis held up Milo's phone. "She lives in Sheboygan, Wisconsin."

"Could you repeat that, please?" Frankie said, a tortilla chip dangling limply from her hand.

"Which part?"

"Everything."

"We found our sister. Her name is Abby Fenn. She lives in Sheboygan, Wisconsin. And oh—" Hollis turned to the waitress. "I'll have the steak tacos."

"She'll have the steak tacos," Milo repeated, and he didn't know why, maybe it was a tension release, but he started to laugh. And once he started he couldn't stop. The waitress left, looking confused, and Hollis and the three moms just sat there, watching him, waiting for him to finish.

"Milo," Frankie said, when he finally stopped snorting long enough to take a sip of water, "you are my son, and no matter what happens . . . no matter how many people you find who share your DNA . . . that will never change. I need you to know that. Because your mother and I . . ." Her voice cracked, but she kept going. "We're the ones who brought you home from the hospital. We're the ones who wrapped you in that little yellow blanket. Remember, Suz? The one with the ducks?"

"I remember," Suzanne said, squeezing Frankie's forearm.

"I still have that blanket," Frankie said fiercely. "I will always have that blanket. Do you understand what I'm saying?" She looked at Milo.

"Yeah," he said.

"You are my boy."

"I know."

"I am your mom."

"I know, Ma."

"Do you?"

Milo started to speak when Suzanne suddenly brought both pinkies to her mouth and gave an ear-piercing whistle.

"Mom, don't—" Milo said, but she was already on her

feet, flagging down the mariachi band. This was a classic Suzanne Robinson move. Imbuing the moment with a theme song, so that Milo would forever associate finding his new half sister with four men in sombreros singing "La Bamba."

"A toast," Suzanne said brightly, lifting her margarita in the air. "To Abby from Sheboygan, Wisconsin. May she be as brilliant and beautiful and open-minded as Milo and Hollis."

"Hear, hear," Leigh said, raising her water glass.

Frankie still looked shell-shocked, but she raised her glass anyway, and so did Milo and Hollis, and everyone clinked, and then Suzanne announced that she only knew one other person from Sheboygan, Wisconsin—Brett Lemmon—and he was a real jackass. And the conversation suddenly veered from half siblings to jackasses, with all of them telling their best jackass stories and laughing. And to the mariachi band—the four mustachioed gentlemen with their vihuelas and maracas—they probably looked just like a regular family.

HOLLIS

SHE WAS IN THE MIDDLE OF A DREAM WHEN MILO WOKE her the next morning. It was a pretty steamy dream. She was hooking up with Gunnar in the janitor's closet at school. (They had actually done this once, in the middle of fifth-period lunch, and it had been rather thrilling.) Anyway, Gunnar had his hand up Hollis's shirt and she had her hand on his zipper and they were making out like crazy among the mops and buckets when she heard, "Hey. Wake up."

Hollis kept her eyes closed and ignored the voice.

"Come on. It's ten o'clock."

She tried to will herself back to sleep, back to the janitor's closet, but a hand was on her arm, shaking it. She opened her eyes and there was Milo. Jeans. Sweatshirt. Rat's nest hair. And there was Pete. Mournful eyes. Doggy breath.

Hollis closed her eyes and groaned. "Go away."

"I can't."

"Why not?"

"Because you're leaving in two hours and we need to do something before you go."

"What?"

"You know how we wrote back to Abby last night?"

Hollis opened one eye. "Yeah."

"Now we have to write back to Noah."

"What?"

Milo flashed her a grin. "You heard me."

Hollis sat up. "We have a brother?"

"Actually, we have two brothers. Noah and Josh are twins."

"Oh my God."

"Yeah. But Josh doesn't want anything to do with this. Apparently, he's really close with their dad, who couldn't have kids of his own because he has low sperm motility, so he feels threatened by the whole donor thing. That's the word Noah used—'threatened.' Noah's not that close with their dad, but their mom, who's the one who got our email, thinks it's important for each of them to make their own decision. So they had some big family meeting and the upshot was . . . Noah wanted to contact us, but Josh didn't."

Hollis stared at Milo. "Oh my God."

"I know."

"Is this really happening?"

"This is really happening."

"Because I feel like I'm on one of those TV shows." Hollis was half serious when she flung her legs over the edge of the pullout couch and looked around the living room. "Am I being punked?"

"No," Milo said. "But you might want to put on some pants."

"Why?"

"JJ's here."

"What? Where?"

"Don't get dressed on my account!" JJ called from somewhere outside the living room. "I don't mind!"

Hollis shot Milo a look. "Seriously?"

Milo grinned. "He is who he is."

*   *   *

From: MiloRobClark@brooklynIDS.org
To: 8007jq3wrhj267lp634@reply
.DonorProgenyProject.org; AbsofSteel3
@sheboygancountryday.edu
Date: Sunday, January 3, at 10:27 AM
Subject: Noah, Abby. Abby, Noah.

Abby Fenn, 15 (Sheboygan, Wisconsin), meet Noah Resnick, 17 (Winnetka, Illinois). Noah, meet Abby.

Hollis is flying home to MN this afternoon and she doesn't have a DPP account, so to include her in any future emails, please cc HollisDarbs @MNPSmail.org. Thanks!

—Milo and Hollis

From: NoahZark.Rez@techHSmail.com
To: MiloRobClark@brooklynIDS.org; AbsofSteel3 @sheboygancountryday.edu; HollisDarbs @MNPSmail.org
Date: Sunday, January 3, at 11:04 AM
Subject: Nice to meet you

Hey Milo, Hollis, and Abby. Showed my mom your email. She's having a spaz. *Ask them for pictures! I want to see what they look like!* Is anyone else's mom flipping out?

—Noah

From: AbsofSteel3@sheboygancountryday.edu
To: NoahZark.Rez@techHSmail.com;
   MiloRobClark@brooklynIDS.org; HollisDarbs
   @MNPSmail.org
Date: Sunday, January 3, at 11:23 AM
Subject: Nice to meet you, too

My mom is unflappable. She's a midwife who's been wearing the same Birkenstocks since 1994, if that tells you anything. And my dad is a research scientist, so he's being very cerebral and scientific about the whole thing. It's my sister who's all, "You're going to break Dad's heart. Our family will never be the same and it will all be your fault." But then, Becca's prone to drama on a daily basis. Does anyone else have siblings?

—Abby

From: NoahZark.Rez@techHSmail.com

To: AbsofSteel3@sheboygancountryday.edu;
MiloRobClark@brooklynIDS.org; HollisDarbs
@MNPSmail.org

Date: Sunday, January 3, at 11:36 AM

Subject: One brother

I have a fraternal twin, Josh. As I told Milo and
Hollis, he doesn't want to make contact with any
genetic siblings or with our donor. He thinks that
would be a slap in the face to our dad. Abby, is
your sister from #9677 too?

—Noah

From: AbsofSteel3@sheboygancountryday.edu

To: NoahZark.Rez@techHSmail.com;
MiloRobClark@brooklynIDS.org; HollisDarbs
@MNPSmail.org

Date: Sunday, January 3, at 11:58 AM

Subject: Nope

Funny story. About 17 years ago, when my mom
was trying to get pregnant, my dad was diagnosed
with oligospermia, which basically means low
sperm count. The odds of them conceiving a baby

together were slim to nil, so they started looking into donor sperm. Enter #9677. My mom got pregnant with me, and then, two months after I was born, surprise! She found out she was pregnant again. Turns out my dad had a few swimmers after all. Becca is 11 months younger than I am. What's weird is I've known her my whole life, and I think of her as my sister 100%, but we only share 50% of our DNA. You guys are just as related to me as she is.

—Abby

From: NoahZark.Rez@techHSmail.com
To: AbsofSteel3@sheboygancountryday.edu;
   MiloRobClark@brooklynIDS.org; HollisDarbs
   @MNPSmail.org
Date: Sunday, January 3, at 12:13 PM
Subject: Even weirder . . .

Josh and I are twins, we have the same biological parents and we're growing up in the same house, and we are NOTHING alike. Riddle me that, Batman.

—Noah

The emailing started in the morning and continued through lunch, through the packing of bags. JJ carried Hollis and Leigh's suitcase out of the living room and was now standing in the front hall, chomping on a Twizzler, while Milo read aloud from Noah's latest email. "*'Riddle me that, Batman.'*" Milo looked up from his phone. "A comic book fan?"

"Or a writer of fan fiction," Hollis said.

"Or one of those guys who paints his face green and throws on some tights," JJ said, "and goes to one of those . . . whaddayacallems."

"Comic-Con?" Hollis said.

"Right."

JJ was grinning, but now, as Milo's moms strode through the doorway and began bustling Hollis and Leigh outside to the waiting cab, his expression suddenly turned serious. "Hey," he said, grabbing Hollis's elbow as she stepped onto the sidewalk.

"What?"

"Let me have your phone real quick."

"Why?"

"So I can put in my number."

"Why would I want your number?"

"In case you can't sleep one night and the urge to call me becomes overwhelming."

"I sleep like a baby," she lied.

"You never know," he said. "There could be an earthquake. Or a tsunami . . ."

"In Minnesota?"

"Stranger things have happened." JJ held out his freakishly large hand. "Come on."

Hollis sighed. She reached into her coat pocket. She gave Jonah Jedediah Rabinowitz her phone.

"If you prefer," he said, punching away with his thumbs, "you can think of this as a bowling hotline. Twenty-four-hour assistance. Next time you're out with your girlfriends, playing a little ten-pin, and you need help with your technique . . . call me."

"Ha," Hollis said, trying to snort but not quite pulling it off. She was smiling. JJ was funny, dammit. She didn't want him to be funny. And she didn't want him to be cute, either. She didn't want him to have big, brown Labrador-retriever eyes or floppy blond hair or ridiculously warm fingers brushing the inside of her wrist as he handed back her phone.

"You won't regret this, Hollis Darby."

Hollis rolled her eyes and walked over to the taxi, where everyone was waiting.

"What was that?" Milo whispered.

"Nothing."

"I beg to differ."

"Beg away."

"He likes you," Milo said.

"Shut up. He does not."

"Want to know what he said?"

"No."

"He said if he ever has a daughter he wants her to turn out like you. Smart and feisty."

"He did not say that."

"I swear to God," Milo said. "Also, you have great gams."

Hollis raised her eyebrows. "*Gams?*"

"Legs."

"I know what they *are*," Hollis said, irritated, "but who under the age of ninety uses the word *gams?*"

"JJ Rabinowitz."

Hollis glanced over her shoulder. JJ was standing twenty feet away, saluting the cab like a soldier.

"Look at him," Milo said.

"Whatever."

Hollis's cheeks were so hot she thought they might burst into flames. She was both relieved and sorry when Frankie announced that they needed to say goodbye or Hollis and Leigh would miss their flight.

Now came the hugging. Hollis was not a big hugger. With the exception of saying good night to her mother and making out with Gunnar Mott in the janitor's closet, she barely touched anyone. She couldn't remember the last time she'd received multiple hugs. Pam's funeral, probably.

All those women from the Family Equality Council, where Pam used to volunteer. And the line cooks from Pam's restaurant. Everyone coming at Hollis en masse, shoving casseroles in her face, patting her head, squeezing the breath out of her just like Suzanne was doing now.

"It was *so* good to see you, sweetheart," Suzanne said, stepping back as she released Hollis.

"So good," Frankie said, moving in for a turn.

"Thanks," Hollis said, nodding like a bobblehead.

"Hey," Milo said, leaning in to give Hollis a quick squeeze and release. "Don't be a stranger."

"I won't," she said.

"Join the group email when you get home."

"I will."

"Who knows," Milo said, "maybe by the time you land we'll have another sibling."

"Maybe."

Milo grinned and Hollis nodded, and it was fine for a few seconds, but then it got weird again. Because really, when Hollis thought about it, even though she and Milo were 50 percent related and had just spent two-plus days together, it wasn't like they *knew* each other. They were still basically strangers. And what was weirder than two strangers hugging on the street?

Answer: Hollis's mother suddenly suggesting that, if Milo and his moms didn't have plans for Presidents' Day weekend, they should fly to Saint Paul and spend a few days at Hollis's house.

"We'll take you on a tour of the Twin Cities," Leigh said brightly. "We'll show you all our favorite haunts."

And before you could say "Mall of America," Milo said, "I'm in."

*　*　*

Hollis and her mother were almost to the airport. Noah's emails had petered out, but Abby's were still going strong.

"She wants to be a writer," Hollis said, looking up from her phone. "A *memoirist*."

Leigh, who was sitting in the front of the taxi, turned around. "Really?"

"The next Augusten Burroughs."

"Who?"

"You know—that author with the bizarre childhood? Who went to live with his mother's psychiatrist?"

Leigh shook her head.

"Doesn't matter," Hollis said, looking down at Abby's email. "Listen . . . 'I guess I want to find my donor not just because I'm curious, but because I need something to write about. Something real. Something raw and heart wrenching and deeply personal. Because how am I ever going to get into NYU, followed by the Iowa Writers' Workshop, by writing about a 16-year-old honors student and her nice middle-class family living in Sheboygan, Wisconsin? No one would read past the first sentence. They would die of boredom. My life is like a pair of khaki pants, clean and pressed with a crease down the middle. If I want to be the next Augusten Burroughs, I need rips and stains, cigarette burns and blood splatters.'" Hollis laughed, a deep, staccato "Ha!"

"Blood splatters?" Leigh said faintly. "Talk about disturbing . . ."

"She's being *metaphorical*, Mom. God."

It bugged Hollis that her mother didn't appreciate literature—that her idea of reading was *Bon Appétit*, the cooking magazine Pam used to subscribe to, and that Hollis's mother continued to renew every year even though she didn't cook. Did she even know what a metaphor was? Did she think that when Thoreau wrote "I wanted to suck out all the marrow of life" he was literally chewing on a bone? Had she even *read Walden*?

Our donor was an English major. The words sprang into Hollis's head without her bidding. Milo had dropped that little nugget on her the day she arrived—when they were up in his room, talking about books. "Our donor was an English major." Followed by, "Our donor is lactose intolerant," and "Our donor can juggle." Milo had shared these bits of trivia casually, as though mentioning a celebrity he'd read about in *Us Weekly*. He stopped sharing when Hollis told him to stop. She didn't want to know anything about their donor. She didn't give a crap that Milo had memorized the "personal profile" for #9677. Hollis's mother had a copy, too, and Hollis never wanted to see it. Her mother could burn it for all she cared. And yet . . . *Our donor was an English major.* This was the news crawl ticking across the screen in Hollis's mind as she stared at her mother.

"I know what a metaphor is," Leigh said, looking wounded.

Hollis felt like a jerk. She never meant to hurt her mother; it just happened. She wasn't even sure what was bugging her. This weekend had been fine. Better than fine, even. Maybe it was all the hugging. Maybe it was finding three new siblings in less than twenty-four hours. Maybe it was too much too soon.

"Why didn't you ask me?" Hollis blurted. Their cab was jockeying for position among the other cabs outside JFK, triple-parking in front of the American Airlines terminal.

"What's that?" Leigh said, but she wasn't responding to Hollis's question. She was thanking the driver. She handed him a bunch of bills. She and Hollis stepped out of the cab and retrieved their suitcase.

"Why didn't you ask me?" Hollis repeated as they walked through the double doors to the ticket counter.

"Ask you what?" her mother said.

"About Presidents' Day weekend. You just went ahead and invited Milo and his moms without even asking."

"I thought you had a good time this weekend."

"I did."

Her mother raised her eyebrows. Pale blond. So light they were almost nonexistent.

"But what if I had plans for Presidents' Day weekend? Did you even think about that?"

"Do you?"

"No. But I could have."

Her mother wheeled her suitcase forward in line. "I'm sorry. I should have consulted you first. It's just . . ." She fiddled with the zipper on her purse. "This weekend was really . . . it's the first time I can remember that I felt . . ." She hesitated, took a breath. "Pam and I used to have people over all the time when you were little. Do you remember?"

"No."

"Pammy loved a full house. She loved laughter and chaos and kids tearing around and everyone eating her food. She wanted us to have *that* house, you know? Where everyone was welcome."

Hollis stood quietly, bracing for impact.

"But that's not even my point." Hollis's mother shook

her head. She fixed Hollis with her eyes. "My point is . . . it's okay to be scared."

"Scared," Hollis repeated. "And what am I scared of exactly?"

"Scared of letting people in. Scared of getting close to anyone you might actually start to care about. Milo, Frankie, Suzanne. Your new half siblings. It's a lot to cope with at once."

Hollis smirked. "Okay, Doctor Phil."

"I'm not just talking about you," her mother said, ignoring Hollis's sarcasm. "I'm talking about me, too."

Ahead of Hollis in line were two shaggy-haired boys with headphones on, plugged into their devices. Zapping aliens, racing through the Mushroom Kingdom, Minecrafting their way into oblivion. Even though she hated video games, Hollis would give anything to be one of those boys right now, just for a few minutes, to disappear into one of their worlds where everything was logical and methodical and no one was trying to climb inside her head.

"Holl," her mother said after a bit, and Hollis realized she'd been spacing out.

"What?"

"I said it's okay to be scared. It's a natural part of the grief process. It's actually very healthy to—"

"Mom."

"What?"

"It's been seven years. I am not grieving."

"There's no statute of limitations on grief."

"You should put that on a T-shirt."

Her mother smiled. "Maybe I will."

"Mom."

"Yeah?"

Hollis hesitated, not sure what she wanted to say until it came out of her mouth. "Can we stop talking about this?"

Her mother's eyes were soft and just a little sad. "Yes. We can."

MILO

IT WAS JJ'S IDEA. JJ—WHO ON SUNDAY NIGHT HAD CALLED
Milo to see if Hollis had made it home safely (she had)
and to see if there were any new emails from Abby and
Noah (there were). Now, on Thursday morning, it was
JJ's idea to turn it into a research project.

Sophomore Science Palooza. It was a stupid name, but
Mr. Bonducci, their third-period Life Science teacher, presented the guidelines with his usual gravity.

This was an eight-week assignment.

Students should choose a topic worthy of intensive
study.

They could work alone or with a partner.

The project would count for 65 percent of their second-
semester grade.

"I am giving you," Mr. Bonducci said, weaving his way

through the classroom, dropping packets onto lab tables, "a list of suggested research topics . . . a list of websites . . . a list of scientific journals . . . and the grading rubric that I will be using to assess your work . . . You will be using today's class period to decide upon an area of study. By the end of the week you should have a working hypothesis . . ."

"You won't be needing this," JJ said, sliding the packet out from under Milo's hand before he could pick it up.

"Why not?"

"I already know what we're doing."

"What *we're* doing?"

"Yes."

"*We.*"

JJ Rabinowitz, laziest lab partner ever, barely scraping by with a C-minus, grinned. "You and me, babe."

"No."

"Are you ready for this?"

"No."

"Because *this* is a kick-ass idea."

"Let me guess," Milo said. "You want to research the effects of daily marijuana use on the teenage brain."

"Nope."

"I'm sorry. You want to research the effects of *hourly* marijuana use on the teenage brain."

"Nope. I want to research your family."

"What?"

116

"A genetics project. You, Hollis, alleles, genotypes, phenotypes, dominant traits, recessive traits, all of it."

Milo stared at JJ.

"Say you had a picture of your donor—"

"I don't."

"Okay, but say you did. And say you had pictures of all your donor's kids. And you had pictures of all of their family members. If someone—Joe Shmoe off the street, who didn't know any of them—if Joe Shmoe tried to sort out who was related to who just by looking at physical traits . . . would he be able to guess which people were a genetic match? I hypothesize that he would."

Milo opened his mouth, closed it, opened it again. "Why are you getting a C-minus in Life Science?"

"Because I don't *apply* myself. Because I don't *work to my potential.*"

"But . . . you actually know what you're talking about. Where did you learn all that?"

JJ shrugged. "I've done a little reading."

"Because of me?"

"No, man. Because of me."

Milo felt like a jackass. This whole time, it hadn't even occurred to him how JJ might be feeling. Besides sharing the fact that he was adopted, JJ didn't talk about it. He'd never mentioned birth parents or long-lost siblings or anything, and Milo had never thought to ask.

"Do you . . ." Milo hesitated. "I mean, do your parents . . . are they open to . . ."

"We don't talk about it."

Milo nodded.

"It's not the same, anyway. Giving away a kid and giving away sperm. They're just . . . not the same."

Milo waited for JJ to say more, but nothing came. What came was tinkling laugher from across the room.

Milo didn't need to look to see who was laughing. He knew that laugh. Just like he knew where Hayley Christenson was sitting (left corner, by the window) and what she was wearing (blue sweater, cowboy boots). Today her hair was braided on the side. Today she was chewing gum. Today she had tiny silver hoops in her ears. Milo didn't need to look to see who was laughing, but he looked anyway. Which was a mistake.

"She's cute, huh?" JJ said.

"Who?"

"That girl Hayley."

Milo shrugged. "If you like the type."

"Your eyes are bugging out of your head."

"She's being loud." Milo looked down at the packet. "Should I start filling out this sheet?"

"What you should *do* is talk to her."

"She doesn't know I exist."

118

"That can be remedied." JJ raised his hand like he was hailing a cab. "Yo, Hayley!"

"What are you doing?" Milo said, panic setting in.

"I'm helping a brother out."

"You're not my brother. I don't need a brother. Seriously. Don't think you're doing me a favor by—"

But she was already standing up. She was weaving her way through the maze of lab tables. She was standing right there in front of him. Blue sweater. Side braid. Lip gloss shimmering in the light. Milo's first instinct was to reach out and touch her, just to see what she felt like, but that would make him a weirdo. His next instinct was to dive under the table and never come out, but that would make him a freak.

"Hayley," JJ said, "you know Milo."

"Sure," Hayley said. "Hey, Milo."

"Hey, Hayley."

Milo's voice cracked. He heard it, and JJ heard it, and Hayley heard it, and no one would mention it, but there it was.

"So," JJ said, "have you come up with a project yet?"

Hayley nodded. "Yeah. Aromatherapy."

"Aromatherapy?"

"It's a hobby of mine. Did you know that different scents can affect your mood and productivity?"

"I did *not* know that. Milo, did you know that?"

Milo shook his head.

"It's true," Hayley said. "Smell is our strongest sense. Lemon, lavender, rosemary, cinnamon . . . inhaling those essential oils can literally change how we feel. They can activate our immune systems and lower our blood pressure."

"Wow," JJ said. "That's cool. Isn't that cool, Milo?"

Milo nodded.

"Speaking of cool," JJ said, "my lab partner here has come up with this kick-ass project, and we wanted to see if you would be willing to participate."

Milo stared at JJ.

"Me?" Hayley said.

"We need someone who doesn't know Milo very well, and I will tell you why. You see, Milo has a unique family situation . . ." JJ turned to Milo. "Permission to divulge?"

Milo nodded again. He didn't trust his voice.

"Did you know he has two moms?"

Hayley shrugged. "Half the kids in Brooklyn have two moms."

"Right. So you know what a sperm donor is?"

"Yeah."

"Have you heard of the Donor Progeny Project?"

Hayley shook her head.

120

"Okay," JJ said. "We'll start at the beginning." He leaned back in his chair, folded both hands behind his head, and kicked his feet up on the table.

"Mr. Rabinowitz," Mr. Bonducci called from across the room.

"Yeah, Mr. B?"

"Feet on the floor, please."

"You got it, Mr. B."

JJ lowered his feet and leaned in. When he finished talking, Hayley turned to Milo, her eyes wide.

"You found four of your brothers and sisters?"

"Half brothers and sisters. Yeah."

"And now you're going to find your dad?"

Milo looked at Hayley. Her eyes were even bluer than her sweater. "My genetic father. Yeah."

"You're going to track down the man who gave you life so you can get a picture of him for this project?"

Track down the man who gave you life. It sounded so Sherlock Holmes. Until that moment, all Milo had really thought about doing was emailing the cryolab to ask for his donor's contact info, which wasn't exactly hardcore detective work. But here he was nodding. Here he was saying, "Yeah."

"Oh my God." Hayley blinked. And for reasons that completely eluded Milo, she leaned over and hugged him. "That's the most amazing thing I ever heard."

In the second before she pulled away, he caught a whiff of her—flowery shampoo, Juicy Fruit, dryer sheets—that made his head spin. Not that he was trying to smell her or anything.

"I will totally help you," Hayley said. Meaning that she would look at a bunch of pictures that Milo A) didn't have, and B) had no idea how to get—and she would guess which of the people in these hypothetical photographs were genetically linked.

"Thanks," Milo said.

"Let me know when you need me."

"Okay."

"Cool," Hayley said, smiling. And suddenly she was gone, weaving her way through the maze of lab tables, back to her spot by the window.

Milo sat there, stunned. Hayley Christenson just hugged him. Hayley Christenson just hugged him and he was going to find his father. He was going to *track down the man who gave him life* in the name of science. He'd given Hayley his word.

"Why did you—" Milo murmured. "How did you—"

"You're welcome," JJ said.

*   *   *

122

From: MiloRobClark@brooklynIDS.org

To: info@twincitiescryolab.org

Date: Thursday, January 7, at 7:37 PM

Subject: Donor #9677

To whom it may concern,

My name is Milo Robinson-Clark. Sixteen years
ago I was conceived by artificial insemination
using donor sperm from the Twin Cities Cryolab.
I have seen my donor's profile and I know that he
was #9677. I also know that he registered himself
as willing to be known. I'm not sure if that still
applies, but if you have his current contact
information I hope that you will share this email
with him.

I am interested in making contact with my donor
mainly for medical reasons. Certain conditions, like
allergies, can be genetically linked. I have only
limited information about my donor's medical
history, and I would like to know more. I would also
like to know what traits and interests we might
have in common.

I'm not sure exactly how this process works,
and my goal is not to violate my donor's privacy,

but if he is still willing to be known, I would like to start by writing him a letter.

Thank you for your time and consideration.

Sincerely,
Milo Robinson-Clark

*   *   *

After he clicked Send, Milo didn't know what to do with himself. Probably he should tell someone. But imagining the look on Frankie's face, and the I-told-you-I-don't-want-to-know-shit-about-him rant from Hollis, didn't make Milo want to share anything with them. Not yet. He didn't want to tell Suzanne without telling Frankie. And he didn't want to get Abby's or Noah's hopes up, either. Not until he actually had something to get their hopes up about. For all Milo knew, their donor could have died in a rock climbing expedition. Or run off to join the circus. The Twin Cities Cryolab might not have his current contact information. And, even if they did, he might not want to be found anymore.

Yes. Milo was doing the right thing keeping this to himself. But he had to tell *someone*. Sending that email had unleashed something inside him, and now he was a bundle of nerves, pacing the room, pulsing with adrenaline.

"How am I supposed to do homework now, Pete? Huh?"

Pete looked up from Milo's bed and yawned.

"Oh, am I boring you?"

Milo grabbed his cell off the bedside table.

"Joe's Pizza." JJ answered on the first ring.

"I did it," Milo said.

"Did what?"

"Emailed the cryolab."

Silence. And then, "Good for you, man."

"Yeah."

"Get anything back?"

"I just sent it. I may not hear back until next week." Milo heard a sharp inhale, followed by a long, drawn-out exhale. "Are you smoking weed?"

"For medicinal purposes only."

"Cancer? Glaucoma?"

"My parents are home," JJ said.

"Ah."

"They're up my ass about school."

"That must be very uncomfortable. Will you need surgery?"

JJ ignored the joke. "They're threatening to get me a tutor. A live-in tutor for when they go away again."

"When's that?"

"Three weeks. Either that, or I have to go with them and get tutored on location."

"Budapest?"

"Glasgow, Scotland. I can get tutored here, or I can get tutored in Glasgow, Scotland. It's my choice."

"What do you want?"

Another sharp inhale. "I just want them to stay home, man." Exhale. "I want them to stay home and be actual parents."

Milo hesitated. He wasn't sure what to say. He'd met JJ's parents briefly, a month or so ago, and they seemed nice. JJ's mom was about as wide as a ruler and wore a lot of scarves and jangly bracelets. JJ's dad spent the whole time talking on his phone to some movie producer in LA, but he stopped long enough to shake Milo's hand. He had a strong grip for someone so short.

"But enough about me," JJ said.

"I don't mind."

"You didn't call to listen to my angst. You called to tell me about your email."

"Yeah, but—"

"I will now consult the Magic 8 Ball."

"What?"

"Oh, Magic 8 Ball," JJ intoned with mock gravity, "will Milo's sperm donor respond to his email?"

"I didn't actually email my donor," Milo said. "I emailed the cryolab—"

"Silence! The Magic 8 Ball is pondering . . . wait for it . . . wait for it . . ."

Milo waited.

"It is decidedly so."

"Oh really," Milo said.

"The Magic 8 Ball does not lie."

Even though JJ was full of it, and Milo didn't believe in Magic 8 Balls any more than he believed in fairies or tarot cards, when he hung up a minute later, he felt strangely calm.

HOLLIS

INSTEAD OF EATING PIZZA DUNKERS IN THE CAFETERIA
with Shay and Gianna, Hollis was making out with
Gunnar Mott in the back of the auditorium. They were
sharing a seat, Hollis on Gunnar's lap. Gunnar's face, half-
lit by the glow of the exit sign, was green. Hollis was kissing the Incredible Hulk.

She wondered briefly what Shay and Gianna would
think if they saw her right now. She'd told them she was
skipping lunch to study for the geometry quiz. *That* they
understood. Shay and Gianna were serious students, a bit
on the nerdy side. The only boys they ever talked about
were book characters. Draco Malfoy. Percy Jackson. As far
as Hollis knew, neither Shay nor Gianna had been kissed
in real life, let alone done the things that she had done
with Gunnar Mott.

Hollis should probably be nervous, afraid of getting caught, but, in truth, that was part of the thrill. She and Gunnar were supposed to be at lunch. They could get busted at any moment. Busted and hauled into the principal's office, where their hands would be slapped (figuratively) and their parents would be called (literally). What would Hollis's mother say? Hollis had no idea. They'd had the Sex Talk, as in, "Most babies are not conceived in a petri dish." And they'd had the Love Talk, as in, "All hearts are created equal." Whether Hollis identified herself as straight or gay or bisexual or transgender, her mother would love her all the same. They'd had that conversation. But they'd never really talked about this: spending your lunch period hooking up in the back of the auditorium with someone you didn't love, just for the hell of it.

Gunnar's lips, Gunnar's hands, Gunnar's smooth, bare chest. Considering they never actually removed any clothing, he and Hollis generated an unholy amount of heat. In the event of a power outage, they could run the school.

Hollis's phone pinged, but she ignored it. Milo, Abby, and Noah could wait. Over the weekend, the group emails had amped up. They'd started sending each other selfies, which was pretty crazy because now they could actually see that they were related. Noah looked even more like Milo than Hollis did. A taller, thicker, shorter-haired version of Milo in preppier clothes. When Abby pointed this out—that Noah appeared to have come straight out of an L.L.Bean catalog—he swore it wasn't his fault. *My mom picks all my clothes*, he wrote. To which Abby replied, *Time for an intervention*. Abby was funny. And prettier than Hollis had imagined she would be. Unlike the rest of them, her hair was straight and shiny, which surprised Hollis until Abby explained that she spent half an hour every morning blowing out her curls. This surprised Hollis even more. In her emails, Abby didn't present herself as a blow-out girl. Or a gold-cross-on-a-chain girl. Or a mascara-and-lip-gloss girl. But, according to her selfie, she was all of these things. If Hollis had seen Abby walking down the hall at school, she might have written her off as a Malory Keener wannabe. But Abby was saved by her caustic wit. Not to mention her double-jointed elbows, garden gnome collection, and self-proclaimed nose fetish. *I'm attracted to guys with really big noses*, she wrote in one of her emails. *Like Owen Wilson and Adrien Brody.*

Noah was harder to read. He played the trombone. He was in the chess club and the French club and the robotics club. His twin brother, Josh—the one who wanted nothing to do with them—was the jock. While the only sport Noah had mastered was Ping-Pong, Josh was some kind of basketball prodigy and this was the big thing that bonded him with their dad, who apparently had played point guard, first in college, and then on some professional European team for nearly a decade, which was Josh's big dream, too. Noah was the odd man out. *Besides living in the same house*, he wrote in one of his emails, *my dad and I have nothing in common.*

All of this was fine with Hollis. She liked getting to know her half siblings. It was the questions about their donor she could do without. What was his medical history? Was he married? Did he play any sports? Did he play any instruments? Was he a Democrat? What did he like to read? Had he ever been arrested? Had he ever had his heart broken? Milo and Abby and Noah were full of hypothetical questions that Hollis never wanted to hear the answers to. She didn't want to know squat. She didn't even want to think about it. All she wanted to do was sit here in the dark, on Gunnar Mott's lap, kissing and kissing until the bell rang.

Which it inevitably did. And they had to come up for air.

They stood. Gunnar tucked in his shirt and said, "See ya." Hollis straightened her skullcap and said, "Later." Gunnar snuck out the side door. Hollis snuck out the back. Well, she didn't *sneak out* so much as *run into* Malory Keener and her size-zero wrecking crew, who were all huddled together outside the door.

"What were you doing in there, Hollis?" Malory asked, narrowing her eyes.

Hollis smiled. "Not that it's any of your business, *Mal*, but I was working on my monologue. Are you familiar with *Our Town*? Thornton Wilder? It's a gem of a play. I'm auditioning for Emily."

This was an amusing lie, but not nearly as amusing as the look on Malory's face, like she'd just sucked on a lemon. "That's not true, and you know it."

"We saw Gunnar go in after you," said one of the Size Zeros. "We know you were hooking up with him."

"How does it feel," asked a girl with a preposterously large Starbucks cup, "being sloppy seconds?"

"Skank," another one murmured.

"What can I say?" Hollis smiled. She opened her arms as wide as they would go. "My lifestyle is an abomination."

This was an in-joke between her and Malory, only Malory probably wouldn't remember because the joke was born a lifetime ago, back when they were friends. Back when there were play dates and birthday parties, a gaggle of giggly girls in the backseat of some mom's Subaru bound for Rice Park or Chuck E. Cheese. Malory wouldn't remember, but Hollis would never forget.

It was second grade, and the worst thing imaginable had just happened. Pam was dead, her ashes scattered by the wind, and Hollis's whole reality was changed forever. She returned to school heartsick. Because Pam was gone.

Because Pam was never coming back. Because once someone you love dies, once you really know loss, you can't unknow it. And the last thing you want to hear, when you are seven years old and devastated, is this: "My mom says your mom's lifestyle is an abomination." But that is what Malory Keener said. She said it to Hollis on the monkey bars, casually, as though she were talking about something insignificant, like ice cream. *My mom says I can buy ice cream at lunch. My mom says your mom's lifestyle is an abomination.*

Hollis hadn't known what abomination meant. But she did know how to read. So after school she looked it up. She used Pam's dictionary. *Abomination (noun): a thing that causes disgust or hatred. Synonyms: atrocity, disgrace, horror, obscenity, outrage, evil, crime, monstrosity.*

Disgust. Hatred. Evil. Those words Hollis knew.

"Oh, honey," Hollis's mother said when Hollis told her. "Malory doesn't know what she's saying."

But that didn't make Hollis feel better. She didn't care if Malory was just a parrot repeating what her ignorant mother said. Malory had called Hollis's family an abomination. This would have been bad enough on its own, but Malory's comment came on top of the fact that when Pam was admitted to the hospital the nurse on duty had refused to let Hollis or her mother into the room because visiting privileges were "family only." Committed lesbian partners were not "family." Non-biological daughters were not "family."

Not family.

An abomination.

That day on the monkey bars, a hard, black seed of shame lodged itself in Hollis's heart and stayed there, like a popcorn kernel stuck in a tooth. Malory might not remember, but Hollis would never forget. Which was why calling herself an abomination now, right after hooking up with Gunnar, right in Malory's face, was so satisfying.

Malory said nothing. She couldn't even think of a comeback.

"Ho," one of the Size Zeros muttered.

But Hollis just grinned. She gave a little Miss America wave as she walked off down the hall.

* * *

Milo called when Hollis was on the bus home. It was well past fifth period, but she was still riding high, picturing the look on Malory's face when she called herself an abomination. *Ha!* Hollis thought, smiling out the window. *In your face, Malory Keener.* Hollis had taken back the power of the word. She owned it now. It was in this warm bubble of invincibility that Hollis was

floating when Milo called, saying that he had their donor's name.

"What?" Hollis said.

"I have his name."

It all came out in a rush. Milo had emailed the Twin
Cities Cryolab last week, he said. He was sorry he hadn't
told Hollis sooner, but he knew how she felt about finding their donor, and, honestly, he thought she might be
mad. Anyway, he hadn't wanted to tell anyone until he actually heard back. Not his moms, because he didn't want
to freak Frankie out. Not Abby or Noah, because he didn't
want to get their hopes up. Because maybe the cryolab
wouldn't be able to give him any information. Maybe
they wouldn't even respond.

"But they did," Milo said. "I got the email this morning.
I sent you, like, six texts. Why didn't you hit me back?"

"I was in class."

"I've been dying here."

"I never saw your texts," Hollis said. This wasn't a lie.
She'd heard her phone ping when she was in the auditorium with Gunnar, but she'd turned it off before she read
any messages.

"I have his name," Milo continued, "and his date of
birth. They couldn't give me a phone number or address
because he lived in student housing at the time and they
don't know where he moved after college, but since he

signed the willing-to-be-known waiver, he gave consent for his name and birthdate to be released upon request from his donor children, so . . ."

"So . . ." Hollis said.

"I know you said you didn't want to know anything about him, and I respect that. I do. I'm not trying to pressure you or anything . . . this is my quest, and I'll do it alone if I have to . . . but if you *did* want to know his name . . . it's not like you'd have to *do* anything with it, you could just—"

"Okay," Hollis said.

"What?"

"You can tell me his name."

"Really?"

"Sure."

Hollis was still floating in her bubble when Milo said the words . . . "William Bardo" . . . *float, float, paddle, paddle* . . . She didn't feel a thing. Not anger. Not sadness. Not panic. Nothing. She didn't feel a thing when Milo said the date of birth either. "September 23, 1978." He might as well have been reading aloud from the phonebook for all it affected her.

"Huh," Hollis said, smoothing Chapstick over her lips. They were still sore, puffy from kissing. Gunnar was a great kisser. Malory must really miss kissing him.

"I haven't done much," Milo continued, "besides

Google his name. Four hundred and twenty-three thousand William Bardos in less than a minute . . . but we could cross-reference the search with his age . . . if he was born in 1978, he must have graduated around 2000, and we know he went to college in or around the Twin Cities, so we could cross-reference that . . ."

"Right," Hollis said. "Uh-huh."

She was being a good friend, she thought . . . *float, float, paddle, paddle* . . . She was being a supportive half sister. Her decision to learn her donor's name may have been hasty, but her intentions were good. Milo needed to do this. He had legitimate medical reasons for doing this. Hollis was just offering her support.

"So, anyway . . ." Milo was still talking as she stepped off the bus. "I wanted to keep you in the loop."

"Thanks," Hollis said.

"I'm going to tell Suzanne and Frankie at dinner. And I'll shoot Abby and Noah an email tonight. I'll cc you."

"Cool." Hollis took out her key, unlocked the front door.

Silence for a second. Then Milo said, "Are you sure you're okay with this?"

"Do I sound like I'm not okay?"

"You sound like you *are* okay."

"Well then," Hollis said, "I'm okay."

"Okay," Milo said. He hesitated. "I'll check in later then."

"Sounds good."

"Keep your phone on."

"Yup."

Hollis opened the front door. She dropped her backpack onto the bench in the foyer. She walked through the hall, stepping over Yvette just like she always did. Idiot cat. It wasn't until Hollis got to the kitchen and poured herself a Coke that she realized Yvette hadn't come running when she opened the fridge. Yvette always came running when she opened the fridge. Every time, even though Hollis refused to give her cheese the way her mother did. That stupid cat was programmed.

Hollis whistled.

Nothing.

Okay, Yvette. You win.

"Eeeeveeee!" she called out. "Cheeeese!"

Nothing.

Hollis knew before she knew. Before she actually walked back to the spot in the hall where Yvette was lying, curled up in a square of pale afternoon light shining through the window. Not moving. Not breathing. Staring into space.

It was like a bowling ball to the gut. Hard, heavy, instant. Pam's dumb, ugly cat was dead. Just like Pam. Hollis couldn't bring herself to touch the body. So she grabbed the closest thing she could find, a checkered dish-towel, and covered Yvette as best she could. She took her phone out of her pocket. Her hands were shaking as she pulled up her contacts.

"Hi, honey." Hollis's mother answered on the first ring. "I'm in the middle of a showing. Can this wait?"

"Yvette's dead," Hollis said. Her voice was high and light. She sounded like a little kid.

"*What?*"

"Yvette's dead, Mom. She's dead. I just found her."

"I'm on my way."

Hollis didn't remember walking into her mother's bedroom. She didn't remember putting on Pam's bathrobe or curling up in a ball on the floor next to Pam's dead cat.

"Honey?"

It could have been five minutes or an hour later that her mother appeared, leaning over Hollis, looking clean and pretty and concerned.

"Mommy?"

Hollis hadn't called her mother "Mommy" since she was a little kid, but here Leigh was, blow-dried and com-petent in her pantsuit, kneeling on the floor and gather-ing Hollis up in a hug, rocking her.

"Holl. Oh, honey. It's okay."

"I was so mean to her." Hollis burrowed her head into her mother's neck, letting out a long, shuddering sob. "I was so mean to her and now she's gone. I never got to say goodbye."

"It's okay." Hollis's mother stroked her hair. "Shhh, baby. It's okay."

But it wasn't okay. It would never be okay. Because this wasn't about Pam's cat—although now that Yvette was gone, Hollis ached for her to be here, hocking up a fur ball on the rug, and that ache was both ridiculous and deep—this was about Pam.

Pam.

It was a lie that Hollis didn't remember Pam. Of *course* Hollis remembered Pam. She remembered everything. Pam's smell, like basil and brown sugar. Pam's hands, a cook's hands, calloused and scarred. At night, Pam used to tell Hollis the stories about her hands. "You see this one?" she'd say, pointing to a mark on her right thumb. "This is from the time I was making tamales and I stabbed myself with a knife while chopping jalapeños . . . and this one?" She'd point to the top of her hand. "This is where I got scalded with caramelized sugar." Pam taught Hollis how to press garlic. How to crack an egg with one hand. The morning Pam went into the hospital, Hollis had wanted to make brownies, just the two of them, but Pam was too tired. She'd lost all of her hair by then. She looked like a garden gnome. Her fingernails were black. Her lips were peeling. But Hollis didn't care what she looked like.

She was still Pam, and they were going to make brownies. Hollis put on her apron. She greased the pan. She walked over to the couch by the fireplace and told Pam she was ready.

"I'm sorry, sweet girl." Pam was wrapped up in an afghan, her bald head propped on a pillow. "I'm too tired."

And Hollis said, "You're always too tired."

"I'm sick." Pam reminded Hollis of what she already knew, that cancer wasn't like a cold. It wasn't like an ear infection.

"I know what it is! I hate cancer!"

"Snuggle with me," Pam suggested weakly. Every word was an effort, like laying an egg. "We can watch TV."

This is where it happened. This is where Hollis said it. "I don't want to snuggle you! I hate you! You ruin everything!" She ran upstairs and locked herself in her room.

A little while later, the ambulance came. Hollis remembered the men in the white coats. She remembered her mother telling her to put on her shoes. She remembered Pam getting carried out on a stretcher. She remembered still being mad about the brownies.

Remembering hurt so much she wanted to scream.

"I never got to say I was sorry." Her voice was strangled now. "I never got to say goodbye."

Hollis's mother pulled away and looked at her. "Oh . . . sweetheart. You're not talking about Yvette, are you?"

Hollis shook her head and swiped at her eyes with her sleeve.

"Listen to me. Pam knew you loved her."

"No she didn't. You don't know. You were in the shower."

Her mother looked confused.

"That morning. Before the ambulance came, you were in the shower. I said terrible things to her."

"Like what?"

"I told her she ruined everything. I told her I hated her . . . I didn't mean it. I was just mad. I wanted to make brownies and she was too tired . . ." A fresh sob burbled out of Hollis's throat.

"Oh, honey." Hollis's mother stared at her. "Have you been holding on to that all this time?"

Hollis nodded.

"You listen to me. Listen to your mother because I am going to keep on saying this until you believe it because this is the truth. Pam knew you loved her. No matter what you said to her that day. And she loved *you*. Every part of you, Hollis. She loved your fighting spirit. She loved that you spoke your mind and you didn't let people push you around, even as a little girl. *Especially* as a little girl. And you know what? You got that spirit from her. You didn't get it from me. If I had been the one with cancer, Pam never would have let that ignorant wench at the

142

hospital tell her she wasn't my family and couldn't go into that room. She would have clawed her way in. She would have gotten a court order and—"

"Did you just say *ignorant wench*?"

Hollis's mother half smiled. "Pam loved the word 'wench.'"

"She did?"

"She did. And that nurse was the worst kind of bigot. That hospital was the worst example of institutionalized discrimination. If I could go back in time . . . the fact that I didn't try harder . . . you not being allowed to say good-bye to Pam is something that will haunt me forever."

It's weird how it happens, how you can be feeling completely sorry for yourself and then someone says something, just a few words, really, and suddenly everything shifts. "Mom," Hollis said, squeezing her mother's hand. "It's not your fault."

"Of course it's not my fault. And it's not your fault. And feeling guilty isn't going to bring Pam back. And it's not going to bring Yvette back either." Hollis's mother flashed a sad little smile at the lump under the dishtowel.

"We should bury her," Hollis said. "In the backyard, by the bench Pam used to sit on."

Her mother nodded. "I think that would be perfect."

*   *   *

As it turns out, digging a cat grave in the backyard in Saint Paul, Minnesota, in the second week of January is harder than you might think. They tried a trowel. Then they tried a shovel. Finally, they tried a chainsaw.

"Since when do we have a chainsaw?" asked Hollis when her mother dragged it out of the basement.

"I can't remember. Pam bought it for something."

"Well . . . do you know how to use it?"

"I think I can figure it out," her mother said.

"Are you sure? Because I don't want you to chop your hand off."

"Holl." Her mother shot her a look. "I've been figuring things out by myself for a while now. I can unclog a toilet. I can change a tire. I'm pretty sure I can work a chainsaw."

And she did. She actually did. It wasn't pretty, but Hollis's mother chain-sawed a hole in the frozen ground and she and Hollis gently lowered Yvette, wrapped in— of all things—Pam's bathrobe.

"Are you sure?" Hollis had said when her mother suggested she take the bathrobe off so they could use it as a burial blanket.

"It's warm," her mother said.

"But you love this robe."

"And Pam loved Yvette."

Well. Hollis couldn't argue with that.

Holding a cat funeral was weird enough, but holding a cat funeral when the person who loved the cat was *also dead* was particularly weird. Yvette was in the ground. Yvette, who had been warm and vital that morning, who had been able to lick herself and purr and stretch in the sun, was now gone forever. Just like Pam was gone forever. It made Hollis's stomach clench, thinking about it. She watched her mother shovel the random bits of frozen dirt and grass that had flown off the chainsaw back into the hole, on top of the bathrobe. "Poor kitty," Leigh said softly.

"Yeah."

Her mother tamped down the dirt with the back of the shovel. She propped the shovel against the bench. Now what were they supposed to do, say something? What did people say at cat funerals?

"Yvette," her mother said, clasping her hands in front of her chest, "I remember the day we brought you home . . . Your fur was so soft. Your tongue was like a tiny scrap of sandpaper . . ."

"This is so weird," Hollis muttered.

"It's not that weird."

"You just chain-sawed a grave for a dead cat wrapped in a bathrobe. And now you're talking about her tongue."

"Yvette wasn't just any cat," her mother said, squashing the dirt with the bottom of her foot. Her boot left a tread mark. "She was a present from me to Pam."

"She was?"

"After our third in-vitro attempt didn't take, and we weren't sure we would ever have a baby, I went out and bought Pam a kitten."

"You never told me that."

"No?" Her mother's face looked calm, almost tranquil, not a tear in sight. Hollis didn't want to say anything to ruin it.

"Was I the fourth in-vitro attempt?"

"You were." Her mother smiled. She lifted her face to the sky. "We got two girls to love, Pammy. Today we say goodbye to one of them. Yvette was a good cat. A loyal cat. And today, she comes back to the earth, back to you."

Hollis snorted. She couldn't help herself. "Don't you think you're being a little cheesy?"

"Pam loves cheese. Don't you, Pammy? Just like Yvette."

Hollis shot her mother a look, which she didn't see because she was still addressing the sky.

Hollis stood in silence, waiting.

Finally, her mother looked at her. "Do you want to say a few words?"

"Like what?"

"There's no right or wrong here, Holl. There are no rules for these things. Just speak what's in your heart."

She didn't plan to say it. She wasn't even conscious of

the thought process, but as Hollis stood there, staring at the mound of dirt, thinking about the three failed in-vitro attempts and Pam's consolation kitten and how, if Hollis's mother hadn't tried a fourth time, Hollis wouldn't even be standing here, the words just popped out. "Milo emailed the cryobank. They told him our donor's name. I thought I didn't want to know anything, and I still don't, really, but now I know. His name is William Bardo and we have his date of birth, and Milo's trying to find him, and none of this would be happening if Pam hadn't gotten sick, and that makes me feel like crap."

"Oh, honey—" her mother started to say, but Hollis cut her off.

"No. I need to say this. The only reason Pam found Milo and his moms is because she got cancer. She knew she was going to die. If we'd never met them, Milo wouldn't have known Pam's email address and he wouldn't have gotten back in touch with me. None of this would be happening. It's all because Pam got sick. Milo . . . Frankie and Suzanne . . . Abby . . . Noah . . . all these people who are suddenly coming into my life are here because of Pam dying. And it's cool. I really like everyone. But I would send them all away, every one of them, if I could have her back."

"Of course you would," her mother said softly.

Hollis wanted to say more, but her mouth wasn't listening to her brain. And now, damn it, she was crying again.

"You're feeling guilty," her mother said, "like you're somehow capitalizing on Pam's death by letting them into your life."

Hollis nodded. She wiped her nose on the back of her hand.

"But don't you see that you're looking at it wrong? Holl . . . this was Pam's *gift*. To you. This was how she made sure you would be okay without her."

"How do you know?"

"I know," her mother said, "because Pamela Barnes was the most generous person I have ever met. And she loved you."

They stood there, Hollis and her mother, looking at each other, breathing in the same crisp air and thinking about all that they had lost, their puffs of breath lingering above the mound of dirt, just for a second, before they disappeared.

HE TOLD HIS MOMS AT DINNER, NOT JUST ABOUT THE
email he'd sent to the cryolab last week, but also about
the response he'd received today.

"Well," Frankie said, slathering butter on a roll. "This
is exciting news."

She was faking it. Milo had known Frankie his whole
life, so he knew when she was putting on an act. Her
reaction—to hearing William Bardo's name, to learning
that Milo was moving forward with the search—might
seem genuine to an outside observer. Warm hug. Jolly
words. But those words didn't ring true the way they had
in sixth grade when Milo discovered he was a finalist in
the New York Public Library poetry contest. *This is exciting news.* Then, she meant it. Now, she wanted him to
think she meant it, but she didn't actually mean it.

Milo had been expecting this. He even started to back-pedal. He started to say, "Listen, Ma, if you're not okay with me—"

But Suzanne cut him off. "No," she said, grabbing Milo's hand across the table, almost knocking over a bowl of peas. "This is important to you, so this is important to us. We are a family and we are in this together . . . right?"

Frankie bobbed her head. "Absolutely." She took a sip of water and set down her glass. Then she turned to Milo. "I just want to make sure that your expectations are realistic."

Right. He knew this was too good to be true. Frankie never just conceded. She had to argue and counterargue every point.

"Just because this man signed a waiver to be known at the time he donated doesn't mean he feels the same way now."

"I know," Milo said.

"What if he has a family of his own? What if he hasn't told them he was a sperm donor? Have you thought about what you actually want out of this, Mi? If it's just medical information, that's one thing, but if you're looking for this man to fulfill some kind of father fantasy . . . if you're looking for this man to suddenly want to be a part of your life—"

"He has a name," Milo cut in. He could feel his body tense. "It's not *this man*. It's William Bardo."

"Frank," Suzanne said gently.

"Okay," Frankie said. "I'm just saying, this . . . William Bardo . . . doesn't know you exist. He doesn't know any of you exist. There will be mental and emotional consequences for him, just like there are for all of us."

"I know that," Milo said.

"Do you?"

"Yes."

"He could shut you out. He could be an asshole."

"Frankie," Suzanne said.

"What? He needs to be prepared." Frankie looked at Milo. "I just want you to be prepared."

"I am."

"Because this could happen really quickly. Now that you have a name, and a birth date . . . with the Internet and social media . . . once you do this . . . once you actually contact him . . . there's no taking it back."

"I know," Milo said. "I want to do this. Can you just trust that I've thought it through? I know what I'm doing. I'm fifteen. I'm not some little kid that you need to protect."

Frankie raised both hands. "I know you're not a little kid. But you're still *my* kid—"

"*Our* kid," Suzanne interjected.

"Our kid. And I—*we*—just don't want to see you get hurt."

Milo looked at his mothers. At Frankie, waving her arms around, subconsciously directing the conversation like a traffic cop, and at Suzanne calmly taking her hand. He thought about all the conversations he'd overheard between them, about how Frankie didn't feel like as much of a mother because she wasn't the "bio mom," and how Suzanne always reassured her that she was. And he thought about walking down the sidewalks of Park Slope, and looking at every dad with a kid, and wondering if that dad could be his. And he thought about how he would always wonder, how he would never stop looking at dads on the sidewalk, and then he heard himself speak. "I don't care if I get hurt. I need to do this. I just . . . do."

Frankie opened her mouth like she wanted to say something more but then thought better of it.

Suzanne squeezed Frankie's hand. "How can we help?"

"Help?" Milo said.

"We could . . . I don't know . . . compile a list of colleges in the Twin Cities or start searching the white pages?"

"No." He shook his head. "I need to do this on my own."

Milo was surprised by how strongly he felt this. It wasn't their quest. It was his. And Hollis's, and Abby's, and Noah's. And—if Noah's brother Josh ever changed his mind—it would be Josh's quest, too. Even if everything blew up in their faces, at least they would be in it together.

*   *   *

From: AbsofSteel3@sheboygancountryday.edu
To: MiloRobClark@brooklynIDS.org; NoahZark
   .Rez@techHSmail.com; HollisDarbs
   @MNPSmail.org
Date: Wednesday, January 13, at 8:33 PM
Subject: Re: Houston, we have a name . . .

I can't stop saying it. *William Bardo. William Bardo.
William Bardo.* It sounds Shakespearean, no? The
Bard? I wonder if he goes by Will. Or Bill. Billy? We
should probably search them all . . .

From: NoahZark.Rez@techHSmail.com
To: AbsofSteel3@sheboygancountryday.edu;
   HollisDarbs@MNPSmail.org; MiloRobClark
   @brooklynIDS.org
Date: Wednesday, January 13, at 8:52 PM
Subject: FB

Facebook is a dead end. There's a William
Bardocz, a William Bardos, a William Bardoel,
a William Bardosson, a Bill Bardon, a Billy
Bardoe, and one Will Bardo, but he's still in high

school. No Instagram, Twitter, or Tumblr matches
either.

From: MiloRobClark@brooklynIDS.org
To: NoahZark.Rez@techHSmail.com;
  AbsofSteel3@sheboygancountryday.edu;
  HollisDarbs@MNPSmail.org
Date: Wednesday, January 13, at 9:11 PM
Subject: Googlin'

There's a Bill Bardo, PhD, with post-doctoral
research in "theoretical and experimental
investigations of the quantum mechanical
behaviour of masers and lasers." But it looks like
he's retired. And British.

From: AbsofSteel3@sheboygancountryday.edu
To: MiloRobClark@brooklynIDS.org; NoahZark
   .Rez@techHSmail.com; HollisDarbs
   @MNPSmail.org
Date: Wednesday, January 13, at 9:16 PM
Subject: Um

What's a maser?

From: NoahZark.Rez@techHSmail.com
To: AbsofSteel3@sheboygancountryday.edu;
   MiloRobClark@brooklynIDS.org; HollisDarbs
   @MNPSmail.org
Date: Wednesday, January 13, at 9:19 PM
Subject: Re: Um

Maser (noun): a device using the stimulated
emission of radiation by excited atoms to
amplify or generate coherent monochromatic
electromagnetic radiation in the microwave
range.

From: AbsofSteel3@sheboygancountryday.edu
To: NoahZark.Rez@techHSmail.com;
MiloRobClark@brooklynIDS.org; HollisDarbs
@MNPSmail.org
Date: Wednesday, January 13, at 9:24 PM
Subject: Thanks Noah

Anyone dealing with masers is clearly A) not an
English major, and B) too smart to have fathered us.

From: HollisDarbs@MNPSmail.org
To: AbsofSteel3@sheboygancountryday.edu;
NoahZark.Rez@techHSmail.com;
MiloRobClark@brooklynIDS.org
Date: Wednesday, January 13, at 9:36 PM
Subject: Speak for yourself

I am wicked smart.

From: AbsofSteel3@sheboygancountryday.edu
To: HollisDarbs@MNPSmail.org; MiloRobClark
@brooklynIDS.org; NoahZark.Rez@
techHSmail.com
Date: Wednesday, January 13, at 9:43 PM
Subject: Hi Hollis!

Nice of you to join us ☺.

From: HollisDarbs@MNPSmail.org
To: AbsofSteel3@sheboygancountryday.edu;
NoahZark.Rez@techHSmail.com;
MiloRobClark@brooklynIDS.org
Date: Wednesday, January 13, at 9:47 PM
Subject: Nice to be here

Sorry I'm late. Weird day.

From: MiloRobClark@brooklynIDS.org

To: HollisDarbs@MNPSmail.org; AbsofSteel3
@sheboygancountryday.edu; NoahZark.Rez
@techHSmail.com

Date: Wednesday, January 13, at 9:51 PM

Subject: Made even weirder by more Googlin'...

Hi Hollis. There's a "John William Bardo" who became
the 13th president of Wichita State University in
2012, but he looks old enough to be our grandfather.

From: NoahZark.Rez@techHSmail.com

To: MiloRobClark@brooklynIDS.org; AbsofSteel3
@sheboygancountryday.edu; HollisDarbs
@MNPSmail.org

Date: Wednesday, January 13, at 10:03 PM

Subject: LinkedIn

And a Will Bardo, "National sales manager at
Australian Autoparts," living in Brisbane, Australia.
Can't see his full profile because I'm not "linked in."

P.S. Hi Hollis ☺.

From: AbsofSteel3@sheboygancountryday.edu
To: NoahZark.Rez@techHSmail.com;
    MiloRobClark@brooklynIDS.org; HollisDarbs
    @MNPSmail.org
Date: Wednesday, January 13, at 10:14 PM
Subject: For your listening enjoyment . . .

Here's a song called "Billy Bardo" by some dead
country singer named Johnny Paycheck. In case
we need a theme song to search by . . . https://
www.youtube.com/watch?v=heZ3Jn7zcz8.

From: HollisDarbs@MNPSmail.org
To: AbsofSteel3@sheboygancountryday.edu;
    NoahZark.Rez@techHSmail.com;
    MiloRobClark@brooklynIDS.org
Date: Wednesday, January 13, 2016, at 10:27 PM
Subject: Wow

I don't even know what to say about that song.

From: AbsofSteel3@sheboygancountryday.edu

To: HollisDarbs@MNPSmail.org; MiloRobClark
@brooklynIDS.org; NoahZark.Rez@techHSmail
.com

Date: Wednesday, January 13, 2016, at 10:35 PM

Subject: You're welcome.

xoxo

10:35 p.m. and they were just getting warmed up.

*   *   *

In the morning, Life Science wasn't in the lab. It was moved to the library so the class could have a research period. Milo found JJ waiting for him at a table in the back.

"So?" JJ said.

"So." Milo pulled up a chair and sat down.

"You look tired."

"I was up late."

"What's new on the donor front?"

"Not much. A lot of dead ends."

What Milo didn't say, what he didn't want to shove down JJ's throat, was how much fun he was having. How—even though they'd had no luck actually locating William Bardo—Milo and Hollis and Abby and Noah had discovered something else they had in common: a sick sense of humor. At some point late last night, they'd switched over from group emailing to group texting, and things had started going off the rails. First Noah texted this: **So I've come up w/ a slogan for our cryolab: U spank it, we bank it.**

Then Milo responded with: **U jack it, we pack it.**

And Abby, without missing a beat, texted back: **Your jiz is our biz.**

Even Hollis, who had been pretty quiet all night, topped it off with: **Thank u for coming.**

Yeah, it was tasteless. But their rapport—their shared ability to laugh in the face of something as momentous as the search for their genetic father—was awesome. Milo didn't tell JJ that. Nor did he share with JJ his revelation that—even though he and Hollis and Abby and Noah hadn't been in contact for long—their connection was instantaneous. Already they'd shared things with each other that they'd never shared with anyone else. Like Noah thinking his father didn't love him as much as he loved Josh, which was part of the reason he wanted to find their donor. Or Hollis feeling like only half a person. Milo didn't tell JJ that the bond he felt with his half siblings had to be genetics at work. How else could it be explained? Milo didn't want to rub JJ's face in it. Because even though JJ barely talked about being adopted, he clearly had some

161

strong feelings on the subject. But here JJ was, grinning and handing Milo a piece of paper. "Look what I made."

"What is this?"

"A chart of physical traits. You get two genes for every trait, one from each parent."

"'Cleft in chin,'" Milo read. He looked up. "What's that?"

"Butt chin. Like Ben Affleck. And Fergie from the Black Eyed Peas."

"Fergie has a butt chin?"

"She does indeed. And look." JJ tapped the paper. "'The presence of a cleft is recessive and represents a homozygous condition.' That means Fergie had to have inherited the recessive gene from both her parents."

"Huh." Milo looked at the list. *Hair curl. Hairline. Dimples. Earlobes. Eye color. Freckles on cheeks.* It went on and on.

"So once you have pictures of everyone . . ." JJ said.

"I have a few."

"Yeah?"

"Well, not of my donor. Or anyone's family. But the four of us have been shooting selfies back and forth for . . . you know . . . comparison purposes."

"Got your phone?"

"Yeah."

"Let me see."

Milo hesitated, fiddling with the paper in front of him. "What?"

He looked at JJ. "Are you sure you're okay with this?"

"What?"

"If this makes you feel . . . I don't know . . . we don't have to do this project—"

"Milo, man. It was my idea."

"I know. I just want to make sure it doesn't bring up . . . stuff for you."

JJ looked at him, reddening slightly. "Of course it brings up *stuff* for me. She gave me away, you know? My birth mother. She gave away her own kid. I've spent my whole life wondering why she gave me up, and where she is, and what she looks like, and who my father is, and whether I have any brothers or sisters . . . but my parents won't let me start searching until I'm eighteen, which feels like fricking forever, so the way I see it, I might as well help you while I wait."

Milo was stunned. This was the most he'd ever heard JJ say about being adopted. "You sure?"

JJ shrugged. "If I can't do this for myself, at least I can live vicariously through you."

"Okay then," Milo said.

"Phone, please."

Milo took his phone out of his sweatshirt, handed it to JJ.

"Okay. Let's see if we have any recessive butt chins."

* * *

Heterozygous. Homozygous. Dominant. Recessive. Square jawline (Milo and Hollis). Oval face (Noah and Abby). Curly hair (all four). Hazel eyes (Milo, Hollis, and Noah). Green eyes (Abby). Straight noses (all four). Then there were all the physical traits Milo's pictures couldn't show. Hitchhiker's thumb. Mid-digital hair. Tongue-rolling ability. Big toe length. There was so much the four of them could have in common that they'd never even considered.

All through the school day, long after his phone battery went dead, Milo's head was spinning. It wasn't until he got home and charged his cell that he saw he had three new voice mails, all from Abby. He called her back while he was sitting on his bed, holding JJ's genetics chart in his lap. She answered on the first ring. "About time."

Milo had never heard Abby's voice before. They'd been emailing and texting for weeks, but this was the first time they'd spoken on the phone.

"You don't sound like I thought you would," he said.

"How do I sound?" she said.

"I don't know."

"Like Clint Eastwood or a life-long smoker? I've heard both."

" 'Go ahead,' " Milo said, giving Abby his best Clint Eastwood growl, " 'make my day.' "

"Funny you should say that. Did you listen to my voice mails?"

"No. I just saw that you called."

"Are you sitting down?"

"Yeah," Milo said. "Why?"

"I think I found him."

"What?"

"William Bardo. I think I found him. I played sick from school today so I could do a little sleuthing. The old thermometer on the lightbulb trick. Ever tried it?"

"No."

"Neither had I. But it works. I gave myself a fever of a hundred and two. I burned my tongue. It still hurts, come to think of it . . ."

"Abby."

"Yeah?"

"Keep going."

"Right. Anyway, I'm home all morning, Googling away to no avail, and then I start cross referencing 'William Bardo' and 'alumni' with every college in the Twin Cities, one at a time, and let me tell you, there are *a lot*. There's Augsburg College and Capella University and Saint Cloud State and North Central—"

"Abby."

"Yeah?"

"You're killing me."

"You don't appreciate that I'm building the dramatic tension to a climax?"

"No, I do not."

"Right. William Harrison Bardo. Macalester College, class of 2000."

"Macalester College," Milo repeated.

"Yup. Right there in Saint Paul. Just a bike ride away from our cryolab. One-point-two miles. I Google Mapped it."

Milo could feel his heart literally thumping in his chest. "Class of 2000. If he graduated when he was twenty-two, that means he was born around . . ."

"1978."

"Right." Milo took a breath. "Did you get his contact info?"

"Nope. Only alumni can log on to the database."

"Crap."

"I know."

Silence for a second. Then Abby said, "What about Hollis?"

"What about her?"

"She lives in Saint Paul, right? Couldn't she just walk into the Macalester alumni office and work her charm?"

"Ha," Milo said.

"I'm serious."

"You haven't met Hollis." Milo pictured Hollis with her barbell tongue and her eggbeater hair, smirking.

"Can you at least ask her?" Abby said.

"I can ask," Milo said. "But I can't promise anything."

"Give it the old college try."

HOLLIS

MILO ASSUMED SHE'D SAY NO, AND HOLLIS WASN'T ABOUT to disillusion him. She told him thanks for the invitation to play Watson to his Sherlock, but she had no intention of walking into the Macalester alumni office and asking for William Bardo's address. Not now, not ever. Of course Milo tried to talk her into it.

"Please?" he said. "You live right there. If you don't want to do it for you, do it for me."

"You can do it for yourself," Hollis said. "Presidents' Day weekend."

"That's a national holiday. I doubt the alumni office will be open."

"So come early."

"I can't," Milo said. "Suzanne already bought the plane tickets."

"Bummer," Hollis said.

Her mother eavesdropped on the entire conversation, sitting at the kitchen table, chin in her hand like she was posing for a JC Penney portrait. After Hollis hung up, she had the nerve to say, "I think you should do it." Then, "I think you should gather all the available information so that you can make an informed decision about whether or not you want to meet him. If you don't want to go alone, I'm happy to go with you for moral support."

Hollis willed her eyes not to roll. What was it with her mother? In the two days since Yvette had died, Leigh had been treating Hollis like someone who had suffered a trauma. Hovering in Hollis's doorway, "checking in" to see if Hollis was hungry or thirsty or wanted to talk. Didn't she know how weird she was acting? Didn't she realize that she'd never acted this way before, not even when Pam died?

Pam, Hollis thought. *Pam's gift. The most generous person I have ever known.*

The things her mother said to her when they were burying Yvette kept running through her head.

"If you don't do it, I will."

Hollis's head snapped up. "What?"

"If you don't go to the Macalester alumni office and ask about your biological father, I'm going to do it."

Hollis stared at her mother. "*Why?*"

"To finish what Pam started. To put some questions to rest. For you. For Milo. And, frankly, for me."

Hollis shook her head in disbelief. "This has nothing to do with you."

"Of course it does," her mother said.

"How?"

"A part of your father was a part of me for nine months."

Hollis made a face. "Gross."

"Gross or not, it's true. You are my daughter because of this man. And I deserve to know the full story of where my daughter came from."

"Well," Hollis said, "what if *I* don't want to know the full story of where I came from?"

"Then I will respect your wishes."

"And not go?"

"No." Her mother shook her head. "I'll still go. I'll just keep the information to myself."

"But you'll tell Milo."

"Yes. I will tell Milo."

*　*　*

Her mother won. It pissed Hollis off to be so blatantly reverse psychologized, but there was no way she was letting her mother walk into the Macalester alumni office *alone* and ask for information about *her* biological father.

Father. The word was like a foreign language. Gibber-ish. Gobbledygook. It didn't even seem real. Even when she texted Milo and Abby and Noah to tell them that she'd changed her mind, she was actually going to do it, none of this seemed real. Not her mother making pancakes for her on a Friday morning. Or calling Hollis's school to say that Hollis would not be in today because she had an "appointment." Or telling her to "dress sharp."

Just on principle, Hollis put on her rattiest jeans, a gray thermal shirt with a rip in the elbow, her shit-kicker boots, and her skullcap.

"Is that the impression you want to make?" her mother asked.

"Yes," Hollis said.

Leigh, on the other hand, looked like she was about to show a million-dollar house. Coiffed, mascaraed, wearing a bottle-green pantsuit Hollis had never seen before. Her mother knew this was overkill, right? Hollis imagined the impression they were making as they walked across the quad of the Macalester campus. Granite countertop mother, derelict daughter.

There were students everywhere. Scuffing through the frosty grass. Smoking. Laughing. Lost in conversation. Some of them were dressed a lot more strangely than Hol-lis was, she realized. A girl in a purple cape. A boy with dreadlocks and a tuxedo T-shirt. Someday, Hollis would be one of them. Someday, she would leave her mother and go off to some crunchy liberal arts school like this, where nobody cared what part of your body you pierced or whether or not you shaved your armpits. Where there were political rallies and sit-ins and Frisbee golf and late-night pizza and everyone could hook up without judgment. Maybe she would even go here, Hollis mused. Macalester College, home of her sperm donor. But no, she quickly corrected herself. Hell no. That would be weird.

"Sixty-two Macalester Street," Leigh murmured, glancing at the map in her hand. "Admissions . . . Financial Aid . . . Alumni Office."

Suddenly, here they were, walking up the stairs. Opening the door. Approaching the front desk. A woman looked up at them. Short-cropped dark hair, funky glasses, orange corduroy blazer. The name tag on her lapel read *Tania Kosiewicz, Alumni Relations*.

"May I help you?"

Tania Kosiewicz, Alumni Relations, seemed nice enough, but Hollis couldn't respond. She felt rooted to the spot, like a mouse caught in a glue trap.

Hollis's mother had no such problem. "I certainly hope so," she said smoothly, stepping forward and holding out her hand. "Hi. I'm Leigh Darby, and this is my daughter, Hollis."

"Tania Kosiewicz."

Handshake, handshake.

Hollis hoped her facial expression didn't convey her desire to evaporate into thin air.

"We're here to get some contact information for a former student named William Bardo," Hollis's mother said. "He graduated in 2000."

"Are you an alum?" Tania Kosiewicz asked.

"No."

"I'm afraid that I can't release any information about our alumni to nonalumni. For privacy reasons. I'm sure you understand."

Right, Hollis thought, *perfectly understandable. Let's go.*

"I'd like to show you something," Hollis's mother said, reaching into her handbag. She pulled out a manila folder. She placed it on the desk in front of Tania Kosiewicz. "My daughter was conceived fifteen years ago using donor sperm from a cryobank right here in Saint Paul. We know that her donor's name is William Bardo and that he was a college student at the time he donated. Based on his date of birth and a little Internet research, we think that William Bardo, Macalester Class of 2000, is our guy."

Tania Kosiewicz's eyes widened behind her glasses. "Are you serious?"

"As you can see from this document"—Leigh opened the folder and tapped the contents with her finger—"he registered as willing-to-be-known, which means that he is open to contact from his donor offspring." She flipped to the next page. "Here is his signature, and here is the seal of notarization."

Holy crap, Hollis thought, staring at her mother. Forget real estate. She should have been a lawyer.

"I'm sorry," Tania Kosiewicz said. And she looked like she actually meant it. "That's amazing. It really is. But I still can't release any contact information to non-alumni."

"Are you sure?" Hollis's mother asked. She tipped her head to the side and smiled. "There's nothing you can do for us?"

Wait—was she *flirting*? Hollis had never seen her mother flirt before. It was bizarre.

"Well . . . ," Tania Kosiewicz said. She was smiling now, too. There was a little gap between her front teeth. "Let me see what I can do."

She stood up. Jeans. It was nice to have a job where you could wear jeans, Hollis thought.

When Tania Kosiewicz walked away, into some back room, Hollis turned to her mother. "You just used your feminine wiles."

Her mother blushed. "Maybe a little."

"Go, Mom."

"Well. Let's see if it works."

A few minutes later, Tania Kosiewicz returned with

something in her hand. "I really can't give you any information, but you're welcome to look at this yearbook from the Class of 2000. At least then you can see his picture and . . ." She glanced at Hollis. "You know . . . see if there's any resemblance." She held out the yearbook.

"Thanks," Hollis said.

"You're welcome." She gestured around the room. "Take a seat wherever."

Hollis and her mother walked over to a couch by a window. Red with blue cushions. Softer than it looked. Hollis sat with the yearbook in her lap. She could feel her pulse quicken. Her hands were moist. God, Hollis hated that word. *Moist.* It was almost as bad as *lozenge.*

"Are you okay?" her mother said.

"I'm nervous," Hollis confessed. Which was stupid. It was just a book. She'd never been nervous to open a book in her life.

"Me too."

"You're kidding, right?"

"No," her mother said. "I feel like I might throw up."

Hollis shot her a look. "Don't."

"I won't. I just *feel* like I'm going to."

"Whatever." Hollis opened the yearbook. "It's only a picture. It's probably not even him."

She started flipping through random pages. *Art History Club . . . Bio Club . . . Mac Activists for Choice . . . Parents*

Weekend . . . Fall Sports. He could be anywhere—any one of these guys in their backward baseball caps and Macalester sweatshirts, hamming it up for the camera, virtually indistinguishable from one another. *Mac Players . . . Mac Protestants . . . Mac Salsa . . . Senior Class Portraits.*

Hollis stopped. Names swam in front of her face. *Lori Aemon. Kenneth Abbott. Elisabeth Acciello.*

"They're alphabetical," her mother murmured.

"I know."

"You're only a page or two away."

"I *know. God.* Could you stop breathing down my neck?"

"Sorry."

Her mother was apologizing when Hollis was the one being a jerk. But she couldn't worry about that right now. All she could do was turn the page. *Marcus Adsuar . . . Gavin Allibrandi.* And turn the page again. *Kelly Archer . . . Arianna Atkinson.* And again. *Rebecca Baker . . . William Bardo.*

Bam.

Hollis sucked in a breath and it caught in the back of her throat. For a second she literally forgot how to breathe. In her peripheral vision she saw her mother's hand fly to her mouth.

Dark, curly hair sprouting out in all directions. Thick brows. Crooked grin. Even without the words printed beneath the picture—*B.A. English Literature*—there was no denying it.

Hollis wanted to deny it, of course she did. Because what was she supposed to do now? There was the obvious: she could take a photo of his photo and text it to Milo, Abby, and Noah, but her body seemed not to respond to this idea. Her hands seemed unable to move to her pocket to take out her phone.

"He's handsome," her mother murmured beside her. "I knew he would be handsome."

Was he? Hollis couldn't tell. His hair was ridiculous. It looked like one of those '70s disco wigs. But then Hollis's own hair often looked like a '70s disco wig.

"You have the same eyebrows," her mother said.

Hollis nodded.

"And the same jawline."

Hollis pursed her lips and nodded again.

" 'B.A. English Literature,' " her mother read aloud. " 'Jazz Ensemble. Ultimate Frisbee Club' . . . I've never played Ultimate Frisbee. Have you?"

Hollis shrugged. "Once. In gym."

"And didn't you say Noah was musical?"

"He plays the trombone."

"Huh," her mother said softly.

Yes, Hollis knew what she was *huh*-ing about: all these little things adding up.

"What's *Chanter*?" her mother said.

Hollis shrugged.

"*Chanter* is the literary magazine." Tania Kosiewicz suddenly materialized in front of them. "How's it going?" she asked. "Are you having any luck?"

Hollis's mother gently removed the yearbook from Hollis's lap and flipped it around for Tania Kosiewicz to see.

"This guy?"

Hollis's mother nodded.

Tania Kosiewicz looked from the picture to Hollis, back to the picture, and then slowly back to Hollis. "Wow."

Hollis gnawed on her lower lip.

"That's remarkable."

"Isn't it?" Hollis's mother said.

Huh. Wow. Remarkable.

"Excuse me," Hollis said abruptly. She had to get off this couch, away from this moment. "I need to use the bathroom."

"Down the hall." Tania Kosiewicz pointed. "Second door on the left."

"Thanks," Hollis said.

She sprang from the couch, miraculously able to move again, and practically ran across the room. What was she doing? She didn't even have to pee. She just stood at the bathroom sink, staring at herself in the mirror. Was her chin always this square? Was her hair really this curly?

Hollis turned on the faucet and splashed her face. The water felt cool against her flushed cheeks. She splashed herself again. Then, without really thinking, she wet her hands and smoothed down her curls. Wet and smooth. Wet and smooth. But who was she kidding? Her hair had a mind of its own. It refused to submit.

Hollis dried her face with her shirt. She walked back to the couch where her mother was sitting. Leigh's eyes flitted from Hollis's damp hair to her damp shirt, but she didn't comment. She just smiled. "I took some photos."

"Photos," Hollis said.

Leigh held up her phone. "His senior portrait and the clubs he was in. Jazz Ensemble. The literary magazine. That way you can take a look at them later. I can text them to you and you can share them."

Hollis nodded.

"Here you go." Tania Kosiewicz suddenly materialized again. Hollis noticed that she was wearing sneakers. Chuck Taylor high-tops. "My card." She held out something small and white.

"Let me give you mine, too," Hollis's mother said, reaching into her purse and rifling around. "In case you're ever looking for a house . . . or know someone looking for a house . . . or looking to sell . . ." She sounded flustered.

Hollis watched this exchange of business cards. Having

never been a lesbian and never seen her mother go on a date, she wasn't exactly qualified to identify whether Tania Kosiewicz, Alumni Relations, was gay or straight, nor was she qualified to interpret the look that passed between Tania Kosiewicz and her mother. But something was happening. That much was clear.

"Thank you, Ms. Kosiewicz," Leigh said. "For all your help."

"Please. Call me Tania."

"Tania." Her mother nodded. "Okay . . . Hollis?" Her mother was looking at her.

"Yeah?"

Leigh widened her eyes.

"Oh," Hollis said. She jerked her chin at Tania Kosiewicz. "Thanks."

"You're very welcome, Hollis. Good luck with your search."

"Okay."

"I'm sorry I couldn't be more helpful."

"That's okay."

"I hope that . . . when the time comes for you to visit colleges . . . you'll take a look at Macalester. It's a great school."

"Oh. Uh-huh."

"I'd be happy to show you around."

"Okay," Hollis said again.

Her mother smiled. Tania Kosiewicz smiled. And that was that.

It wasn't until they got home and Hollis's mother took the business card out of her purse that they saw what was written on the back. Blue pen, block print, slanted to the right.

HE LIVES IN EDEN PRAIRIE.

MILO

HE WAS WALKING HOME FROM SCHOOL, SCUFFING THROUGH the snow in Prospect Park—snow that hadn't existed that morning—when his phone rang. Milo saw Hollis's name and answered. "Hey. It's snowing!"

"It's him."

"What?" Milo tipped his face to the sky. He opened his mouth and caught two fat flakes on his tongue.

"I saw his picture in the Macalester yearbook. It's him."

It took a second for Hollis's words to register. "Wait—" Milo stopped. "You have his *yearbook*?"

"No. But we looked through it in the alumni office. My mom took photos of what we found. I have one on my cell. Do you want to see him, or . . ."

Milo gave the tree in front of him an incredulous look,

as though it were Hollis. "Why wouldn't I want to see him?"

"I don't know."

"What are you waiting for?"

"I don't know."

"Take your time, Hollis," Milo said. "It's not like I care what my father looks like or anything."

"I'm getting a sarcastic vibe here."

"Hollis," Milo said firmly. "Text me his picture."

"Fine."

*　　*　　*

Milo couldn't stop looking at him. He tried, several times on the way home, to shove his phone in his backpack and think about something else: homework, war in the Middle East, Hayley Christenson. Nothing worked. He kept stopping to pull it out again. He kept staring at the picture. *This is my father. This is my dad.* It wasn't just that Milo saw parts of himself, because of course he did. The hair. The eyebrows. The chin. It was that . . .

His phone was ringing again.

Crap. It was probably Frankie, wondering why he wasn't home yet. Milo glanced at the screen. Not Frankie. Hollis.

He answered. "Hey."

"Conference call," Hollis said. "Noah's having a breakdown."

"It's not a breakdown," came another voice. Low, husky . . . Abby. "It's a break*through*. Right, Noah?"

There was a snuffling sound, a few murmured expletives.

"You okay, man?" Milo said.

"It's a catharsis," Abby said. "He's fine."

"I am not fine." Noah's voice was thick.

"Break*down*. Break*through*."

"I look just like him!"

Right, Milo thought, connecting the dots. Noah had seen the picture.

"You and me both," Milo said. Was he missing something here? Wasn't looking like their biological father to be expected?

"Yeah," Noah said, "but I didn't think it would be so obvious." He and Josh were twins, he reminded them, but they were fraternal. Josh looked just like Noah's mother—same face, hair, everything. Until this moment, Noah hadn't realized how much he looked like his father—not the dad who raised him, who never wanted him to search for his sperm donor in the first place, but William Bardo, Macalester Class of 2000. "Josh was right," Noah said. "It would kill my dad if he saw this picture. I'm basically rubbing his face in the fact that he couldn't have kids."

"Josh isn't *right*," Abby said. "And no one is rubbing anyone's face in anything. You just want to know where you came from."

That's what they all wanted, wasn't it? Milo thought. To know where they came from? It wasn't right, it wasn't wrong; it just was.

"Speaking of where we came from . . ." Hollis said.

Milo waited.

Nothing.

"Yes?" he said.

"Well . . ." Hollis hesitated. "I kind of found out where he lives."

"You *kind of found out where he lives*?" Abby practically shouted.

"It's a funny story, actually. There was this woman in the alumni office. She said she couldn't tell us anything because we weren't alumni, but then my mom started flirting with her and she gave us the yearbook, and *then* they exchanged business cards, and then, when we got home—"

"Hollis," Milo said.

"Yeah?"

"Does this story have a point?"

"Yes."

"What is the point?"

"William Bardo lives in Eden Prairie."

Milo took a measured breath. He let this information sink in. Then he said, "What's Eden Prairie?"

"Not *what*," Hollis said. "*Where*. It's outside Minneapolis."

"Hang on," Abby said. "I've got my laptop. I'm Googling . . ."

"Noah?" Milo said while they waited. "You still with us?"

"Uh-huh."

"How're ya doin'?" Hollis said.

"I'm . . ." Noah paused. "Wait. Let me blow my nose . . ." There was a rustling noise. Then what sounded like a foghorn. Finally, "I'm full of snot."

"There are worse things to be full of," Hollis said.

"I guess."

"Noah," Hollis said.

"Yeah?"

"You're not the only one, you know. We're all freaking out a little."

Hollis was a good egg, Milo thought. Once you got past the crusty exterior, she had a gooey center.

"Okay, listen," Abby said. " 'Eden Prairie is an edge city. Twelve miles southwest of downtown Minneapolis in Hennepin County, and the twelfth-largest city in the state of Minnesota. It is on the north bank of the Minnesota River—' "

"We get the picture," Hollis said.

"I'm setting the *scene*," Abby said.

"Why?"

"Because she's a writer," Milo said. "The next Augustus Burroughs."

"Augus*ten*," Abby corrected him. "Not Augus*tus*."

"Potato, potahto."

"Come on," Abby said. "*The north bank of the Minnesota River*? Think of the symbolism. Water is the universal sign of *change,* people. The turning point in a story. Purity. Cleansing. Rebirth . . ."

"Death," Hollis said.

"Okay, Mary Sunshine."

"Ophelia? Captain Ahab? 'Rime of the Ancient Mariner'? 'Water, water every where—' "

"Okay," Milo interrupted. "I thinking we're getting off track. We need to decide what to do next."

"Easy," Abby said. "We write him a letter."

"Or not," Hollis said.

"Don't we need an address?" Noah said.

"Abby?" Milo said.

"I'm on it. Give me a sec." Abby muttered to herself as she typed. "White pages dot com . . . first name . . . William . . . last name . . . Bardo . . . city . . . Eden Prairie . . . state . . . MN . . ." And finally, "Ding, ding, ding!"

"All aboard," Noah deadpanned.

"William H. Bardo," Abby said. "17 Kerry Lane, Eden Prairie, Minnesota."

Milo let out a deep breath. "Whoa."

"Yeah."

"I can't believe we have an address."

"And a phone number," Abby said.

"Holy crap."

"I know."

"How do we know it's him?" Noah said.

"According to whitepages dot com," Abby said, "there is only one William Bardo in Eden Prairie, Minnnesota, and this one is between thirty-five and thirty-nine years old."

"I see," Noah said.

"*I see,* said the blind man," Hollis said.

"One of my all-time favorite expressions."

"Mine, too."

"I hereby nominate Milo to write the letter," Abby said.

"Me?" Milo said. "You're the writer."

"Yeah, but you brought us this far. You're our fearless leader. Our Captain Ahab."

"You know he dies, right?" Hollis said.

"What?" Abby said.

"Captain Ahab. He drowns at the end of *Moby Dick.* Tangled in the line of his own harpoon."

"Thank you, Debbie Downer."

"You're the one who wanted cigarette burns and blood splatters."

"Hollis has a point," Noah said.

Noah was sounding better, Milo thought.

"Do you guys not think Milo should write the letter?" Abby said.

"I think Milo should do what Milo wants to do," Hollis said.

"Agreed," Noah said.

"Let me rephrase," Abby said. "Milo, do you want to write the letter?"

Yes, Milo did. He wanted to write the letter to William H. Bardo—17 Kerry Lane, Eden Prairie, Minnesota—telling him about the four of them. He wanted to write it bold and proud: *We are your kids.*

"Okay," he said.

"Go forth," Abby said.

"And may the forth be with you," Noah said.

Hollis groaned. "Please tell me you're not a *Star Wars* fan."

"Hollis." Noah breathed raspily into the phone. "I am your father."

"Oh God."

"God is not your father," Noah rasped. "*I* am your father."

"Go blow your nose, Darth Vader."

Milo wanted to write the letter. He really did. And yet he couldn't.

As he sat in Starbucks, sipping a blackberry Izze—one of the few flavors he wasn't allergic to—he scrolled through the Donor Progeny Project website on his laptop. There was this page he remembered from the FAQ section. *I Just Found My Donor. Now What?*

If Milo decided to initiate contact, the page advised, he should "proceed slowly." He should offer only "basic information." He should "wait and see" what kind of response he received before "taking things further." The page read more like a list of warnings than helpful hints. Milo should "exercise caution" and "maintain limited expectations." He should prepare himself for his donor's "ambivalence" and avoid asking any "loaded questions" that might put his donor "on the defensive."

The more Milo read, the less confident he felt. He'd opened a new Word document and tried to get started, but he wasn't even sure how to begin. *Dear Donor? Dear Mr. Bardo? Dear William?* Another son might have known exactly what to write to the father he'd never met. Another son might have read the FAQ section—scanned through *I Just Found My Donor. Now What?*—and said, screw it, I'll write whatever I want. Another son might have started his letter with *Dear Dad* because he wasn't afraid of the consequences.

Milo was not another son. Milo was at a loss.

JJ would know what to write, he thought. Something comic and irreverent. Something to make his donor laugh. *Yo, yo, yo, Willy B. What up, dawg?*

Milo thought about texting him. Was Jonah Jedediah Rabinowitz really the best person to help write this letter? Probably not. But Milo texted him anyway. **Starbucks 7th Ave STAT.** Then he texted Frankie and Suzanne to let them know where he was. **Doing homework at Starbucks on 7th.**

It wasn't the whole truth, but the whole truth could wait. Later, he would tell them. After he mailed the letter.

After he mailed the letter? Ha! He didn't even know how to start. How was he supposed to start? Milo sucked down his blackberry Izze. He angled his chair so he could see the door. He waited for JJ.

HOLLIS

MILO GROUP-TEXTED THE LETTER ON SATURDAY MORNING.
Dear Mr. Bardo, it began, which struck Hollis as funny,
as though Milo were addressing the school principal or an
elderly neighbor. Not that she would know how to greet
the guy any better. **Dear #9677?**

Anyway. **Dear Mr. Bardo,** it began.

My name is Milo (age 15), and I'm writing not just for
me but also for my half siblings, Hollis (14), Noah (17),
and Abby (15). We were all conceived using donor
sperm from the Twin Cities Cryolab in Minneapolis,
MN. Our Donor was #9677. We are writing to you
because our research suggests that you may be Donor
#9677 and that, if you are, you registered with the TCC
as willing-to-be-known by your future offspring (a.k.a.

us). All we are asking at this point is to hear back from you. We don't want to disturb your life or freak you out or anything, but we would like to know that you are A) alive and B) open to contact. Whatever you want to share with us is great. If you don't want to share anything . . . well, we will respect your feelings. But we hope this is not the case because we would really like to hear from you.

Sincerely,
Milo, Hollis, Noah, and Abby

P.S. You can email us anonymously by registering with the Donor Progeny Project and posting on the Twin Cities Cryolab message board under #9677. Or, if you want, you can email us directly: MiloRobClark @brooklynIDS.org; HollisDarbs@MNPSmail.org; NoahZark.Rez@techHSmail.com; AbsofSteel3 @sheboygancountryday.edu. Thanks again.

Milo texted one other photo—a crop shot of his hand, dropping the envelope into the mailbox. **Signed, sealed, and delivered**, the caption read. Followed by, **Hey, Hollis, if u want to watch him open it, u could stake out his house for the next 3 days, LOL.**

Hollis did not LOL. She knew Milo was joking, but she

also knew exactly how close 17 Kerry Lane, Eden Prairie, Minnesota, was to her house. It was 23.6 miles. Yes, she'd Google Mapped it. Yes, this had been a stupid thing to do. She *knew* she shouldn't Google Map William Bardo's house. She told herself not to do it, and then she went ahead and did it anyway. Why hadn't she *listened* to herself?

Now, Hollis was plagued by the thought that she might have crossed paths with William Bardo any number of times in her life and not even realized it. They could have passed each other in the shampoo aisle of Target or the shoe department of Kohl's. They could have sat in adjoining booths at the Original Pancake House, poured syrup from the same bottle, bought gumballs from the same dispenser on their way out. Had he noticed her? Had he thought she looked familiar? *23.6 miles.* It was screwing with Hollis's head.

Milo had mailed the letter, and that was fine, but Hollis needed to pretend that it was bound for somewhere else—somewhere far, far away. She needed to clear her mind of it completely.

"*Thelma and Louise?*" her mother said. "*Little Women? . . . Delivery Man?*" She read aloud from the pay-per-view description: " 'An affable slacker discovers that he has fathered 533 children through anonymous sperm donations to a fertility clinic twenty years before—' "

"Seriously?" Hollis said.

"What? We love Vince Vaughn."

"Mom."

Her mother smiled. "I think it sounds funny. And apropos."

17 Kerry Lane, Hollis thought. *23.6 miles.* Her mother knew this. Her mother was well aware because Hollis had told her. "This isn't a joke to me," she said.

"I know it's not." Her mother was grimacing now. "Sorry . . . I was aiming for levity."

"Ha," Hollis said. A nonlaugh.

"I'll make the popcorn," her mother said. "You pick the movie. Okay?"

"Fine."

* * *

At 11:58 p.m., Hollis was in bed but not asleep when she heard something hit her window. Once, twice, three times before she got up to investigate. There, standing in her ice-encrusted backyard, half-lit by the moon, was Gunnar Mott.

"Hey," he stage-whispered when she opened the window.

"Hey."

"Want to come out?" He tossed a handful of pebbles in the air and they hit the ground in a silvery spray.

194

Come out? Hollis thought. It was midnight. It had to be 15 degrees. But what else was she going to do, sleep? She couldn't sleep. Her head was spinning. *17 Kerry Lane. 23.6 miles.* The movie had distracted her for a little while, but as soon as it was over she went right back to thinking about William Bardo.

"Hang on," she said.

Hollis went outside in pj's and her skullcap. Without saying a word, Gunnar reached for her. He stuck his tongue in her mouth: Doritos. Hollis liked Doritos well enough but not in someone else's teeth.

She pulled away. "What are you doing here?" Gunnar lived nowhere near this neighborhood. He rode a different bus to school.

"Sleeping over Fitzy's."

Fitzy's, Hollis thought. She was drawing a blank. Then she remembered Michael Fitzgerald. He was a sophomore like Gunnar—a tall, skinny kid with bad skin. He lived three blocks down and was always dribbling a basketball.

"Oh," Hollis said. Her mind was a tornado, twisting and rising. If she didn't let some pressure out, she might be swept away. But talk about her feelings with Gunnar Mott? She and Gunnar didn't talk. The most scintillating words in their repertoire were *hey* and *see ya*.

"Hey," Hollis said softly.

"Hey." Gunnar reached up under her pj top. His hands were freezing.

Hollis shivered. "Did I ever tell you about my father?"

"Hmmm?" He was kissing her again. Tongue probing. Teeth scraping. Hands pressing her back against the side of the garage.

Hollis pushed him away. "My father."

"Oh shit." Gunnar dropped his hands and looked around the yard like a crazy person. "Where?"

"He's not *here*. I've never even met him."

"Oh . . . shit." Gunnar laughed, a puff of relief. He stuck his tongue back in Hollis's mouth.

She pushed him away again.

"What?"

"I'm trying to talk."

"Talk," he repeated.

"Yeah. You know . . . *words*? Strung together to form *sentences*?"

Gunnar didn't say anything, which Hollis took as a "please continue." So she did. She told him she was donor-conceived. She told him she had a half brother named Milo. She was just about to explain what the Donor Progeny Project was when Gunnar cut her off. "Hey," he said.

"What?"

Gunnar lifted her pj top, ran his fingers along her bare side.

Hollis flinched.

"What's wrong?"

"Your hands are freezing."

"Well," Gunnar said low, "why don't we warm each other up?" He inched his hand higher.

Hollis folded her arms against her chest, blocking him.

"What?" He sounded annoyed.

"I'm trying to *tell* you something."

"I didn't come here for you to *tell* me something."

"What did you come here for then?"

Gunnar shook his head. "Forget it."

"No. I want to hear you say it."

Silence.

"Whatever," Hollis muttered. She stamped her feet. Her toes were going numb. The air was biting through her pj's. She should just go back inside—quit while she was ahead. But she couldn't seem to leave.

"I'm not your boyfriend," Gunnar said finally.

Hollis snorted. "Who says I want you to be?"

"I mean . . . I like you."

"OMG. You *like* me? I feel sooooo special."

"Don't be that way."

"What way?"

"Hey," Gunnar said. He leaned in and gave her a different kind of kiss. Soft and slow, no tongue.

"Go away," Hollis murmured.

"You don't want me to kiss you?"

"Not particularly," she said, kissing him back, grabbing his belt loop.

"You sure? Because it seems like you do."

"Shut up."

Lips, hands, skin.

Twenty-three point six miles popped uninvited into her head. *No,* she told herself, pulling Gunnar toward her, back against the garage. *I am not going to think about that. I am not going to think about anything.*

* * *

I have been behaving carelessly.

Hollis sent the text at 12:47 a.m. It's not like she expected Milo to answer, but she felt the need to send it anyway. She needed to do something. Hooking up with Gunnar had only distracted her for 47 minutes.

Hollis held her phone in her lap. No text back from Milo and she wasn't the least bit tired.

Then she remembered.

She scrolled through her contacts. It took a while to find—not because she had so many friends but because he hadn't listed his number under "R" or "J" like a normal person. He'd listed it under "B" for "Bowling Hotline."

He answered on the fifth ring.

"It's Hollis," she said. "Darby."

"Hello, Hollis Darby."

"Hello, JJ Rabinowitz."

He yawned loudly.

"I woke you up. I'm sorry."

"It's okay. What's going on?"

What's going on? How was she supposed to answer that? *Well, I've been hooking up in the backyard with a boy who's not my boyfriend, about ten feet away from the spot where I recently buried Pam's dead cat. A cat I thought I hated, but now that she's gone, it turns out I miss her. Although not nearly as much as I miss Pam. But I'm trying not to think about that. I'm trying not to think about a lot of things. Like fathers. And letters. And towns on the north bank of the Minnesota River. But the more I try not to think about those things, the more I think about them. Hence my need to distract myself by hooking up in the backyard with a boy who's not my boyfriend.*

"Nothing," Hollis said. "Just couldn't sleep."

"What time is it?" JJ said.

"Twelve fifty-two . . . Well, one fifty-two for you."

"Oh." He yawned again.

"Sorry. This was dumb. I shouldn't have called you."

"No. I'm glad you did."

"You are?"

"So glad."

Hollis smiled in the dark.

"Tell me something," JJ said.

"What?"

"Anything. What were you doing before you called me?"

"Nothing."

"You must have been doing something."

"Fine," she said. "If you must know, I was hooking up with Gunnar Mott in my backyard."

"Gunnar Mott?"

"Yeah."

"What kind of a name is *Gunnar Mott*?"

"What kind of a name is *Jonah Jedediah Rabinowitz*?"

"Touché."

There was a moment of silence during which Hollis could hear JJ breathing, deep and slow. "Okay," he said finally. "Tell me about Gunnar Mott."

"What about him?"

"How did you get together?"

"We're not *together*."

"Okay . . ."

"You're going to think this is whacked," Hollis said.

"Try me."

Hollis thought back to the night of the Snowflake Formal. She almost hadn't gone because A) she couldn't dance, and B) she hated getting dressed up. But her mother's real estate agency was having their annual holiday party that night, and Hollis didn't feel like spending her Friday alone on the couch, watching Yvette lick herself a fur ball. So she asked her mother to drop her off at the high school. "It's on your way to the party," she said. "I'll take a cab home."

Leigh was surprised. "Really?"

"Why not?"

"You're going to a formal?"

"Yup."

"By yourself?"

Hollis shrugged. "Shay and Gianna study on Friday nights."

"Are you—" Her mother hesitated. "Do you think that's the most appropriate outfit for a school dance?"

Hollis had on a slinky black dress that she'd found in the back of Leigh's closet. And combat boots—because, well, she loved her combat boots and she didn't give a shit what anyone thought.

"What's wrong with my outfit?"

Her mother shook her head. "Nothing. I'm just—"

"You said I could wear your clothes any time."

"I know. You can. But that *body*. With your curves . . . Hollis, you look about twenty-five in that dress."

"So?"

Her mother shook her head. "Just wear a coat, okay?"

"Fine."

There were a few stares and snarky comments when Hollis took off her coat and walked into the gym, but not as many as she would have predicted. It was dark. Most people were dancing. Some of them looked drunk. Hollis made her way to the bleachers and sat with a few of the fringier kids she'd known since elementary school. Jenn Mattias. Grace Sung. They talked about what books they were reading and watched the other kids dance.

Hollis couldn't remember exactly when it happened— it was toward the end of the night and she was starting to think about calling a cab. But then she saw Malory Keener on the dance floor. Malory Keener in a silver sequined dress and light-up Christmas ball earrings. Her arms were draped over Gunnar Mott's shoulders and her hips were swaying side to side. Hollis knew who Gunnar Mott was; of course she did. In a school where football reigned supreme, you had to be living under a rock not to know who he was. Gunnar Mott, #24, Sophomore Quarterback Phenom. He had enough social currency to date any girl in school, including the seniors, and he'd chosen Malory, a freshman. Hollis didn't know why this pissed her off, but it did. Watching the two of them on the dance floor, latched together and swaying, all she could think about were those words: *My mom says your mom's lifestyle is an abomination.* It didn't help that a few minutes earlier, when

Hollis had gone to get a drink, one of Malory's glittery friends had smirked at Hollis's boots and said, "Nice shoes."

"Nice face," Hollis said.

"Dyke."

Malory didn't say it, but Malory might as well have said it, and that word started a fire in Hollis's chest. As she watched Malory hanging all over Gunnar Mott, the fire crackled and spit. After the song ended, Gunnar said something in Malory's ear, Malory nodded, and Gunnar walked away.

Hollis still didn't know what possessed her. She hadn't been drinking. She hadn't been smoking pot, like some of the upperclassmen she'd seen in the parking lot when her mother dropped her off. But something—some unknown force—compelled Hollis to get up off the bleachers and follow Gunnar Mott. She followed him down the hall to the boys' bathroom. She waited until he came out. And when he did, she said, "Hey, Gunnar."

He turned around, raising those golden eyebrows. "Yeah?"

"I'm Hollis," she said.

"Hey," he said. His eyes moved up and down her dress.

"Hey," she said. Then, "Want to go for a walk?"

If Gunnar was surprised by the offer he didn't show it. He just shot her that killer smile and said, "Sure."

Hollis took charge. She led him into the science lab.

They made out like a couple of horny teenagers in a movie, and it was actually *really* fun. They kissed up against the Bunsen burners, and—even though Gunnar was the first guy Hollis had seduced, or maybe *because* Gunnar was the first guy Hollis had seduced—she was incredibly turned on, and so was he, and one thing led to another. Not everything. But . . . things.

And then, just as they were leaving the science lab, they ran into Malory Keener at the water fountain. She was standing with the same glittery friend who had called Hollis a dyke. Gunnar was straightening his shirt, and Hollis was fixing her hair, and the look on Malory's face when she saw them together was perfect. *Perfect.* That look would have been enough, but Gunnar coming back for more—all those hookups that followed, and now, showing up in Hollis's yard when he was still going out with Malory? Priceless.

"You're right," JJ said, when she finished the story. "That is whacked."

"You wanted to know."

"So you're hooking up with this guy for revenge? Against some girl who hurt your feelings when you were little?"

"I wasn't that little," Hollis said. "And she didn't just hurt my feelings."

"Okay."

"She insulted my family. She basically called my mom repulsive because she's a lesbian. No—worse than repulsive. *Evil.* And she said it right after Pam died. Which . . . by the way, did you know I wasn't even allowed into her hospital room to say goodbye? Because—guess what? *Other* people besides Malory's mother think that being gay is an abomination, and they won't even let a seven-year-old into the room to say goodbye because the person dying in there isn't *family.*"

"Okay," JJ said. "I get it."

"Do you?"

"I think so. Yeah."

Hollis sighed. "I know it doesn't make a lot of sense. Malory probably didn't even know what she was saying. But I did. *I* knew what she was saying. And my mom was so sad, and there was nothing I could do to bring Pam back. And *I* was so sad, and all that sadness kind of . . . I don't know . . . morphed into anger. I've been angry for a long time, I guess. Hooking up with Gunnar—okay, yeah, at first it was for spite, but now it's . . . I don't know . . . being with him makes me feel . . ."

"Less angry?"

"Yeah."

"Less lonely?"

"Uh-huh. *And* it's fun."

"Fun," JJ repeated.

"Let's just say that Gunnar Mott is exceedingly easy on the eyes. I think he was a baby model."

"A *baby model?*"

"So the rumor goes. He was on the cover of *Parenting* magazine or something when he was, like, six months old."

JJ was quiet for a long time. At first Hollis thought he'd fallen asleep, but then he blurted, "I was an ugly baby."

"What?"

"I was an ugly baby."

"No you weren't."

"I was. Trust me. I looked like Winston Churchill."

"Don't most babies look like Winston Churchill?"

"I'm serious. I had the world's biggest head. And five chins."

"I bet you were cute."

"I wasn't. For the longest time, I thought that was why my birth mother gave me away. Because she didn't want an ugly baby."

Hollis swallowed. Hearing JJ say that made her throat hurt. "You know that's not true."

"How do I know that's not true? It's as good a reason as any."

Hollis hesitated. "I want to say something to make you not feel that way . . . but I don't know what to say."

"That's okay."

"I like the way you look," she said.

"Thanks. I like the way you look, too."

"I wouldn't give you away."

"I wouldn't give you away either."

It was suddenly very quiet, like the whole world was asleep except for them.

"I feel like I can talk to you," Hollis said.

"Me too."

It was so quiet. She closed her eyes and listened to JJ breathe.

"Hello darkness, my old friend," he suddenly belted out.

"What are you doing?"

"Breaking the sound of silence with 'The Sound of Silence.' You know—Simon and Garfunkel?"

"You're so weird."

She could hear him smile. "You're pretty weird yourself."

"I'll take that as a compliment."

"You should," he said. More silence and then, "Is it weird to say I'm jealous of Gunnar Mott?"

"Because he was a baby model?"

"Because he got to hook up with you tonight."

Oh God, Hollis thought.

"I wanted to kiss you the first time I saw you."

Oh God oh God oh God.

"Sorry," JJ said. "Did I say that out loud?"

"Uh-huh."

"I have this problem. I just say what's in my head without really thinking . . . do you want me to take it back?"

"No . . . I don't know." This was crazy. She and JJ barely knew each other. An hour ago, she'd been hooking up with Gunnar. And yet. And yet. Why was her stomach doing funny things?

"I feel stupid now," JJ said.

"Don't feel stupid."

"Let's pretend I never said that."

"If that's what you want."

"It is."

"Okay."

"Do you want to get off the phone?"

"No."

"Are you sure?"

"I'm sure."

"So . . ."

"So . . ."

"How 'bout those Mets?" he said.

Hollis smiled. "I'm a Twins fan."

"Right."

"Also, it's January."

"Good point . . . how 'bout that letter?"

Crap, Hollis thought. "What letter?"

"Ha, ha. Did Milo tell you I helped him write it?"

"No."

"I tried to get him to ask William Bardo if he could fold his tongue into a four-leaf clover, but he didn't go for it."

"What are you talking about?"

"Cloverleaf tongue. It's a genetic trait. Very few people can do it. I've been trying to teach myself, but so far no dice."

"Huh."

"You're thinking I'm weird again."

Hollis smiled. "Maybe."

"Can you do it?"

"Fold my tongue?"

"Yeah."

"Two-leaf clover, three-leaf clover, four-leaf clover, roll, and flip."

"Damn," JJ said. "Some people have all the luck."

"I must have good genes."

"Yes you do. Want to hear another one?"

"Yeah."

Hollis closed her eyes and listened to JJ talk about widow's peaks and hitchhiker's thumbs and detached earlobes. And after a while she stopped thinking about the letter. Well, she didn't stop thinking about it exactly, but it became background noise. JJ's voice was deep and soft. Each word was a wave, rolling toward her, rolling away.

After a while, she was too tired to participate in the conversation. She just listened. Wave in, wave out. Wave in, wave out.

"Hollis?"

"Hmm?"

"You're snoring."

"Nomnot."

JJ laughed. "Good night, Hollis Darby."

Barnes, Hollis thought from the bottom of the ocean. *Barnes.*

MILO

I have been behaving carelessly.

Milo didn't read Hollis's text until Sunday morning. She'd sent it in the middle of the night, and he thought maybe she was making a *Gatsby* reference, but he couldn't be sure.

Carelessly how? he texted back.

Three hours later he got **Forget it. I'm good.**

U sure?

Yup.

Milo wasn't dense. He knew Hollis had issues. Issues with her dead mom, issues with the search for their donor. He wanted to tell her, "It's okay. I'm a little effed up, too." But Milo wasn't one for deep confessionals. This was a guy thing, maybe. Or was it? Noah seemed to have no trouble pouring his heart out. Sharing his doubts about his father's love—his fear that Josh was the favored son and that finding their donor would only deepen the rift in his family. Was Milo kidding himself? Could sending the letter have been a terrible mistake?

Well. It was too late now.

He'd told Suzanne and Frankie last night at dinner. "We found William Bardo's address. He lives in Eden Prairie, Minnesota."

Frankie, attuned to every nuance of every word that came out of Milo's mouth, said, "We?"

"Uh-huh," Milo said. "Me, Hollis, Abby, and Noah. It was a group effort."

"I see."

"We—well, technically, *I*—just sent him a letter."

"Just?"

Milo took a casual sip of water. "I mailed it this afternoon."

"Oh, Mi," Suzanne said, rushing around the table to give Milo a hug. "Congratulations."

"Congratulations?" Frankie said.

And Suzanne said, "Is there an echo in here?"

Frankie pressed her lips together.

"Ma," Milo said gently. "It *is* kind of a big deal."

"You think I don't know that?" Frankie said.

God, it sucked. Hearing Frankie use that tone. Seeing the look on her face, like she'd just been slapped. Even after she hugged him. Even after she apologized for her reaction.

"He may not even write back," Milo said. "He may not want anything to do with us."

"One step at a time," Suzanne said.

One step at a time.

Sunday afternoon, twenty-four hours after he'd dropped the letter in the mailbox, Milo was still waiting for the next step. And waiting. And waiting. Even though he knew that he'd missed the noon mail pick-up yesterday and that no mail would go out today. He didn't know what to do while he waited. Trawling the Internet was no help. Each link was more discouraging than the last.

New Study Shows Sperm Donor Kids Suffer.

Sperm Donor Kids Are Not Really All Right.

Children of Sperm Donors Met With Hostility, Ridicule.

"Listen to this," Milo said when JJ called. " 'Regardless of socioeconomic status, donor offspring are twice as likely as those raised by biological parents to report problems with the law before age twenty-five.' "

"Huh," JJ said.

" 'They are more than twice as likely to report having struggled with substance abuse. And they are about 1.5 times as likely to report depression or other mental health problems—' "

"Dude."

"I know. Who *are* these people? Don't they think about the kids who might be reading their blogs? I mean . . . come on. Don't they feel any—"

"*Dude.*"

"Yeah?"

"How long have you been reading that crap?"

"I don't know. A while."

"Stay where you are."

"What?" Milo said.

But JJ had already hung up.

Twenty minutes later, he appeared on Milo's front stoop. "This is an intervention."

"I don't need saving," Milo said.

But JJ ignored him. JJ brushed right past him and into the kitchen, where Frankie was sitting at the counter, doing the *New York Times* crossword puzzle, and Suzanne was pouring herself a cup of coffee.

"Hey, Milo's moms," JJ said. "I'm taking Milo skating."

Frankie looked levelly at JJ. "Skating?"

"Ice-skating. At Rockefeller Center."

"Well," Suzanne said, taking a sip of coffee. "That sounds like fun."

"Good clean fun." JJ nodded. "No controlled substances."

Frankie shot him the hairy eyeball.

JJ held up three fingers. "Scout's honor."

Oh, God, Milo thought. *Not Scout's honor.* He braced

himself for Frankie's rant about the Boys Scouts of America and their historically ass-backward stance on homosexuality, but Suzanne made the save. "JJ," she said. "Frankie and I have been meaning to invite your parents over for dinner. We'd like to get to know them."

Frankie shot Suzanne a look.

"Cool." JJ grinned.

Suzanne squeezed Frankie's shoulder. "We'll give your mom a call and find a night that works. Right, babe?"

Frankie gave a noncommittal grunt.

On their way out the door, JJ said to Milo, "I'm growing on them. Admit it."

*   *   *

JJ rented Milo skates. He held Milo up by the hood of his sweatshirt because Milo couldn't stand without falling. JJ used to be a hockey player. He showed Milo moves.

"Whoa," Milo said, watching JJ spray ice through the air with a fancy stop. "You're good."

"I used to play for the NYC Cyclones," JJ explained. "Premier league. Right wing."

"What happened?"

He shrugged. "I got kicked off the team."

"Why?"

He shrugged again.

"Weed?"

"Something like that."

It occurred to Milo that JJ could be living a completely different life if he weren't a pothead. He'd still be at the Buckley School. He'd still be playing hockey. He'd probably have a girlfriend, because—not that Milo had been checking him out or anything—JJ was a good-looking kid. He wasn't dumb either. His grades definitely didn't reflect his potential; they reflected his propensity to get high every day after school.

"Not to sound like your dad," Milo said, "but do you think you should lay off the ganja?"

"You don't sound like my dad."

"No?"

"My dad has no clue."

Milo nodded, but nodding threw him off balance and he had to grab the handrail.

"We don't really talk, you know? Or when we do he just . . . doesn't get it."

"Right."

"Anyway," JJ said, "you don't have to worry. Hollis already talked to me."

"Hollis talked to you?"

"Yeah. We made a deal."

"You made a deal . . . with Hollis."

"Yeah."

"Am I missing something?" Milo said.

Which is when JJ explained how Hollis had called him last night and they had talked for a long time, and how he had called her this morning and they had talked for an even longer time. And how they had discussed, among other things, "numbing" their feelings—JJ with weed, Hollis with Gunnar Mott, the football player she'd been hooking up with for the past month.

"Gunnar Mott," Milo repeated.

"Yeah."

"She's getting busy with a guy named *Gunnar Mott*?"

"I know. I said the same thing. Anyway, we made a deal. She'll stop hooking up with him and I'll stop smoking weed."

"Just like that?" Milo said. He was dubious, not because he questioned JJ's word, but because he remembered learning about drug withdrawal in health class. Going cold turkey was no joke.

"We're making a plan," JJ said.

"A plan."

"A four-week de-numbing plan. We're sponsoring each other."

"Huh."

This whole time, they had been skating. Correction: JJ had been skating; Milo had been wobbling painfully along the perimeter of the rink, clutching the handrail for dear

217

life. There were four-year-olds skating with more grace. Why hadn't his mothers ever taught him how to skate? Or bowl? Or master anything remotely athletic?

"So?" JJ said.

"So?" Milo clutched the rail.

"What do you think?"

"I think you have a crush on Hollis."

JJ spun around suddenly and started skating backward, grinning like an idiot. "I think you're right."

Hollis and JJ, Milo thought. It made sense, in a way. They were both a little odd. They were both a little broken. If being odd and broken together helped JJ stop smoking weed and Hollis stop hooking up with a guy whose name sounded like a soap opera character, who was Milo to argue?

JJ was looking at him, eyebrows raised.

Milo thought, *He wants me to approve. He wants me to give my blessing.* Milo nodded. "Cool."

"She's a whack-a-doo." JJ did a spin move, spraying ice through the air. "But so am I."

"Yes you are," Milo said.

"And she's smart. *God*, is she smart. She was telling me about all the books she's read."

"She's a big reader."

"I dig her, man. I know it's too soon to tell, but I think

she might dig me, too." JJ's grin widened. "She's calling me tonight."

"That sounds promising."

*   *   *

When he got home and saw Suzanne and Frankie curled up together on the couch, Milo realized something. Everyone had someone but him. Suzanne had Frankie. Hollis had JJ. Noah and Abby—even if the relationships with their siblings were complicated—had Josh and Becca.

"How was skating?" Suzanne said, smiling and patting a spot on the couch. "Tell us about it."

"It sucked," Milo said. Then, "Why didn't you ever get me skating lessons? I was the only person in all of Rockefeller Center who couldn't skate."

This was immature and also untrue. There had been at least a dozen Indian college students in NYU sweatshirts, wiping out all over the ice. But Milo was suddenly consumed with self-pity. He flopped onto a chair opposite the couch and dropped his messenger bag—with its stupid EpiPen and Benadryl inside—onto the floor. Why did he have to be allergic to everything? Why did he have to be so skinny? Why did girls like Hayley Christenson never notice him unless guys like JJ Rabinowitz waved her over and asked her for help on their stupid science projects? Milo's stomach churned.

"You want skating lessons?" Frankie asked.

Milo snorted. "*Yeah*. Because I'm *six*."

"Hey," Suzanne said, looking at him. "What's with the voice?"

"It's the only voice I've got, Suzanne."

"Since when am I 'Suzanne'?"

"Mi," Frankie said gently. "What happened?"

"Nothing *happened*. I just had a crappy time."

It wasn't even true. He'd had an okay time; he was just in a crappy mood because he was jealous. Okay, there. He'd said it. He was jealous of JJ and Hollis because—sometime in the past twenty-four hours, before Milo had even had a chance to respond to Hollis's text—the two of them seemed to have made a connection that didn't include him. Was it juvenile? Yes. Did it make any logical sense? No. But there it was.

"Want to talk about it?" Frankie said. She was using her *My heart is open* voice, her social worker voice. "We're here for you."

Milo said nothing. Of course he didn't want to talk about it. When did he ever want to talk about anything with his mothers?

"You've got a lot on your mind," Suzanne said. "We get it."

"No, you don't," Milo said. The words came out so low even he didn't hear them.

"What, honey?" Frankie said.

"You don't get it."

"What don't we get?"

"What if he doesn't write back?" Milo said. He didn't mean to say it; he wasn't even consciously thinking about it. The question just slipped out. "What if he doesn't want anything to do with me?"

"Oh, Mi," Suzanne said softly.

He shook his head. "I shouldn't have sent that letter. It was stupid."

"It wasn't stupid," Frankie said. "It was brave. I think it's the bravest thing I've ever seen anyone do."

"Really?"

"Yes."

Frankie was probably just saying that. Trying to make him feel better. Because, come on, how brave was it to write a letter and stick it in the mailbox for someone else to deliver? It wasn't like he'd appeared on William Bardo's front porch and rung the doorbell. It wasn't like he'd picked up the phone and called him. Still, Milo felt slightly less sorry for himself. Even though he didn't have an athletic bone in his body. Even though he didn't have a Someone. When Suzanne asked if he wanted meatballs for dinner he said yeah. Meatballs sounded good.

HOLLIS

"LET ME SEE YOUR TOES," JJ SAID.

"My *toes*?"

"Yeah."

"Why?"

"Just let me see them."

Hollis pulled off her socks and propped her feet on the desk in front of the computer.

JJ squinted. "Mm-hmm."

"What?"

"See how your second toe is shorter than your big toe?"

"Yeah. So?"

"Look at mine."

JJ disappeared from view for a minute. Then his freakishly large feet appeared and completely filled the screen.

Hollis laughed. "All I can see is your heels."

"Hang on." He backed up. "Can you see them now?"

"Yeah."

"See how my second toe is longer than my big toe?"

"Yeah."

"Genetics, baby. Longer second toe is dominant. Shorter second toe is recessive."

"Huh." She stared at JJ's feet. "What size are those bad boys?"

"Fourteens."

"Do you have to shop in a special store? Do you have to have your own team of elf shoemakers?"

"You know what they say about men with big feet . . ."

"Don't even—"

"Big hearts."

Hollis tried not to smile but couldn't help herself.

It was Wednesday afternoon and they were Face-Timing. It wasn't their first time. They'd tried it a few nights ago, in the middle of one of their marathon phone calls. "I want to see your face," JJ had said. And Hollis said, "Why?" And he said, "Because I do." So they'd Face-Timed each other from their separate bedrooms, which somehow felt way more intimate than talking on the phone. They toured each other around. They showed each other their stuff. Like JJ's vintage hockey posters (chosen by his mother's decorator, which Hollis thought was weird) and his solar system mobile (built by JJ during his fourth-grade astronaut phase, which Hollis thought was cute).

Hollis told him about the books she loved. He told her about the TV shows he was hooked on. (How had she not seen a single episode of *Breaking Bad*? Blasphemy!)

Hollis didn't know why talking to JJ was so easy. Was it his lack of pretention? His goofiness? His angst? *My mother gave me away. I was an ugly baby.* Whatever it was—whatever walls had been knocked down over the past week to allow them to confide in each other—it was a tender thing. Like a newly hatched butterfly or a mung bean sprout. Hollis had a distinct memory of sprouting mung beans with Pam. It had taken a long time. There were many steps. It involved some kind of a cloth bag.

"Agh, my legs are cramping." JJ lifted his feet and lowered them to the ground. "I have the flexibility of a ninety-year-old."

"You should do yoga."

"Do *you* do yoga?"

"No. But I am extremely flexible." Hollis was about to demonstrate her flexibility by pulling a foot behind her head when her cell phone pinged. She picked it up.

Did u c the email?

"Tell me that's not Gunnar Mott," JJ said.

Hollis shook her head. "It's Milo. He wants to know if I saw the email."

"What email?"

"I don't know."

What email? Hollis texted. Her stomach felt funny. Had Milo heard back from William Bardo? Was this actually happening? Crap. She wasn't ready.

Her phone pinged almost immediately. **Abby's.**

Abby's. Hollis exhaled. **Didn't c it. Sup?**

She found where he works. There's a bio on the site.

Hollis took another breath.

"Everything okay?" JJ said.

"Abby found where he works." She hated the tremulous note in her voice.

"Your donor?"

Hollis nodded. "Milo says there's a bio."

"Did Abby send a link?" JJ said.

"I don't know."

Is there a link? she texted.

Yup, Milo texted back. **Check it out.**

Hollis's chest felt tight, like someone was sitting on it.

"Are you okay?" JJ said.

"Yes."

"Breathe."

"I am."

"Do you want to check your email?"

"I don't know."

"Do you want *me* to check your email?"

"I don't know."

"Why don't we call Milo?" JJ suggested. "He can fill us in."

Hollis closed her eyes. She tried to breathe. *In through the nose, out through the mouth. In through the nose, out through the mouth.*

"Or I could go . . . and you could call him yourself. Maybe it's better if you two—"

"No!" Her eyes snapped open. "Stay. Call him."

"Okay." JJ picked up his phone and tapped the screen. "Hey," he said as soon as Milo answered. "I'm FaceTiming with Hollis. She got your text and she's wondering if you could tell her about Abby's email . . ." Silence for a second. "Because she seems to be having a little trouble breathing."

"I can breathe fine," Hollis said sharply.

"She says she can breathe fine. Hang on—" JJ said. "I'm putting you on speaker . . . okay, you're good."

"Can you hear me?"

Hollis could hear Milo's voice coming out of JJ's phone, which JJ was holding up to the computer screen like a lighter at a rock concert. It was bizarre. This whole thing was bizarre.

"Hollis?" Milo said.

"I can hear you."

"Okay, so he's a teacher."

226

A teacher. It felt as though her insides were being squeezed through a very tiny hole.

"He works at a Montessori school," Milo continued. "The Eden Prairie Cooperative Learning Center. Abby found the website . . . Do you want me to read you his bio?"

"Yes," Hollis said with more conviction than she felt.

JJ nodded encouragingly from the computer screen. He looked warm and rumpled in his plaid shirt: Paul Bunyan relaxing after a day of log rolling. Even though he wasn't actually here, Hollis was glad she had him to look at while she listened.

" 'Hi. I'm Will,' " Milo began.

"Will?" JJ cut in. "What kind of a school—"

"Shhh," Hollis said.

"Sorry."

" 'I'm Will,' " Milo repeated. " 'This is my eighth year teaching Language Arts at the EPCLC. I grew up in a small town outside Indianapolis, Indiana, and received my BA in English from Macalester College in Minnesota. I have an MA in Education from Minnesota State University, Mankato. Before I went into teaching, I was an Outward Bound instructor at Colorado Outward Bound in Denver, which is where I met my wife, Gwen—' "

"He's married?" Hollis blurted.

"He called her his wife," Milo said, "so yeah."

Hollis didn't know why this surprised her. Maybe because, ever since she saw the Macalester yearbook, she'd been picturing William Bardo as a college student. But of course, that was sixteen years ago. He'd be—what? Thirty-eight by now? Thirty-eight wasn't an unreasonable age to be married.

"Can I keep going?" Milo said.

"Yes."

"Okay . . . 'which is where I met my wife, Gwen, who teaches biology and outdoor ed right down the hall. We both love it here. The Eden Prairie Cooperative is a lovely learning community, both environmentally and socially conscious . . . '"

Hollis almost snorted. *Lovely learning community?* But somehow she managed to contain herself and let Milo finish.

" '. . . which meshes with our philosophy that a teacher's job is not just to teach children how to read and write and solve equations, but also how to make the world a more humane and sustainable place. Gwen and I have a little house just a few miles from the school, with a yard big enough for three Nigerian Dwarf goats, a dozen chickens, and a wolfhound named Max. In my spare time I like to read, mountain bike, noodle around on my saxophone, and play Ultimate Frisbee. I look forward to getting to know you this year and learning what makes you tick. Sincerely, Will.'"

"He actually sounds it," JJ said.

"What?" Hollis said.

"Sincere."

"Yeah," Milo said. "He seems like a decent guy."

Sincere? Decent? Hollis was at a loss. She knew what the words meant, obviously, but how was she supposed to feel? Hollis had spent the better part of her life hating this man. She spontaneously combusted just thinking about him—how he'd profited from her conception while taking zero responsibility for her life. He was a bad guy. A careless person. And now . . . what? He was some sincere and decent Montessori-teaching, Nigerian-Dwarf-goat-raising husband with a social conscience? This was bullshit! It was too late! He couldn't just suddenly change his story and expect Hollis to forgive him. It didn't work that way!

"You should check out his page," Milo said. "There's a picture of him in his backyard."

"Nigerian Dwarf goats?" Hollis said weakly. "Really?"

*   *   *

"He sounds like a cool cat," Abby said.

"Define cool cat," Hollis said.

It was her second FaceTime of the day. Hollis needed

perspective, and she was hoping that Abby Fenn—sperm sister, aspiring memoirist—could provide some. Abby Fenn of the shiny hair and the gold cross necklace, lounging on a frilly canopy bed, eating a container of yogurt with a fork. Abby Fenn of the smoker's voice and the disturbingly familiar eyebrows, who seemed unfazed by Hollis's face popping up on her computer in real time.

"Cool cat," Abby said. "Noun. One who enjoys noodling around on his saxophone."

"*Noodling.*" Hollis snorted. "Who *says* that?"

"Jazz musicians. Wordsmiths."

"Pfff," Hollis said.

"You're aware, I assume, that the proverbial apple does not fall far from the tree? Noah's trombone? My writing? You and Milo and your billions of books? Hellooo. He loves to read!"

Hollis gave a noncommittal grunt.

"You have to admit," Abby said. "This is pretty wild."

"What is?"

"This." Abby waved her hands in front of the computer. "All of it. Us finding each other. All these crazy little connections."

Hollis couldn't decide whether to agree with Abby—because on some level she did—or whether to confess that everything she'd assumed about her existence was suddenly being called into question. And it was freaking. Her. Out.

"Hollis?" Abby said.

"Yeah?"

"I think your phone just pinged."

Hollis looked down at her desk. *Crap*, she thought.

"Maybe it's Milo," Abby said. "With news."

Crap, crap, crap. Hollis closed her eyes. *I'm not ready.*

She made herself pick up her cell. She made herself look.

Bitchslut. Stop hooking up w/ other girls boyfriends.

"Ha!" Relief washed over her.

"What?" Abby said. "Is it Milo?"

Hollis shook her head.

"Noah?"

"No."

"Why 'ha'?"

"It's a funny text." *Bitchslut.* It *was* pretty funny. A compound insult.

"What does it say?"

"You don't want to know."

"Yes," Abby said. "I do."

It took Hollis a long time to tell the Malory Keener story. It took her all the way back to second grade. Back to the monkey bars. Back to *My mom says your mom's lifestyle is an abomination.* Hollis told the whole thing, and Abby listened. Hollis described how it felt to see the expression on Malory's face at the Snowflake Formal when she and Gunnar exited the science lab. And the expression on Malory's face outside the auditorium when Hollis called herself an abomination. And the rush she felt every time she pressed her body up against Gunnar's, her lips on his lips.

"That's not okay," Abby said when Hollis finished.

"I know," Hollis said. "I can't explain it. I just like hooking up." *Numbing*, JJ had called it. As though making out in the janitor's closet was anything close to smoking pot in the basement.

"I'm not talking about hooking up," Abby said. "That's just hormones. I'm talking about what those girls are doing."

"What?"

"They're slut shaming you."

"Well. I *did* hook up with Malory's boyfriend."

"That's no excuse."

Hollis shrugged.

"Are they slut shaming *him*?"

"I don't think boys get slut shamed."

"You're making my point," Abby said. "Calling in the middle of the night? Posting those things on Instagram? That's harassment."

"I don't feel harassed."

"Maybe you should."

"I don't want to dignify their behavior with my outrage. Besides . . ." Hollis hesitated.

Abby cocked her head, waiting.

"I kind of like messing with Malory. Every time I see her I remember what she said about Pam in second grade and I get mad all over again."

"Hollis."

"Yeah?"

"Second grade?"

"Yeah. So?"

Abby removed the fork from her yogurt and stabbed the air. "You know what you need, Hollis?"

"What?"

"A resolution to this story."

"You know what you need, Abby?"

"What?"

"A spoon."

*   *   *

It was five o'clock by the time Hollis logged off the computer. Her mother wouldn't be home for another hour, so Hollis pulled her bike out of the garage. It was too cold for a bike ride, but the frigid air felt right for the occasion. Like when you're crying hysterically and what you really need is a slap in the face.

I am on the Arctic tundra, Hollis thought as she ped-aled. *I feel nothing. Feeling nothing is good.*

And it was good. Until she turned onto Reeder Street and there was Gunnar Mott, shooting baskets in Fitzy's driveway.

The universe, Hollis thought as she pedaled, *is messing with me.*

Hollis wanted to avoid Gunnar, but she also wanted him to notice her. Just like she wanted the bitchslut mes-sages to stop, but she also enjoyed getting under Malory's skin. She knew it made no sense. These stupid, weird, needy, competing urges that she justified with Malory's comment about Pam from a million years ago.

Let's make a deal, JJ had said. *Let's break our self-destructive habits together.* Hollis had agreed, more for JJ's sake than for her own. She wasn't sure she bought JJ's theory that Gunnar was her drug of choice. Hollis just liked hooking up. Hooking up made her feel good. Was that really so bad?

Whatever. Her legs *were* tired. She *had* been pump-ing hard. She wouldn't look over. She wouldn't call his name.

But now he was calling hers. "Yo, Hollis!"

She slowed down.

"Hollis!"

He was running now, dribbling the basketball down the street toward her.

"Hey," she said, stopping the bike and putting one foot on the ground.

"Where've you been?" He was sweating a little, even in the cold. His hair stood up in tufts.

"Around."

He spun the basketball on one finger. "Cool."

Cool that she'd been around, or cool that he could spin a basketball on one finger?

"I've been FaceTiming," she blurted. She didn't plan to; it just slipped out. "With my half siblings. We just found out our donor's a teacher."

Gunnar slapped the ball, keeping it moving.

"You know, the father I've never met? He works for some hippie school. And he's *married*."

"Cool."

Hollis stared at Gunnar. *Cool?*

Gunnar caught the ball. "You wanna . . . ?" He cocked his head in the direction of a thicket of trees.

"What?"

He smiled. Great teeth. So white. "You know."

"Do I want to hook up with you in that thicket of trees?"

He shrugged, still smiling.

God, that smile. Part of Hollis wanted to grab him and kiss him right here on the street. But the other part of her was still talking. "Did you not hear what I just said?"

"What?"

"My *father*. We sent him a letter. Like five days ago. We could hear back from him at any second. I'm trying to decide how I *feel*." Hollis was on a roll. The words were just pouring out of her. More words than she had ever spoken to Gunnar Mott.

"*I* know how you feel," he said, tossing his basketball onto the grass.

"You do?"

Gunnar pulled Hollis toward him, bike and all. "Mm-hmm." His lips were on her lips. "You feel soft."

Hollis pulled away. "That's not what I—"

"And warm." His hands were under her shirt. "You feel really warm."

"Hey," Hollis said sharply. This wasn't making her feel good. This was pissing her off.

"What?"

"I was telling you something," Hollis said. "If you want to listen, great. If you want to give me advice, great. But if all you want to do is stick your hands up my shirt . . . well . . . I think I'm going to keep riding my bike."

"Oh." Gunnar stepped back. He looked embarrassed— for her or for himself, she couldn't tell.

Lucky for him, this was the moment when Fitzy hollered down the street, "Yo, Mott! We playin' or what?"

"So, listen," Gunnar said, bending to retrieve his basketball. "I should go."

"Me too."

"I'll see you around, I guess."

"Yeah," Hollis said. "See you around."

WILL BARDO TAUGHT LANGUAGE ARTS.

Will Bardo hailed from Indiana.

Will Bardo owned farm animals.

Will Bardo played Ultimate Frisbee.

Will Bardo was married.

Will Bardo's wife was a knockout.

This last fact was brought to Milo's attention by Noah, who had apparently looked up Gwen Bardo's bio page on the Eden Prairie Cooperative Learning Center website and then sent this text: **Check out WBs wife.**

Milo tapped the link, and suddenly there was Gwen Bardo, holding a surfboard and wearing a wet suit. Her hair was slicked back and hung nearly to her waist. Her legs were long and tan. She was laughing.

There was only one word to text back: **Whoa.**

Ikr? Noah texted.

And Abby texted, **Where does one surf in Minnesota?**

And Hollis texted, **One doesn't.**

And Noah texted, **Missing the point.**

And Abby texted, **& the point is . . .**

She looks like a supermodel, Milo texted.

And Hollis texted, **Hello. She also has a brain.**

It was true. According to Gwen Bardo's bio, she had double-majored in earth sciences and chemistry at Dartmouth. She held a master's in science from Trinity College in Dublin. Her field of interest was biodiversity and conservation.

Thank u, Hollis, Abby texted.

And Hollis texted, **It's not like looks and brains r mutually exclusive.**

And Noah texted, **WB hit the jackpot.**

And Milo texted, **Srsly.**

If a man with Milo's mushroom hair and crazy eyebrows could get a woman like that to marry him, there had to be hope. Gwen Bardo gave Milo hope.

When Will Bardo writes back, Milo thought, *I will ask him how it happened.*

*   *   *

When Will Bardo writes back.

It had been seven days and, so far, nothing. No letter. No email. Nada.

"Did the mail come yet?" Suzanne asked Milo on Friday afternoon.

"Uh-huh," he said.

"Anything interesting?" Frankie asked. Casually, as though she were wondering if the new *National Geographic* had arrived.

Milo shook his head.

*   *   *

Any word? Noah texted on Saturday afternoon.

Nope, Milo texted back.

Maybe he's trapped under something heavy, Abby texted.

And Hollis texted, **Maybe he's too busy noodling on his sax to write back.**

And Noah texted, **Maybe a Nigerian dwarf goat ate his letter.**

And Milo texted, **Maybe he sent his letter by carrier pigeon.**

Or by chicken.

Maybe his house caught fire and the letter burned.

Maybe he was abducted by aliens.

Maybe he's in a witness protection program and has a whole new identity.

Maybe he doesn't actually exist.

Maybe he's a figment of our imagination.

Maybe none of us exist.

Maybe the moon is made of green cheese.

It all degenerated from there.

*　　*　　*

On Sunday night, JJ and his parents came for dinner. Milo didn't know why Suzanne and Frankie had felt the need to invite them, but they had.

Roz and Abe Rabinowitz arrived at seven thirty sharp— she in tight leather pants and teetering heels, carrying a houseplant, he in a black T-shirt and jeans, carrying a bottle. JJ shuffled behind them, wearing a plaid shirt and a pained expression. He had to be a foot taller than both his parents. And about twenty shades blonder.

"Welcome, welcome," Suzanne said. She was wearing a multicolored tunic that made her look like a tropical fish.

"Come in, come in," Frankie said.

Why his moms were saying everything twice Milo

couldn't comprehend. Nor could he fathom why Frankie was wearing a gay pride sweatshirt—as though the fact that she and Suzanne were lesbians wasn't obvious.

"We brought you a bamboo palm," JJ's mother said, holding out the plant. Her nails were long and painted purple.

"How lovely!" Suzanne exclaimed.

"And a Glenmorangie single malt," JJ's father said, holding out the bottle. He was completely bald. His scalp shone in the overhead light.

"You shouldn't have," Frankie said.

"It's our pleasure."

Could this be any more awkward? Milo wondered, as the six of them gathered around the coffee table for allergy-friendly, gluten-free appetizers. Cilantro chicken satay. Vietnamese salad rolls. Ham-wrapped asparagus.

"So," Frankie said, helping herself to a satay. "I hear you both work in film. That must be exciting."

Milo groaned inwardly, but JJ's dad nodded and dipped a salad roll in soy-free duck sauce. "It is indeed."

"Tell us what you're working on," Suzanne said, placing a bowl of olives on the table.

"Well." Abe Rabinowitz cleared his throat. "About a year ago, a gem of a script fell into my lap . . ."

JJ's dad talked about his gem of a script. Suzanne poured wine and ginger ale. They drank. They munched.

Well, most of them munched. Roz Rabinowitz—screen name "Roz Rabin"—took one bite of asparagus before putting it down. The camera adds twenty pounds! Milo kept eating. He could use twenty pounds. JJ kept checking his watch. Twice. Thrice. Four times. Everyone moved to the butcher-block table. More movie talk. More drinks. More hypo-allergenic cuisine. Suzanne and Frankie had gone all out for this dinner. It felt good to be eating new things; it felt *amazing*. Letter? No letter? What did it matter? These stuffed peppers were the bomb. Milo could eat all night. Will Bardo could take his sweet time. The parents could talk about film noir and production budgets and digital cinematography until the cows came home. Milo was going to eat six of these bad boys.

"You know who would be a natural on screen?" Abe Rabinowitz boomed, hoisting his glass in the air. "Jonah. If he would ever listen to his father and give acting a shot."

Milo looked over at JJ, who was looking blankly at his dad, as though to say, *In your dreams*. JJ's mom squeezed JJ's arm and leaned in to kiss his cheek. "Look at this face. Can you believe this face?"

"Mom," JJ whispered. "I'm eating."

"He's eating." Roz Rabin smiled. Her teeth were a little purple from the wine. "Always eating, this one."

"This one, too," Frankie said, jutting her chin at Milo. "Bottomless pit."

"When my brother and I were teenagers," JJ's dad said, "we used to eat a whole loaf of bread for breakfast. And a whole jar of peanut butter. Our mother would come downstairs and say, 'Where's all the food? I just went to the market.'"

The parents shared a chuckle. They were hitting it off.

*　　*　　*

"I'm sorry," JJ said later.

The two of them were in Milo's room while Abe and Roz and Frankie and Suzanne were having "digestifs" by the fire.

"What for?" Milo said.

"My parents."

"What about them?"

JJ frowned. Happy JJ, golden-retriever JJ—frowning. "They're so . . . I don't know."

"I thought they were pretty cool."

JJ shook his head. "They just . . . don't get it."

"Get what?"

"Anything. Life outside the movie set. Me. We're just . . . nothing alike."

"And what—?" Milo said. "You think your biological parents would be different? You think they'd 'get' you more because they're six-foot Swedes instead of five-foot Jews?"

"Maybe. Yeah."

This sentiment wasn't lost on Milo. He'd had similar thoughts for a long time, although his were less about genes and more about gender. *Suzanne and Frankie don't get me. My father would get me because he's a guy.* But how much could Will Bardo get him if he couldn't even be bothered to write back? How much did Noah's father get Noah? How much did Leigh get Hollis?

"None of them get us, dude," Milo said to JJ. "They're parents."

HOLLIS

NOT HOOKING UP WITH GUNNAR MOTT REALLY OPENED UP Hollis's schedule. She was back to eating lunch with Shay and Gianna. She was no longer pleading for bathroom passes to meet Gunnar during class, or lingering behind the bleachers after school, waiting for him to finish practice. The good news was, Hollis had nothing but time. The bad news was, she was bored. All Shay and Gianna talked about was school. Sitting through class after class without a single kissing break was mind numbing. Hollis was thinking too much.

Ten days. Ten days since Milo sent the letter to Will Bardo, and still nothing. She didn't know how to feel. If he never wrote back, well, then he was the jackass she'd always assumed him to be and she could just go back to thinking the way she had always thought about him. Or could she? Now she had *information*. Now she had a *visual*. Will Bardo in his backyard with his stupid goats. Hiking boots, jeans, gray hoodie. Curls, eyes squinting into the sun, crooked grin. Crap. Hollis wished Abby had never found out where he worked. Hollis wished she'd never seen his bio page. Now he was real. Real and choosing not to write back.

"What are you hoping to hear?" JJ had asked when they were talking on the phone last night. "If he did write back, what would you actually want him to say?"

Hollis didn't know.

She didn't know how to feel about Will Bardo, and she didn't know how to feel about her mother going on a date.

A date, Hollis thought as she sat in Algebra II, pretending to care about logarithmic functions. *My mother is going on a date.*

It had happened Sunday afternoon. Tania Kosiewicz, Alumni Relations, called, allegedly for news about William Bardo, but then, as soon as she discovered that there was no news to speak of, she asked Leigh out. Dinner and a movie. Maybe some live music. Hollis's mother had been giddy when she got off the phone. She was talking so fast, Hollis had to tell her to take a breath. *Breeeeeeeathe.* Leigh had promised herself, when Pam died, that she wouldn't go on a single date until she felt "the spark." She felt it right away, she admitted to Hollis, that day in the alumni office,

247

the moment Tania Kosiewicz smiled. It was instantaneous.

"The spark?" Hollis said.

"The spark."

Hollis didn't know how she felt about the spark. Or about Will Bardo. Or about JJ being so sweet. Or about Gunnar blowing her off in the hall this morning. All Hollis knew was that she couldn't sit through one more second of logarithmic functions.

She raised her hand and asked for a bathroom pass.

* * *

Wandering the empty halls gave Hollis even more time to think. How was this helpful? She considered walking down to the language lab, where Gunnar had Español, and trying to flag him down through Señora Lopez's window. But no. God, no. What was *wrong* with her? Hollis reversed direction.

As she ambled past the computer lab, a thought ambled into her brain. If Jonah Jedediah Rabinowitz went to school here, would she be trolling the halls looking for *him*? But before she could contemplate an answer, Hollis saw the vice principal turn the corner and start walking toward her. The last thing she needed was detention. Hollis veered left into the girls' room. There, standing at the sink, applying mascara with a vengeance, was Malory Keener.

Well. Hollis hadn't expected this. Neither, apparently, had Malory, whose mouth made a little "oh" of surprise in the mirror.

Hollis glanced around. She waited for a toilet to flush, for one of Malory's Size Zeros to slink out of a stall. Nothing happened.

"Well," Hollis said, "go ahead."

Malory stared at her in the mirror. "What?"

"Call me a slut. Or a ho. Or a ho-bag bitchslut. Whatever you've got."

Malory's mascara wand hovered in the air, and her face morphed. She looked . . . how did she look? Uneasy. In all the time Hollis had known her, which was basically since kindergarten, she couldn't remember a time when Malory Keener had looked unsure of herself. She was always surrounded by friends. She always had a buffer. This unfamiliar expression, Hollis realized, was her cue. "What—?" she said, taking a step forward. "You can't say it to my face? You need a phone to help you?"

Malory's phone, in its aggressively pink, bejeweled case, was perched on the edge of the sink. Instinctively, Malory reached out and clutched it to her heart, as though Hollis might steal her lifeline. She glanced over Hollis's shoulder, presumably contemplating her escape.

"Tell me something," Hollis said, widening her stance. "Is it fun, calling me names?"

"Is it fun, hooking up with my boyfriend?"

"Actually, yeah. He's a really good kisser."

Malory's pretty face twisted. "God, you're awful."

"*I'm* awful?"

"Yes."

Now that they were facing each other, Hollis noticed something. Malory's annoyingly blue eyes were bloodshot. Puffy.

"What's wrong with you?" Hollis asked.

"What's wrong with *you?*"

"No, I mean . . . you look like you've been crying."

"What do you care?"

I don't, Hollis thought. *I don't care about you, Malory Keener, because you are a careless person.* And yet . . . goddamn it, look at those baby blues welling up.

"Let me guess." Hollis yanked a paper towel out of the dispenser and handed it to Malory. "Boyfriend troubles?"

"Shut up," Malory said, setting down her mascara and dabbing at her eyes with a tiny corner of the towel. "I had a fight with my mom."

"Does she find your lifestyle abominable?"

"What?"

"Nothing." Hollis shook her head. "Go on."

"She thinks I'm getting fat. I came downstairs this

morning wearing these jeans and she said they looked like sausage casings."

Hollis stared at Malory. Tall, yes. Curvy, yes. *Fat*? Not even close. "Are you serious?"

"I've gained ten pounds in the past year."

"Yeah," Hollis said. "It's called puberty."

Malory shook her head. "She doesn't see it that way. My mom's, like . . . super judgmental."

"No shit," Hollis said.

Malory raised her eyebrows.

"I recall."

"You recall what?"

"Second grade? The monkey bars?"

Malory gave her a blank look.

"My mom had just died," Hollis said. "We were up on the monkey bars and I was crying, and you turned to me in your little plaid dress, and you said, 'My mom says your mom's lifestyle is an abomination.'"

Malory's pretty brow crinkled. "I did?"

"Direct quote."

"I don't remember that."

"Right," Hollis said, like she didn't believe Malory. But she did, a little. It was a long time ago.

"I swear," Malory said.

"Well, *I* do. You said it with such conviction. Like being gay was a crime against humanity."

"I don't think that."

"Well . . . you thought it in second grade."

"I was *seven.*"

"So?"

"I was quoting my mother!"

Hollis knew this was true, but she wasn't ready to concede the point. "You can't blame your mother for everything."

"I'm not—"

"I was grieving! You made me feel like shit! You still do!"

"Wait—" Malory blinked at Hollis. "*That's* why you've been hooking up with Gunnar? Because of something I said to you in *second grade?*"

Hollis shrugged. "If the shoe fits."

Malory opened her mouth, closed it, opened it again.

"I believe the word you're looking for is 'bitchslut'?"

Malory's lips twitched. "For the record, I have never called you any of those things."

"Right. You just set your dogs on me."

"They're not dogs. They're my friends."

"Well, would you mind calling them off?"

"Would you mind not hooking up with my boyfriend?"

Hollis shook her head in amazement. "How are you still going out with a guy who cheats on you?"

Malory stared at Hollis. "I love him."

"Seriously?"

"I don't expect *you* to understand. But yes."

Hollis had to grit her teeth to avoid saying something snarky. What did Malory Keener know about love? Then Malory blew her nose into the paper towel, a big, wet honk, and suddenly, against all her better judgment, Hollis didn't hate her anymore. "Just for the record . . ."

"Yeah?"

"You're not fat."

Malory looked surprised. "Thanks."

Hollis turned around. It was the perfect word to leave on.

*　　*　　*

A date. My mother is going on a date.

Leigh was trying to decide what to wear. It was a Tuesday, not a Saturday. Casual, right? She didn't want to overdo it.

Hollis felt both elated and devastated. Her mother was going on a date! But there was Pam, hanging over the fireplace, watching Leigh iron her palazzo pants and her jean skirt with the funky border. Pants or skirt? Pants or skirt? She couldn't decide.

Hollis stared into Pam's wide, hazel eyes and said, "Mom."

"I know," her mother said.

And Hollis thought, *Do you?*

"Pam and I talked about it. After her diagnosis, when we knew it wasn't good. She told me she wanted me to fall in love again."

Hollis swallowed. "She did?"

"Well, first she wanted me to grieve for a while. Cry, drink a lot of wine, eat a lot of cheese. But eventually, yeah. She wanted me to fall in love and get married. Because we never could. Because she believed that someday the law would change."

Hollis remembered when it happened. It was the summer before sixth grade. She had been riding her bike around the house and she'd just wiped out on the driveway. She ran into the house to get a Band-Aid for her scraped knee, and there was her mother on the couch, crying.

"What's wrong?" Hollis said. And Leigh had pointed to the TV—where a video montage was playing. Couples kissing; couples laughing; couples throwing their linked hands in the air. Then the newscaster came on. A guy with helmet hair and Day-Glo teeth, standing on the steps of the capitol building to announce that today was an historic day for the state of Minnesota. Same-sex marriage was now fully legal and recognized, not just in the Twin Cities, but in every city and town from Owatonna to Roseau.

Her mother had gone from crying to laughing. From laughing to whooping. From whooping to busting out the champagne flutes and pouring the sparkling cider. She toasted Pam's picture hanging over the fireplace. *We did it, Pammy.* Those were her words. *We did it.*

And now . . . now her mother was looking up from the ironing board, not at Pam, but at Hollis. "Pants or skirt? Be honest."

"Are you going to marry her?" Hollis blurted.

"What?"

"Tania Kosiewicz. Are you going to marry her?"

Her mother laughed, a single "Ha!"

"What's so funny?" It was all well and good for her mother to go on a date tonight, but if things got serious, Leigh's life wouldn't be the only one to change. Hollis's life would change, too. What if Tania Kosiewicz moved in? What if she wanted kids? What if she already *had* kids?

"Hol," her mother said. "We just met."

"I know, but—"

Leigh held up a hand to stop her. "One step at a time. Please. It's taken me seven years to get to the point where I would even *consider* dating. Anyway, we may not hit it off."

"You'll hit it off."

"You think so?"

Hollis looked at her mother—the mixture of doubt and

255

hope on her face. Her mother was going on a date and she was nervous. This was so *weird*.

"Pants," Hollis said. "You'll be more comfortable in pants."

"You're right," her mother said. She looked relieved. She held up the palazzos and nodded. "Thank you."

"You're welcome."

Her mother went upstairs to get dressed, leaving Hollis alone in the living room with Pam. She could feel Pam watching her. Wherever she went in the room, Pam's eyes followed. Hollis wasn't a nut job. She had never been so crazy as to talk to a picture on the wall. To do so now would be stupid and unnatural. But here she was, looking at Pam. And here was Pam, looking at her.

Hollis cleared her throat.

"Mom's going on a date," she said softly.

Pam didn't respond.

Hollis tried again, louder. "I found my father. He lives in Eden Prairie. His name is Will."

Finally, "I don't hate Malory anymore."

Nothing.

Of course nothing; Pam was a freaking picture on the wall. Hollis held her gaze anyway. Just for a second. Even though she knew it was dumb.

MILO

MILO AND JJ WERE IN MILO'S BEDROOM WORKING ON
their Science Palooza project. Frankie brought snacks.
First, rice chips and bean dip. About twenty minutes later,
sliced pears and black cherry seltzer. Maybe she was doing
this out of the goodness of her heart. Or maybe—despite
Milo's assurances that JJ had quit smoking, and despite
Frankie deeming JJ's parents "perfectly respectable"—
she still half expected to open the door and find JJ rolling
a joint. Milo didn't know what Frankie was thinking. All
he knew was that JJ was crunching rice chips all over their
poster board.

"Dude," Milo said, brushing off the crumbs.

"Sorry," JJ said, spraying out a few more. "How many
pictures do we have?"

Milo counted. They had photos of him, Suzanne, and

Frankie. The three Hollis had emailed of herself, Leigh, and Pam. They had the four Fenns: Abby, her mom, dad, and sister Becca. They had the four Resnicks: Noah, his mom, dad, and twin brother Josh, who looked surprisingly blue-eyed and fair-haired. And they had two pictures of Will Bardo: the Macalester yearbook portrait, circa 2000, and the photo from his bio page on the Eden Prairie Cooperative Learning Center website. Last night Milo had resized them all on Suzanne's computer and printed each one on her color printer. They now lay on the floor next to the poster board, dealt out in rows like playing cards. Sixteen.

"You think that's enough?" JJ said.

"I don't know."

JJ picked up the photo of Will Bardo in his backyard. "I wish we had a close-up."

"We do." Milo pointed to the yearbook portrait.

"A *recent* close-up. To compare to the other parents."

Milo shrugged. "Not for lack of trying."

Two weeks and two days. Two weeks and two days since he sent the letter to Will Bardo, and *still* nothing. The only new development was Noah finding Will's name on a website for the Twin Cities Ultimate League. Every Saturday, apparently, Will Bardo tossed around a Frisbee with a bunch of other guys who called themselves the Floppy Discs. Interesting fact, but so what?

He is never writing back, Milo thought. *He is never writing back, and I will never know why.* Then he thought, *Screw it.* He guzzled some black cherry seltzer and shoved a chip loaded with bean dip into his mouth. At least after he glue-sticked these photos onto the poster board he could call Hayley Christenson and tell her he was ready for her help. He could invite her over and—

"Dude," JJ said, pointing to the rug, onto which Milo had just plopped some bean dip.

Milo scooped the beans up with a napkin. *Hayley Christenson.* Just thinking about her made his stomach flip.

"Maybe we should throw in a few decoys," JJ suggested. "Someone who's not related to anyone. Like me. Or Will's wife."

"Sure," Milo said. He didn't care what photos they used. He grabbed his glass, took another slug of seltzer.

There was a knock on the door. "Mi?"

Milo twisted around. Frankie. Again. Obviously she didn't trust them in here. He was about to call her on it, but then she said, "Your phone is blowing up."

"What?"

She held up his cell, which had been charging on the kitchen counter. "You're very popular today." She walked over, handed it to Milo. "Ping, ping, ping."

"Thanks," he said.

Milo waited until Frankie left. Then he looked at his

phone, and his stomach flipped again. Hard. There were Hayley Christenson flips, and there were half-sibling group-texting flips.

Did u c the email???

One word: lame.

What family stuff?

R we not family stuff?

Not opposed to future contact. WTF.

Marinate???

Excuse me, r we steak tips?

Srsly.

Milo r u out there?

Milo check your email!!!

Milo felt his insides churn.

"Hey." A rice chip hit him in the elbow. JJ. "Are you okay?"

Milo nodded, barely. "I have to check my email."

"Okay . . ."

"I think he wrote back."

*   *   *

From: 873rt0sjo2908dklsklmw3@reply
.DonorProgenyProject.org
To: MiloRobClark@brooklynIDS.org; HollisDarbs
@MNPSmail.org; AbsofSteel3
@sheboygancountryday.edu; NoahZark.Rez
@techHSmail.com
Date: Monday, February 1, at 3:13 PM
Subject: Sorry for the delay

Hi, Milo, Hollis, Abby, and Noah.

I apologize for not responding sooner. My wife,
Gwen, and I had some family stuff going on and
were out of town. But we're back now, and I
wanted to let you know that A) I received your
letter, and B) I am indeed Donor #9677.
   Wow. I knew this would happen one day, but
still. This is a real head trip. I'm glad you guys
reached out, and I'm not opposed to future
contact, but if you don't mind, I'm going to let this
marinate for a bit. I'll be in touch.

All best,
Will

Without a word, Milo handed his phone to JJ. He waited for JJ to finish reading.

" 'Not opposed to future contact,' " JJ said. "That's promising."

Milo said nothing.

"He'll be in touch, he says. After . . . you know . . . he puts his thoughts in a ziplock bag with some Thousand Island dressing."

Marinate for a bit, Milo thought. How long was a "bit"? A week? A month? A year? A "bit" wasn't good enough.

"Hey," JJ said. "I was kidding—"

Milo held up his hand. An idea was unfurling inside his head. A crazy idea.

"LET ME GET THIS STRAIGHT," HOLLIS SAID, SQUEEZING the phone to her ear. "You want Abby and Noah to come for Presidents' Day weekend, too."

"Yes," Milo said.

"Under the guise of a half-sibling reunion."

"Not *under the guise* of a half-sibling reunion. It will actually *be* a half-sibling reunion."

"The purpose of which will be to stalk our sperm donor."

"'Stalk' is a strong word."

"Okay . . ."

"We will not be stalking him. We will be observing him in his natural habitat."

Hollis snorted. "What is this—Animal Planet?"

"JJ's words," Milo said.

"You shared this plan with JJ?"

"Yes, and he thinks it's brilliant."

Hollis pictured JJ, standing outside Milo's apartment saluting the cab. She pictured his giant bare feet on her computer screen. "You're using JJ Rabinowitz as your gauge for brilliance?"

"Why not?" Milo said.

"He's . . ." Hollis hesitated.

"What?"

"JJ will do anything. He doesn't care what people think."

"He cares what *you* think," Milo said. "He cares big-time."

Hollis felt her cheeks flush. "Shut up. That's not what I mean."

"What do you mean?"

This, Hollis thought, was always the hardest question to answer. "I mean . . . come on. We're just going to show up on our sperm donor's porch and peer through his windows?"

"No," Milo said. "We're going to show up at the Recreational Sports Dome at the University of Minnesota and watch him play Ultimate Frisbee."

Hollis blinked. "Are you serious?"

"It's the Indoor Hat Tournament."

"What?"

"I checked out the website. There's a tournament that weekend and the Floppy Discs are registered. February thirteenth. Open to the public, and we are the public."

"Okay," Hollis said slowly. "But don't you think we should . . . I don't know . . . give him a heads-up?"

"Did he give *us* a heads-up when he donated his sperm? Did he give us the chance to say, *Hey, actually, number 9677, I prefer not to be conceived in this manner*? He didn't consider *our* feelings. Aren't you the one who raised that point to me?"

"I may have been," Hollis admitted.

"Hollis," Milo said. "We're not going to ambush him. We're just going to watch him play Frisbee. He won't even know we're there."

Hollis shook her head. It was a ridiculous idea. Harebrained. Was she actually going to agree to this? Was she really that malleable? "Fine."

"Fine what?"

"I will ask my mother if Noah and Abby can come. She'll probably be thrilled."

"You think?"

"She's been reminiscing a lot, about these parties she and Pam used to throw. She says our house is too quiet."

"Okay," Milo said. "Just ask about Noah and Abby, though. Don't mention the Will thing."

"Why not?"

"If you tell your mom we're going to watch him play Frisbee, she'll tell Suzanne and Frankie, and Frankie will want to go with us. She'll probably want to talk to him. Have a whole heart-to-heart. She could scare him away."

"Fine," Hollis said. "I'll just ask about Noah and Abby."

"Thank you."

"You're welcome."

"Oh, and JJ wants to come, too."

"*What?*" Hollis's throat was suddenly dry.

"You heard me. He wants to be the event photographer."

"The event photographer—"

"You know, that project we're working on for school? The one you emailed me the photos for? Genetic traits. He wants to take pictures of everyone's widow's peaks and tongues and . . . I don't know . . . knuckle hair. Really, I think he's just looking for an excuse to see you."

"Oh." JJ coming to Minnesota. To see her.

"Think about it," Milo said. "No pressure or anything."

"Right." Hollis huffed out a small snort. "No pressure."

* * *

Her mother said yes, as Hollis had known she would. Hollis asked her the next morning at breakfast, waiting until Leigh had finished recapping Date #2 with Tania Kosiewicz because that was more pressing business. It wasn't so much that Hollis wanted to hear details—how good the spaghetti Bolognese was, or how the two of them talked through the whole movie, or how Tania loved jazz. It was the look on her mother's face.

Hollis tried to remember the last time she'd seen her mother truly happy. She thought back to before Pam got sick—before the stomachaches, before the pill bottles, before the sleeping all day on the couch. Hollis remembered her two moms sitting at the kitchen counter, drinking French-press coffee, eating Pam's lemon-poppyseed scones and laughing. Pam always made her mother laugh.

Leigh didn't exactly laugh when she told Hollis about her second date, but she did smile. Which was almost as good.

"I'm glad you had fun," Hollis said. They were eating frozen toaster waffles. Hollis found this oddly comforting. Seeing her mother cook was just wrong.

"Me too."

"Do you think you'll go out again?"

Her mother smiled. "I think so. Yeah."

"So . . ." Hollis cleared her throat. "I have to ask you about something."

Leigh's fork hovered above her plate. "What? Is it weird for you that I'm dating?"

"No. I mean, yes—it's weird that you're dating, but my question is unrelated. It's about Presidents' Day weekend."

"What about it?"

"I know Milo and his moms are coming. But I was wondering . . . well, Milo and I were both wondering . . . could we invite Noah and Abby, too? They wouldn't have to stay here or anything. They could get rooms at the DoubleTree or whatever, but we just thought, since it's a holiday weekend, and since the four of us have been getting to know each other—"

"Oh, honey," her mother said.

"What?"

Her mother's eyes were shiny. There was Nutella on her lip. A clump of mascara in her lashes from last night. "A party."

"Well, it doesn't have to be a *party* per se—"

"Pam would love this. Do you have any idea how much Pam would love this?"

"Yes," Hollis said.

"Can you get me their numbers? Noah's and Abby's parents? They'll need to buy tickets. When is Presidents' Day weekend again?"

"February twelfth."

"February twelfth . . . February *twelfth*?"

"Through the fifteenth."

Her mother's eyes widened. "That's ten days from now."

"I know," Hollis said.

"Oh my God. We need to start *planning*."

MILO

HOLLIS HAD DONE IT. IF YOU'D TOLD MILO SIX WEEKS AGO
that Hollis Darby-Barnes would be organizing a half-sibling
reunion/sperm-donor stakeout on her home turf, he would
have laughed in your face. But here it was: February 12.
And here they were: Milo, Suzanne, Frankie, and JJ on a
plane to Minnesota.

Part of Milo was glad his moms were with him. He
could pretend this was just another vacation—like the one
they'd taken to the Bahamas when Milo was ten. Or
the ski trip to Vail for Frankie's forty-fifth birthday. His
moms made him feel grounded. And yet a part of Milo
wished it could be just the four of them: him, Hollis,
Noah, and Abby. Well, the *five* of them if you counted
JJ. JJ Rabinowitz, honorary sperm sibling—or, if you
were Frankie, JJ Rabinowitz, "lost soul." That's what she

called him when Milo told his moms JJ wanted to come on the trip. "Poor kid," Frankie said. "He's a bit of a lost soul, isn't he?" Then she went into social worker overdrive, talking about identity formation in adopted children and how the turbulent teen years invite complicated feelings about self. Milo had wanted to call BS. *Attachment theory? Self-identification?* JJ wasn't looking for a *new family* by coming with them to Saint Paul. He was looking for a way to hook up with Hollis! But Milo hadn't argued. He'd kept his mouth shut. Because honestly, he felt a little guilty. JJ, at least, was in on the plan, which was more than Milo could say for his moms.

Milo wondered what would happen tomorrow. Would he see Will Bardo standing there in the Recreational Sports Dome and feel compelled to walk up and introduce himself? And if he did, what would happen? Would Will Bardo flip out, like one of those meth heads who got busted on *COPS*? "I told you I wanted to let this marinate, man!" Would he run? Would he throw his Frisbee like one of those circular swords? Milo's head was spinning. Whoa. He needed to get a grip.

"Ladies and gentlemen, welcome to Minneapolis–Saint Paul International Airport. Local time is 4:22 p.m."

HOLLIS

OHMYGOD. OHMYGOD. OHMYGOD. THIS WAS HOLLIS'S BRAIN in the middle of the Minneapolis–Saint Paul International Airport baggage claim, where she and her mother stood side by side, holding up a ridiculous piece of poster board that read *Robinson, Clark, Resnick, Fenn* in black Sharpie.

This was actually happening. She had agreed to this. She, Hollis Darby-Barnes, had made this weekend possible. What had she been *thinking*?

Hollis reminded herself that she was doing this out of half-sisterly love for Milo. That seeing their donor in person could lead to meeting him, to developing a relationship, to genetic testing, which—down the line—might, in some convoluted way Hollis didn't fully understand, help

Milo find a cure for his allergies. She told herself she was doing a good thing. She told herself to breathe.

"Are you nervous?"

Hollis looked at her mother. "Why would I be nervous?"

"You're scowling."

"So?"

"You scowl when you're nervous."

"I scowl when people ask me stupid questions."

Her mother smiled. Smiled! "You'll be fine."

Hollis did not think she would be fine. But then planes started arriving and swells of people filled the escalator, and suddenly, she was swept up in it all. Everything happened at once. Abby—Hollis knew it was Abby because her shirt read *Careful what you say, or I'll put you in my memoir*—ran over and hugged her, then whipped out a small, spiral-bound notebook and said, "Tell me what you're feeling, right now, in this moment."

Noah, who seemed to arrive nearly simultaneously, was a taller, wider, shorter-haired version of Milo, a fact that Hollis's mother commented on immediately.

"You're smaller than I thought you'd be," Noah said, hooking an arm around Hollis's neck. He smelled like cologne.

"You're bigger than I thought you'd be."

"Nice shirt," Noah said to Abby, giving her the same elbow-neck hug, but with his other arm.

272

"Careful what you say," Abby said. "I'll put you in my memoir."

Leigh introduced herself to Noah and Abby. Abby offered everyone Dubble Bubble. Leigh asked after Noah's and Abby's parents, with whom she had spoken several times on the phone, and whom she now wanted Noah and Abby to call, to let them know they'd arrived safely.

At some point a whistle pierced the air. When Hollis looked up there was Suzanne at the top of the escalator, waving. Frizzy hair, long crocheted sweater. She was flanked by Milo and Frankie—jeans, beat-up leather jacket—and they were working their way down, which of course meant teary-eyed mom hugs and exclamations about facial features. "Look at the eyebrows! Look at the jawlines!"

Suddenly, Hollis was surrounded on all sides. Noah and Milo were fist bumping and back slapping. Frankie was squeezing Hollis's arm. Suzanne was kissing her cheek. Hollis was just trying to breathe, lifting her chin for a little oxygen, when she saw JJ working his way through the bodies.

"JJ Rabinowitz," he said, pumping Noah's hand up and down. "No relation to anyone."

Hollis watched him move from Noah to Abby to Leigh, plaid arm pumping, hair flopping in his eyes. "JJ Rabinowitz, honorary sperm sibling." "JJ Rabinowitz, event photographer." God, he was weird. Hollis watched him introduce himself and she thought about how he didn't have any of this, how he didn't know who his birth parents were, or where they lived, or whether they were even alive. He didn't know if he had brothers or sisters, or, if he did, whether he would ever meet them, and how it must feel even weirder for him to be here than for anyone else. And she heard herself saying, "Look what the cat dragged in."

When he turned around and saw her, he grinned, shaking his head like he couldn't believe what he was seeing. Like, what were the odds he would run into her in the Minneapolis–Saint Paul International Airport on February 12? "Hollis Darby," he said.

"JJ Rabinowitz."

"I'm here to take a picture of your clover tongue."

"Oh, really."

"And your hitchhiker's thumbs."

"I don't have hitchhiker's thumbs."

"Prove it."

Hollis gave him two thumbs-up and he grabbed both of them in his big warm hands and squeezed. "It's good to see you," he said.

"It's good to see you, too."

And they stood there, grinning like idiots, thumb-holding in the baggage claim until Milo came over and thumped Hollis on the back. "How do you feel?"

Hollis thought for a moment. "I feel okay."

"Good." He thumped her again. "We're going to pick up the rental car."

*　　*　　*

It was weird having all these people in her house. Perched on chairs, leaning against counters, nibbling on the snacks Hollis's mother had put out. But it could have been weirder, Hollis reminded herself as Suzanne walked around the kitchen taking drink orders. Abby and Noah could have brought along their parents and siblings. Meeting Becca and Josh—Hollis's half-siblings-in-law, or half siblings once removed, or whatever they were? *That* would be weird. When Hollis thought about it, she was impressed that Noah and Abby came alone. The only time Hollis had traveled anywhere alone was to sleep-away camp in Iowa. She was eleven. She'd *hated* it—a fact that her mother seemed to have forgotten because this very morning, while she was unrolling sleeping bags in the basement in anticipation of everyone's arrival, Leigh exclaimed, "This will be just like camp!" Suzanne and Frankie would have Hollis's room, and the five kids would get the basement all to themselves. Their own bunk! What could be better?

"I hated camp," Hollis felt free to remind her mother. "I didn't have any friends."

"This will be different," her mother said. "The friends are built in."

The friends are built in.

Until her mother had said that, Hollis hadn't really thought of her half siblings as friends. But she supposed they were. In the past month, she'd talked to Milo and Abby and Noah more than she'd talked to Shay and Gianna. Which begged the question . . . was JJ Rabinowitz, honorary sperm sibling, a friend, too? The thought of JJ sleeping in the same room filled Hollis with . . . what? She didn't know. She and JJ had been talking on the phone—and FaceTiming and texting—for nearly four weeks. They had never hooked up. They had never even hugged. But that didn't mean nothing was happening between them.

"What do you think?" Leigh called out in the middle of the hubbub. "Should we order some pizza?" She had found—in consultation with Suzanne and Frankie—a restaurant in Saint Paul that made a gluten-free, dairy-free, soy-free pizza, so Milo could have his own pie.

Yes! They all agreed. Pizza!

Pizza was ordered. Pizza was delivered. Pizza was consumed. JJ ate five slices of Hawaiian. Five!

"Where do you put it all?" Hollis asked.

"Right here," JJ said, tapping his thigh. "My hollow leg."

Milo, who was sitting on JJ's other side, knocked on JJ's head. "What about in here? Isn't this hollow, too?"

"Hardy har har."

"Why don't we play a board game?" Hollis's mother suggested.

A board game? Hollis nearly groaned. But Noah had Trivia Crack on his iPad and Abby said she was unbeatable in Trivia Crack.

"Is that so?" Noah said.

And Abby said, "Try me."

They gathered around the coffee table. It was the Darby-Resnick-Rabinowitzes versus the Robinson-Clark-Fenns. The competition was fierce. At some point, Abby busted Noah in the kitchen, texting his brother Josh for an answer to some obscure basketball question. "Cheater!" she cried, dragging Noah by his elbow back into the living room. "I call for a disqualification!"

"In my defense," Noah said. "If Josh had agreed to come here and support his brother, he would be on my team."

"Oh no," Abby said. "You are *not* going to pull on our heartstrings right now."

*　　*　　*

Later, when the lights were out and the five of them were scattered around the basement in their separate sleeping bags, but no one was actually sleeping, the subject came up again. Noah texted Josh one of the pictures JJ had taken of the four half siblings on the couch. Josh didn't text back.

"Maybe he's asleep," Abby said.

"He's not asleep," Noah said. "He's conflicted."

"Do you think he wishes he came?" Milo said.

"Part of him. Yeah."

"Does he know what we're doing tomorrow?" Milo said.

"He knows."

"What does he think?" Abby said.

"He thinks we're crazy."

"He has a point," Hollis said. "Who stakes out their sperm donor at an Ultimate Frisbee tournament?"

"Crazy people," Noah said.

And Abby said, "I'm not going to be able to sleep."

"Me neither," Milo said.

They agreed that they were too wired to sleep. Hollis turned on the lights. She passed around the snacks again.

"This floor," Milo said, propping himself on one elbow and taking a few baby carrots from a bowl, "is harder than it appears."

"Surprisingly hard," JJ agreed, chomping on a handful of potato chips.

"Should I be drinking this Mountain Dew with its fifty-five milligrams of caffeine?" Abby said. "Probably not."

"Are there potato chip shards all over my sleeping bag?" Noah said. "Making the likelihood of a good night's sleep even less likely? Yes there are."

"Mine too," JJ said. "Shards everywhere."

"Who should we blame for this sad state of affairs?" Abby said.

"I blame Milo," Hollis said.

"Hey." Milo chucked a baby carrot at Hollis. "I didn't bring the potato chips. I'm *allergic* to potato chips."

Hollis chucked the carrot back. "We wouldn't be here *eating* potato chips if it weren't for you, Bilbo Baggins."

"Milo's a hobbit?" Noah said.

"Yes he is," Hollis said. "And tomorrow he will lead us to Smaug the dragon, whom we will observe in his natural habitat."

"You're welcome," Milo said.

It was almost one a.m. In a matter of hours, they would see Will Bardo for the first time. They would watch him throw a Frisbee.

"Oh my God!" Abby suddenly exclaimed. "I almost forgot. I brought you guys something!" She rifled through her duffel and came up with a paper bag, the contents of which she dumped on the floor. Plastic noses and hats and

279

glasses and what appeared to be a pile of furry caterpillars.

"What *is* all that?" Hollis said.

"Disguises!"

"Disguises," Milo repeated.

"So we can go incognito tomorrow." Abby picked up one of the furry caterpillars and held it to her lip. "We've got mustaches." She sifted through the pile. "Beards . . . dark glasses . . . fake teeth."

"Let me see those," JJ said. He stuck the teeth—yellow and rotting—into his mouth and leered at everyone.

Hollis laughed. She grabbed a platinum-blond wig from the pile and tucked her curls inside. "Do I look like Lady Gaga?"

"Better," JJ said.

"Milo." Abby was trying to get his attention. She was holding something up, waving it in the air.

"What?"

"Try this on."

Milo did as instructed. The beard was long and bushy and made him look like an Amish farmer. "You realize," he said, "that we're just going to draw *more* attention to ourselves if we wear these."

"Where's your sense of dramatic irony?" Abby said.

"It's actually not dramatic irony. If it were, the audience would get the joke, but the players would not."

"Yes, but in this case, *we're* the audience. Will's the player."

"We look like a bunch of weirdos."

"We *are* a bunch of weirdos," Noah said.

"Speak for yourselves," Hollis said, fluffing her wig. "I'm Lady Gaga."

* * *

It was four in the morning when JJ woke Hollis up by whispering in her ear. "Hollis Darby." He had pulled his sleeping bag next to hers, so his head was just inches away.

"JJ Rabinowitz," she whispered back.

"You awake?" His breath was warm—a little sour, but not awful.

"I am now."

"I need to tell you something," he said.

"Okay."

"I wanted to kiss you in the airport."

"You did?"

"Yeah."

"So why didn't you?"

"I don't know. I was nervous."

"Why?"

"There were a lot of people looking . . . and I wasn't sure you'd want me to. So I grabbed your thumbs instead."

"Ah."

They lay there in silence, looking at each other. There was just enough moonlight shining through the basement window for Hollis to see JJ's face. The plane of his cheekbones, the curve of his chin. Hollis studied him for a long moment. She thought about the phone call where he'd gotten choked up talking about his birth mother, and she thought about him shaking everyone's hands at the airport. She thought about what Milo had said—how JJ was just looking for an excuse to come see her. She knew that boys were mostly after one thing and would say anything to get it, but if Hollis was really honest she would announce to the world, *I like hooking up, too, so sue me.*

"No one's looking now," Hollis said softly.

"What are you saying?"

"What do you think I'm saying?"

JJ smiled. "Come here."

His arms, big and warm, pulled her closer, and she could feel the heat from his mouth as he pressed his lips to the top of her head. Her head! It was a tender, unexpected gesture.

"That's sweet," Hollis murmured.

"You're sweet."

"No I'm not."

"What are you then?"

Hollis smiled and pulled his face down to meet hers.

JJ's kiss was softer than she expected—not that she'd been expecting him to kiss her at all, necessarily, although he *had* mentioned being jealous of Gunnar hooking up with her, and that had been weeks ago, when she and JJ first started talking on the phone, so really, what did she think would happen this weekend? It was a little weird that they were kissing here, on the basement floor, with her three half siblings sleeping just feet away. But it was fairly innocent. No clothing was removed. No body parts were touched except for lips and tongues and chins and cheeks and ears and necks.

"I like you, Hollis Darby," JJ whispered when they finally came up for air.

She felt that familiar ache in her chest. "Barnes," she whispered back.

"What?"

She asked JJ to come upstairs with her. She asked him to sit on the couch in front of the fireplace. "JJ Rabinowitz," she said, gesturing to the wall, "Pam Barnes. Pam, this is JJ." Then she sat on the couch and told him about Pam. How, the minute Pam woke up, she would make herself a cup of hot water with lemon. How she could stand on her head for ages. How she loved the Beatles, and the taste of real butter, and walking around barefoot. The memories tumbled out of Hollis's mouth, one after the other. A few times, she could feel the tears well up, but they never actually dropped. Mostly what she felt was JJ's hand, warm and sure on top of hers. And when she finished talking, that hand pulled her off the couch and led her back down to the basement, where they kissed some more.

MILO

HE WOKE UP WITH A JOLT OF ENERGY, LIKE HE'D JUST chugged a can of Red Bull. Today was the day!

Milo looked around the basement. Hollis and JJ were curled up next to each other like puppies. When had this happened? Hadn't they gone to sleep on opposite sides of the room? Abby was a lump inside her sleeping bag. Noah was snoring. Milo thought about waking them all. *Rise and shine, kids! It's Donor Day!* But this, he decided, was a bad idea. It would be better for everyone to be rested. Besides, they had time. The Indoor Hat Tournament lasted all day.

Milo crept upstairs, closing the basement door behind him. Hollis's mom was sitting alone at the kitchen table, holding a flowered coffee mug.

"Good morning," Milo said.

"Good morning." Leigh smiled. She looked better than she had when she and Hollis came to Brooklyn. Milo wasn't sure what the difference was. A haircut, maybe? Makeup? "Anyone else awake down there?" she asked.

"Not yet," Milo said, taking a seat.

"Can I get you some tea? The water's still hot."

"No, thanks."

"Not much of a tea drinker?"

"Not much of a tea drinker."

"Are you hungry? I picked up some rice-flour waffles that your moms said were okay for you. And there's fruit . . ."

"Thanks," Milo said. "I think I'll wait until everyone gets up."

Leigh nodded and took a sip from her mug. Milo glanced around the kitchen. The walls were painted a soft, buttery yellow. The curtains on the window had little red checks. The counters shone. It was basically the opposite of Hollis's bedroom, which looked like a Tim Burton movie set with its tapestries and gargoyles and black light. Even the soap in Hollis's bathroom was Goth. Milo had noticed it yesterday when she gave them the tour. Hollis washed her hands with black raven-wing soap.

"Thank you," Leigh said suddenly.

Milo looked at her.

"Hollis would never tell you this herself, and she would probably hate me for saying it . . . but this weekend . . . all of you being here . . . it means a lot to her."

He nodded. "It means a lot to me, too."

* * *

There were truths and there were half-truths. Everyone ate breakfast together (truth). The rice-flour waffles were delicious (half-truth). Abby's pre-blow-dryer hair was even crazier than Hollis's (truth). The siblings wanted to take a "bonding trip" after they ate (half-truth).

"A bonding trip?" Suzanne said, looking at Milo across the table.

"Uh-huh." He took a sip of apple juice.

"Quality sibling time," Abby said.

And Hollis said, "I thought I'd show them the sights." She turned to her mom. "You know . . . the Peanuts characters in Rice Park. Find the Elf at Lake Harriet. Maybe the Mall of America for lunch."

"Sounds great," Frankie said, starting to rise. "I'll just go brush my teeth—"

"Ma," Milo said.

"What?"

"Babe," Suzanne said, putting a hand on Frankie's arm. "The kids want to go off on their own."

"On their own?" Frankie said. "But . . . how will they get around?"

"I have my driver's license," Noah said (truth). Then, "I have a clean driving record" (half-truth). Last night in the basement, Noah had told them about backing his mom's Volvo out of his driveway and into a lamppost, denting the rear fender.

Frankie shook her head. *Of course* she shook her head. "The only people who can drive the rental car are Suzanne and myself. It's not that we don't trust you, Noah, but if there were an accident . . ."

Right, Milo thought. *Go directly to the worst-case scenario.*

"They can take my car," Hollis's mom said.

Hollis's mom saved the day (truth).

*　　*　　*

As the five of them walked through the front doors of the Recreational Sports Dome at the University of Minnesota, preparing to see Will Bardo for the first time, Milo could have had any number of thoughts, but for some reason he was thinking about Hayley Christenson. Probably because—just as they were walking in—a pair of girls was walking out, and one of them had long, blond hair. And great legs. And a killer smile. All of which reminded Milo of Hayley and made him temporarily forget that he was wearing a bushy gray beard. Which was obviously why the girl smiled at him: because he looked ridiculous.

They all looked ridiculous.

Hollis in her platinum wig. Noah in his Groucho Marx glasses. Abby in her porkpie hat and prosthetic nose that made her sound like she had a sinus infection. Even JJ, who had no reason to disguise himself, insisted on wearing the rotten teeth, which looked even more disgusting inside the dome, under the fluorescent lighting.

"Huh," Hollis said, looking around when they got inside. "This place is weird."

It *was* weird. They'd walked into a big, white bubble—an alternate universe. The turf was an unnatural shade of green. There was a huge maroon-and-gold *M* painted in the middle of the field. Men of all shapes and sizes were running every which way, and Frisbees were flying, so Milo assumed that the Indoor Hat Tournament was in full swing, but the dome was not exactly packed with spectators.

"So much for blending in with the crowd," Noah murmured, as they made their way around the edges of the bubble, as inconspicuously as possible, until they were standing in a corner with a handful of other people.

"What color do you think they are?" Abby asked.

Milo shook his head. "I don't know. I just know they're the Floppy Discs."

"Are you looking for the Floppy Discs?" a woman said. She was wearing a blue bandana and holding a squirmy toddler on her hip.

"Yeah," Noah said.

"Over there." She pointed to the other end of the bubble. "Field four. The tie-dyed shirts. My husband's team just played them."

"Thanks," Milo said.

The woman smiled. "Is this some kind of fraternity/ sorority thing?"

"Pardon?" Milo said.

"The costumes. My sorority sisters used to make me wear all sorts of crazy getups."

"Yes," JJ interjected with his rotten teeth. "We're being initiated."

"Well." The woman shifted the toddler to her other hip. "Enjoy it! These are the best years of your life."

They all nodded like doofuses in their disguises.

As soon as the woman walked away, Milo turned to Hollis and Abby and Noah and JJ. "What do you guys think? Do we go over or watch from here?"

"We go over," Abby said.

And Noah said, "Let's do this thing."

290

HOLLIS

FIELD FOUR. TIE-DYED SHIRTS. WAS THAT HIM—THE TALL guy in the yellow shorts? She squinted as they made their way in the other direction, feeling her pulse quicken. Or was it the guy in the sweatpants?

What, Hollis wondered suddenly, would this moment mean to her in twenty years? Would it become just one more chapter in her crazy story—something to share at dinner parties or to tell her own kids someday? *Your grandfather was a hippie Frisbee player.*

"You okay?" JJ whispered.

Hollis nodded, assuming the look of someone who wasn't about to pass out. JJ reached over and grabbed her thumb. She felt her nerves settle slightly.

But now here they were, standing at field four, just yards from the Floppy Discs. Hollis closed her eyes, as though this would make her invisible. She listened. Everyone was whispering.

"I don't see him." (Abby)

"The guy in the yellow shorts?" (Noah)

"Nah." (Abby) "His hair's too straight."

"He could have gotten a haircut." (Milo) "My hair looks straighter after a haircut."

"Mine, too." (Noah)

"Yeah, but look at his nose." (Abby) "It's way too big."

"What about the guy in the sweatpants?" (Milo)

"He has no eyebrows." (Noah)

"Really?" (Milo) "I can't tell."

"He has eyebrows." (JJ) "They're just sparse."

"There." (Abby)

"Oh my God." (Milo)

Hollis felt someone grab her elbow. Her eyes flew open. The light made her blink. "What?"

"That's him," Abby said. "Coming out of the bathroom."

Hollis squinted. Jogging toward them, red-cheeked and sweaty, was a man. She sucked in a breath. That *was* him, wasn't it? But lots of men had thick eyebrows. Lots of men had dark, curly hair. So what if he was wearing a tie-dyed shirt. They were all wearing tie-dyed—

"Yo, Bardo!" someone hollered. "Sub!"

Yo, Bardo.

Hollis's legs were Jell-O. She could feel her heart thump against her throat. He was *here*, ten feet in front of her, running onto the field. If she had a Frisbee, she could bean him in the head.

"Oh my God," Milo murmured again.

Hollis felt Abby's hand, damp and hot against her skin, and she saw that Noah was crying a little, and Milo's mouth was hanging open, and the only one who wasn't having any kind of fight-or-flight response was JJ, who had taken out his camera and was casually clicking away. While JJ moved into open space, the rest of them unconsciously inched closer together and were now standing motionless, like a family of deer in the road. Silently breathing in and out, watching their sperm donor lurch and trip around the field. How preposterous he looked. Hollis would laugh about this later. Hollis would laugh about all of this, just as soon as she got out of here.

"Wow," Noah said finally, shaking his head. "He's *really* uncoordinated."

"And yet surprisingly effective," Milo said.

"You think?" Abby said.

"Watch. He's going out for a pass . . ."

Hollis watched as Will Bardo clomped the Frisbee between both hands, then pitched his whole body forward to make a remarkably wobbly but accurate pass up the field to the guy in the yellow shorts before he stumbled, then quickly righted himself.

"Every time," Milo said, "he looks like he's going down like a ton of bricks."

"But he doesn't," Noah said. "He defies gravity."

"He's a Weeble," Abby said.

Hollis found her voice. "A what?"

"A Weeble. Remember Weebles? You could push them over as hard as you wanted, but they rolled right back up."

"Well." Noah half smiled. "I see where I got my athleticism."

Who knows how much time went by. Two minutes? Twenty? But they were still standing there, and Hollis was just getting used to the idea that she was related to this Weeble-like man, staggering and heaving his way around the field, when Milo dropped a bomb.

"I want to talk to him."

MILO

"WHAT?" HOLLIS WAS STARING AT MILO.

"I want to talk to him," he repeated quietly. "When the game ends. I want to go over and introduce myself."

Noah shook his head. "I don't think that's a good idea."

"Why not?"

"It wasn't the plan."

"Plans change."

"I think it's a great idea," Abby said.

And Hollis said, "You just want writing material."

"I don't *just* want writing material."

"No one else has to come," Milo said. "I'll do it alone if I have to." And he realized, as he spoke the words, that he meant them. He was feeling a surge of courage—of resolve. Will Bardo was his father. He deserved to meet his father, and he would do it with or without approval.

"Don't," Noah said.

"Why not?" Milo persisted. "Give me one good reason."

"I think it will backfire."

"How?"

"He said he wasn't ready."

"And I quote," Hollis said, " 'I'm going to let this marinate for a bit.' "

"Yeah," Abby said, "but he was happy to hear from us." She scratched quote marks in the air with her fingers. " 'I'm glad that you guys reached out.' "

"We haven't heard from him in eleven days," Noah countered. "If he wanted to 'be in touch,' he would 'be in touch.' "

"More 'family stuff,' no doubt," Hollis said.

"We all have family stuff." Milo kept his voice low but gestured for emphasis. "*This* is family stuff."

"Okay," Noah said. "I'm just saying . . . what if he gets mad? He could cut ties completely."

"What if he has a heart attack tomorrow?" Abby said. "This could be our only chance to meet him."

"He's not going to have a heart attack," Hollis said.

"How do you know?" Milo said. "People have heart attacks every day."

"If we go up and introduce ourselves," Noah said, "*that* could give him a heart attack."

"Guys." JJ was walking back over, holding his camera. "You might want to see something."

"A heart attack would be tragic irony," Abby said.

"Can we stop talking about heart attacks?" Noah said. "My point is—"

"I know what your point is," Milo said. "And you don't have to—"

"Why are we arguing?" Hollis said. "We're supposed to be—"

"*Yo!*"

Everyone looked at JJ.

"You might want to check out Will's wife."

HOLLIS

IF HOLLIS HAD BEEN OUTSIDE HER BODY, OBSERVING THIS scene—if she had watched the four of them turn simultaneously, if she had heard the collective intake of breath and seen their eyes bug out of their heads like Wile E. Coyote—she might have laughed.

But she was not outside her body.

She was here, watching Gwen Bardo—dark jeans, high boots, Rapunzel hair—kiss Will Bardo on the lips. She was here, watching Will smile and place a hand on Gwen's belly.

"What the . . ." Noah spluttered. "Is that . . . is she . . ."

"I believe the word you're looking for is 'plot twist,'" Abby said.

Hollis blinked. Will's wife *was* pregnant, right? She hadn't just eaten a really big lunch?

No. Hollis shook her head. That belly was freakishly large. Unlike the rest of Gwen Bardo, which looked pretty much the same as it had in the wet suit, on her bio page for the Eden Prairie Cooperative Learning Center. Now, she just looked like she'd swallowed a watermelon. A ginormous watermelon. A ginormous watermelon that Will was gazing at, rubbing with both hands.

"What is he *doing*?" Abby said.

And JJ—JJ Rabinowitz of all people—said, "He's communing with the baby."

Communing with the baby.

A thought popped unbidden into Hollis's head. Pam had done this, too. When Leigh was pregnant with Hollis. There was a photo somewhere, of Leigh in a butt-ugly maternity shirt—God, what had been on that shirt? Cowboy hats? Sombreros? Hollis couldn't remember. But she could picture that photo in her mind's eye: Pam's hands on Leigh's belly, both of them gazing down, smiling.

"We can't go over there," Hollis blurted.

Milo looked at her. She realized that he hadn't spoken a word. That he was still not speaking.

"I mean—" Hollis hesitated. "Look at them."

Will and Gwen. She was handing him something now. It looked like one of those insulated lunch boxes.

"Aww," Abby said. "She brought snacks."

Hollis imagined Gwen standing at the kitchen counter

of their little farmhouse, chopping up apples. Scooping Goldfish crackers into a baggie. And in that moment of imagining, something loosened inside her.

"They have a life," she said softly.

Milo nodded. "I know."

"We can't just—"

"I know."

MILO

THEY WALKED TO THE DINER OUTSIDE THE UNIVERSITY of Minnesota student center—not because any final decision had been made about Will, but because A) Abby thought they needed to "regroup," and B) JJ Rabinowitz, event photographer, was so hungry he could "eat his camera."

Milo was just glad to take off his beard. The worst thing about the beard was that it itched. He'd wanted to rip it from his face the entire time he was in the dome, but now he was glad that he hadn't. He was glad to have been a fly on the wall when Will's pregnant wife showed up.

A baby, Milo thought as they stood in line to order.

He didn't know how to feel. Gwen Bardo's belly had brought everything to a screeching halt. Her belly had appeared without warning, announcing to the world that

Will was going to be a dad. A *real* dad. A dad who would push strollers and change diapers and read bedtime stories and throw baseballs and have awkward conversations about sex.

"How far along is she?" Noah said. His head was down. His thumbs were moving rapid-fire across his phone. "Josh wants to know."

"Far," Hollis said. "Did you *see* the size of her belly?"

"If the baby's born by February eighteenth," Abby said, "it'll be an Aquarius, like me."

"Aquarius," JJ said. "Which sign is that?"

"The water bearer," Abby said. "We are witty and clever. We dislike anything ordinary."

"Clearly," Hollis said, flicking Abby's porkpie hat with her finger. Abby was the only one still wearing a disguise.

"Do you think he told her?" Noah looked up from his phone. "About being a sperm donor? Do you think she has any idea we exist?"

"I was wondering the same thing," Abby said.

"So was I," Hollis said.

The musings continued as Milo ordered. He wasn't very hungry. His stomach was churning just like the thoughts in his head. He didn't want to eat, but he wanted something comforting. Like cocoa.

"Do you have rice milk?" Milo asked the girl behind

the counter, who was wearing a baseball cap and a U of M sweatshirt.

"Sure do," she said.

"Do you have plain cocoa powder—the kind without milk?"

"Yup."

"Could you please make me a nondairy hot chocolate?"

"You got it," the girl said.

The cocoa was too hot to drink, so Milo sat at a table with JJ, who had ordered a double cheeseburger, fries, and a strawberry milkshake. Milo blew into his cup.

"How you doin', man?" JJ asked, stuffing a fry into his mouth.

"Okay."

"Want to see pictures?"

Milo wasn't sure he wanted to see pictures, but JJ was already wiping his fingers on a napkin and reaching for his camera. "I got some great close-ups of Will. You can really see his bone structure . . ."

"Let me see," Hollis said, arriving with a grilled cheese and a Coke and peering over JJ's shoulder.

Good, Milo thought. Let Hollis marvel at Will Bardo's cheekbones. He would sit here and think.

Gwen Bardo and her stupid belly, Milo thought, taking a careful sip of cocoa so as not to burn his tongue. He hated her belly for showing up and ruining everything. He had been *ready*. He had *wanted* to meet Will. He *still* wanted to meet Will. And if not today, at the Indoor Hat Tournament, then when?

Milo took another sip, a bigger one. It burned the tip of his tongue, but he didn't care. He took another sip. He was starting to feel warm.

"I'll tell you another thing about Aquariuses," Abby said as she and Noah sat down with their food. "We are rebels."

"Hey, rebel," Hollis said, holding out the camera to Abby. "Tell me this doesn't look like Milo in twenty years."

"Wow," Abby said, looking and nodding. "It really does."

She passed the camera to Noah, who did a double take—"whoa"—before passing the camera to Milo. "Want to see yourself in twenty years?"

Milo blinked at the camera in front of him, but he couldn't see the picture clearly. His eyes were itchy. He could tell that Noah was saying something but he couldn't hear the words because he was starting to cough and his arms were hot and everything seemed to be moving in slow motion. Milo could see the cup falling out of his hand. He could see that Hollis was turning and pointing, and that JJ was shouting and gesturing to Noah, but there was no noise, no noise at all, not even the sound of his own breath, and Milo was wondering why this was, and he tried to ask but there were no words because there was no air, and he needed air, because oh shit he couldn't breathe, and he suddenly realized, as he slid off the chair and his head hit the floor with a sickening thunk, that someone had turned out the lights.

HOLLIS

IT TOOK HOLLIS A SECOND TO REGISTER WHAT WAS happening. Milo was on the floor; his lips were blowing up. Brown liquid was everywhere. The hot chocolate. The effing hot chocolate! She didn't have time to think about why, exactly, he was having a reaction. She had to . . . she needed . . . Milo's backpack! Hollis pointed and shouted. EpiPen! Frankie's tutorial came at her in one big rush, a tsunami of instructions. *Orange tip down make a fist pull safety release outer thigh 90 degree angle hold hold hold.* She was moving too fast to panic. She was rubbing Milo's thigh too vigorously to consider how weird it was to be rubbing Milo's thigh.

* * *

Only after the paramedics came, after JJ called Frankie and Suzanne, after Milo was rushed to Abbott Northwestern Hospital with a tube in his throat, after the girl behind the counter had her breakdown about mistaking almond milk for rice milk (*The containers look the same! He said nondairy! All I was thinking was nondairy!*)—only after, when they were sitting in the waiting room and the doctor came to tell them that Milo was going to be fine—did Hollis finally cry.

MILO

HE DIDN'T WANT TO WAKE UP. AT FIRST, THE IMAGES in his head had been sort of disturbing. Flying Frisbees. Giant bellies. Will Bardo's widow's peak coming at him, magnified a hundredfold. But now, here was Hayley Christenson. What was she doing, floating above his head like an angelfish? He couldn't imagine. But she was smiling. Smiling at *him*, amazingly. And she was so beautiful. The side braid, the sapphire eyes, the shiny lips. She was reaching out to him, beckoning . . . beckoning . . .

He woke up in a hospital bed, attached to an IV drip. The only person floating above him was Frankie, looking spiky haired and pale. Suzanne was straightening his blanket. Hollis, JJ, Abby, and Noah were across the room, sitting in a row along the window ledge.

"Mi," Frankie said softly. She bent down to kiss his cheek and then started to cry.

"Ma," he said. He could barely get the words out, his throat was so sore. "I'm okay."

Suzanne leaned over, kissing his other cheek, wiping her eyes with the cuff of her shirt.

Then Hollis and Abby came sprinting across the room. "You're awake! He's awake!"

Followed by JJ, squeezing Milo's shoulder. "Dude. You sure know how to make an exit."

Everyone was gathered around him, like a force field.

"Sorry," Milo croaked.

"*Don't* apologize," Hollis said fiercely. "We're just glad you're okay. You are okay, right?"

Milo nodded. His head hurt.

Noah patted his foot. "Do you remember what happened?"

Milo nodded again, slowly. He remembered being hot. He remembered everything moving in slow motion. He remembered hitting the floor.

"That bonehead behind the counter?" Hollis said. "She made your hot chocolate with almond milk instead of rice milk."

Milo raised his eyebrows.

"She said the containers looked the same. Can you believe that shit?"

"You should have seen Hollis in action," JJ said. "She was a rock star."

"EpiPen?" Milo rasped.

"Yeah, yeah," Abby said. "She stabbed you in the leg and saved your life and everything, but you should have seen her when we got *here*, and the nurse was like, 'family only,' and she was all, 'That's our brother in there. And these are his moms. And if you don't let us in that room—'"

"Please." Hollis smirked.

"What?" Abby said.

"I did *not* sound like James Earl Jones. 'That's our brother in there.'" Hollis made her voice deep and booming. "'And these are his moms.'"

Abby laughed. "You totally did. You went Darth Vader on her ass."

"Don't listen to her," Hollis said to Milo. "She's exaggerating for effect."

"You think she's exaggerating *now*?" Noah said. "Wait until you read her memoir."

"Artistic license," Abby said.

Hollis rolled her eyes. Then, out of nowhere, she leaned down and kissed Milo's nose. Lightning quick.

He stared at her.

"What? You almost died. I can't kiss you?"

"Speaking of kisses . . ." Milo swallowed past the pain

in his throat. He glanced from Hollis to JJ and back to Hollis.

"You look tired," Hollis said. "Doesn't he look tired?"

JJ grinned. "We made out."

"Hey!" Hollis cuffed JJ's ear.

"What?" JJ grinned wider. "It's true."

Milo smiled. "Good."

Frankie, puffy-eyed but no longer crying, reached out to smooth Milo's hair back from his forehead. "You should be resting."

And Suzanne said, "They're keeping you under observation for another few hours. Just to be safe." She squeezed his arm through the blanket. "You sleep, honey. We'll be back in a little while."

"Thanks," Milo murmured. It wasn't a bad idea, actually. Maybe, if he closed his eyes, Hayley would appear again.

"We love you," Suzanne said. "You know that?"

"I know."

*   *   *

The next time Milo woke up, it was just Frankie, sitting in a chair next to his bed.

"Hey, bud," she said. She held up a plastic cup. "You thirsty? The doctors want you to hydrate."

Milo drank. And drank. And drank.

"More?" Frankie asked when he'd finished.

He shook his head. He glanced around the room. "Where is everyone?"

"Down in the cafeteria . . . how're you feeling now?"

"Better."

Frankie heaved a sigh. "You gave us a real scare, kiddo."

"I didn't mean to."

"I know you didn't." She grimaced. "That girl should be fired. Who mistakes almond milk for rice milk? If Hollis hadn't found your EpiPen . . ."

"She did."

"But if she *hadn't* . . . we didn't even know where you *were* . . . you could have been anywhere . . . Rice Park . . . Lake Harriet . . . the Mall of America—" Frankie's voice broke.

Her concern was so palpable that Milo felt bad—he felt *horrible*—for lying.

"Ma."

"What is it, sweetie?"

"That's not . . . we didn't go any of those places."

"What?"

It took him a long time to tell Frankie what she didn't know. About the Eden Prairie Cooperative Learning Center. About the Twin Cities Ultimate League. About Will's lame email asking for time to "marinate." About the

312

plan they'd made to see him, even if he didn't want to be seen. About Milo wanting to go rogue and meet Will.

Frankie couldn't believe it. Milo would actually do that? Put himself out there? Take that kind of emotional risk?

Well, Milo said, yeah.

And finally, Gwen Bardo's belly. The showstopper.

"I did *not* see that coming," Frankie said.

"Neither did I."

Silence for a moment and then she looked at him. "That must have been hard for you, seeing her pregnant. It must have brought up some complicated feelings."

Milo nodded.

"I'm sorry."

"I am, too . . . for not telling you the truth."

Frankie cocked her head. "Why didn't you?"

"I don't know. I was afraid you would . . ." Milo hesitated.

"What?"

"Freak out. Think I didn't love you or something. Just because I want to meet Will doesn't mean I want to replace you or anything. I mean . . . you're my mom."

"Right." Frankie nodded and cleared her throat. "So . . . there was this girl."

"What?"

313

"There was this girl, in college."

"And the non sequitur award goes to . . ."

"Bear with me," Frankie said. "This story has a point."

"It does?"

"Humor your mother, okay?"

"Okay."

"So, Julie Catalano. She was in my sociology class sophomore year, and I had a massive crush on her. Huge. She was a senior, and she had this long, brown hair. Big, blue eyes. Great legs. I thought I would die if she didn't go out with me."

"Yeah," Milo said. He sat up straighter in the bed.

"Wayyy out of my league, though. Sorority girl. Came from money. Her father donated a wing of the library, that kind of thing. And here I was, a scholarship kid. Working in the cafeteria just to pay for books. Living in the dorms because I couldn't afford to live off campus. You get the picture."

"Yeah."

"So I'm nursing this crush on Julie Catalano all through sophomore year, until finally spring rolls around, and I realize . . . this is it. She's about to graduate, and I need to make my move, you know, or I'll never forgive myself."

"You need to make your move."

"Right. And it needs to be big. A *grand romantic*

gesture. But to execute this grand romantic gesture, I needed to pull out all the stops. So I took all the money I had out of the bank, all my work-study money—"

"Seriously?"

"Yup. And I bought every romantic thing I could think of. Champagne, roses, caviar, stinky French cheese. I borrowed my roommate's car, and I drove Julie Catalano out to this beautiful picnic spot by Lake Harriet, and I paid the marching band—"

"Wait, the *marching band*?"

"Oh, yes. I paid the marching band to show up and play 'Baby, Baby' by Amy Grant while I sang the lyrics."

"No."

"Yes. And then, when I was opening the champagne, I popped her in the eye with the cork."

"No," Milo said, laughing. He couldn't help it.

"I swear to God. She had a black eye for graduation and she never talked to me again."

"Shit," Milo said.

"Yup."

"I'm sorry."

"I'm not," Frankie said. "Because you know who I met that night?"

"Who?"

"Erin Anderson. She was playing the snare drum in the marching band."

"Erin Anderson who introduced you to Mom?" Milo said.

"Yup. Erin and I became friends. And then roommates in grad school. And then . . . she introduced me to your mom."

"Huh," Milo said.

"The love of my life. The mother of my child. Are you getting my point?"

"Huh?" Milo was back on the roses and caviar and stinky French cheese. He was thinking about grand romantic gestures. He was thinking about Hayley Christenson.

"My point," Frankie said, reaching out for Milo's hand, "is that sometimes . . . when you take a great emotional risk . . . when you put yourself out there and make yourself most vulnerable . . . you hit pay dirt. It just may not be the pay dirt you expected to hit."

Milo nodded—he got it. Then he swallowed the lump in the back of his throat, wondering why it was there. The answer was obvious, of course: he was still dehydrated and Frankie was being cheesy.

"Are you ready to get out of here?" she said.

"You have no idea."

HOLLIS

MILO LOOKED OKAY. BY NINE O'CLOCK THAT NIGHT HE was sitting on the couch in Hollis's living room, and JJ was making him laugh. Noah was texting Josh. Abby was writing in her notebook. There was so much to write about. They'd seen their *father* today. His wife was having a *baby*. Milo could have *died*. Whenever Hollis thought about Milo lying on the floor of the coffee shop, barely breathing, she wanted to barf. Milo drove through life without a seat belt—without a crash helmet. The worst part was that it could happen again. He could eat the wrong thing. He could—

No. Hollis shivered. She wasn't going to think about that now. She was going to put this bowl of popcorn that her mother had asked her to make on the coffee table, in front of Frankie and Suzanne, who were flipping through Hollis's baby album. God, that thing was so embarrassing. She was naked in half the pictures. Naked and wearing a Kleenex box. Naked and riding a tricycle.

"You were adorable," Suzanne said, looking up at Hollis and beaming.

It was all she could do not to roll her eyes. "Thanks."

She perched on the arm of the couch next to JJ. He squeezed her knee. "Hello, Hollis Darby-Barnes."

"Hello, JJ Rabinowitz."

He grabbed her thumb.

She felt herself smile. She couldn't help it.

Hollis looked around the room and thought, *Everyone is here. In my house.* She felt an odd sense of calm. But she felt something else, too. An almost panicky feeling underneath. *Don't leave!*

They had only one day left. By Monday afternoon, everyone would be gone. Milo and Frankie and Suzanne. JJ. Abby and Noah. What was Hollis supposed to do then? Just go back to her stupid life? Homework? Quiet lunches with Shay and Gianna? She was no longer hooking up with Gunnar. She was no longer receiving slut mail. Ever since that day in the bathroom with Malory, everything had stopped. The texts. The voice mails. The posts. It wasn't that Hollis missed being called a slutbag ho—she wasn't that messed up—but still. School was dullsville. Maybe she needed some new friends.

An image popped into her head then, of Milo and JJ and Abby and Noah walking down the hall with her— all in a row the way Malory and her friends walked— taking up all the space in the world. The image twinged Hollis's heart.

"This sucks," she announced.

"What sucks?" Milo said.

"We only have one full day left."

"I know. It's a bummer."

Move to Saint Paul, Hollis thought. *Go to my school! JJ and I can hook up in the janitor's closet! Everyone can live in my basement!*

"We'll just have to come back," Abby said.

"You're welcome anytime," Hollis's mom said.

And Noah said, "If we do this again, Josh wants to come."

Everyone looked at Noah.

"Seriously?" Hollis said.

"I texted him so many pictures, I think I wore him down."

"*I* know," Abby said, closing her notebook and sticking her pen behind her ear. "You should all come to Sheboygan this summer. We have a lake house."

"Or Brooklyn," Milo said. "We could sit around sweating and wishing we had a lake house."

"Or Chicago," Noah said. "We could go to a Cubs game."

It wasn't until later, when everyone was asleep, and JJ lay heavy and warm beside her on the basement floor, that Hollis thought about Will Bardo. In all the drama surrounding Milo, they'd forgotten to debrief.

"You guys?" Hollis said.

There was no response.

"Anyone awake?"

Nothing. Breaths and sighs and gentle snores. Hollis didn't have the heart to wake them.

MILO

AT BREAKFAST, SUZANNE HUGGED MILO FOR AN EMBAR-
rassingly long time. When she finally released him, she
said, "We are going to figure this out, with or without
Will Bardo."

"Figure what out?" Milo said.

"Your allergies," Suzanne said.

She had talked to one of the doctors yesterday, when
Milo was in the hospital. There was a new therapy they
might consider when they got back to New York. Immu-
notherapy. By introducing each of Milo's allergens into his
system in very small increments—over the course of many
months—the hope was that his immune system could
begin to create antibodies to fight the allergens.

"One allergen at a time?" Milo said.

"One allergen at a time," Suzanne said.

"Several months for *each one*?"

"Or more. It can take up to a year."

"I'll be Rip Van Winkle by the time I'm allergy free!"

"You want your beard back, Rip?" Abby said. "You rocked that look yesterday."

Milo laughed. "I am *never* wearing that thing again."

*   *   *

They decided to go to the Mall of America to ride the roller coasters. This was Milo's idea, and since he had defied death and everyone was freshly, poignantly aware of the tenuousness of life, this is what they did.

They took two cars. Frankie and Leigh drove. They wasted half an hour searching for parking spots. They walked through the food court and past the shops and up and up and down escalators while Hollis spouted random facts: "Did you know you could fit seven Yankee Stadiums inside the Mall of America? Did you know the Mall of America has its own counterterrorism unit?"

When they got to the bottom of Rock Bottom Plunge, JJ insisted on taking a picture. "Everyone get together. Moms, too."

They got together in a wobbly line.

JJ lifted his camera. "Say sperm."

"Sperm!" Milo said.

"Sperm!" Abby said.

"Sperm!" Noah said.

"Sperm!" the moms said.

JJ lowered his camera. "Hollis?"

"Seriously?"

"Humor the event photographer."

"Sperm," Hollis said.

JJ snapped the picture.

"That," he said, "is one good-looking family."

The moms opted out of the roller coaster ride, but the rest of them filed into the first car of the Rock Bottom Plunge. Milo and Hollis. Abby and Noah. JJ.

"Crap," Milo said, as they began to move. "I forgot how much I hate roller coasters."

Hollis looked at him. "You're the one who suggested it. You wanted to sit in the front."

"I know," Milo said, shaking his head incredulously. "I don't know what I was thinking."

"Staring death in the face after your near-death experience?"

"Something like that," Milo said, squeezing the restraint bar. "I don't know. It was either this or eat a peanut."

Hollis shot him a look. "Don't joke about that."

Milo shrugged. "Gallows humor."

The car jerked forward, beginning its ascent.

"So," Abby called out behind them, over the squeak of metal, "I need to tell you guys something!"

"What?" Hollis said.

"Last night, when you were all asleep, I posted another message to Will!"

"What?" Milo said.

The car jerked some more. The squeaking got louder.

"I told him we were here until tomorrow! I gave him my cell number! He could call at any second!"

"And you waited until now to tell us?" Noah said.

"Dramatic tension!" Abby said. "Building to a climax!"

They were ticking their way straight up, lying flat on their backs, gazing through the skylights at the staggeringly blue sky.

Milo squeezed the restraint bar so hard his knuckles were turning white.

"Just in case!" Abby yelled. "You know—we all have heart attacks on the way down! At least he'll know we tried!"

"Again with the heart attacks!" Noah yelled.

Milo's back was braced against the seat. His heart was leaping.

"Hollis Darby-Barnes!" JJ called from two rows back.

"Yeah?"

"Come sit with me!"

"I'll be right there! Let me just take off my seat belt!"

"Don't joke," Milo murmured through clenched teeth. Then, "Oh, shit." The car peaked, pausing at the very top.

He looked at Hollis.

"It's okay." She was laughing. "Just wait. It's kind of a rush."

He couldn't see what came next, but he could sense it: the air below them, charged with possibility.

"Ready?" Hollis said.

They plunged.

ACKNOWLEDGMENTS

FIRST AND FOREMOST, I'D LIKE TO THANK JON YAGED, president of Macmillan Children's Publishing Group, for entrusting me with his story seed; and Joy Peskin, my exceptional editor/literary doula, for helping me birth this baby.

Thank you to Morgan Dubin, my publicist, for her enthusiasm and hard work.

Thank you to Elizabeth H. Clark, designer of this spectacular cover; to Maya Packard and Katie Cicatelli-Kuc, copy editors extraordinaire; and to Johanna Kirby, my wonderful marketing manager.

I am grateful to Rebecca Sherman, my agent at Writers House, for her advocacy and continued support.

A special thank you to Dr. Jonathan Stein, for helping

with my allergy and genetics research, most of which took place on the Little League sidelines.

Thanks to Taco Pacifico, for providing dinner for my kids when I was too busy writing to cook.

A big hug to David Wick, who gave me Sheboygan. A shout-out to the real, live Tania Kosiewicz, who does not work at Macalester College, nor does she date Hollis Darby-Barnes's mother, but I am happy to call her my friend and the inspiration behind "Tania Kosiewicz, Alumni Relations."

Last, but certainly not least, enduring love and gratitude to my other f-word: Jack, Ben, Emma, Kuj, Beckett, Bobo, and Swish. And to my parents, Beebo and Geo, who believed in me from the very beginning, when all I wrote about was rainbows.

GOFISH

NATASHA FRIEND

What did you want to be when you grew up?
An Olympic gymnast.

When did you realize you wanted to be a writer?
At age six, as soon as I could read.

What's your most embarrassing childhood memory?
Riding my bike into a school bus in front of the boy I had a crush on.

What's your favorite childhood memory?
Playing baseball in the park with my dad.

As a young person, who did you look up to most?
Mary Lou Retton and Judy Blume.

What was your favorite thing about school?
Writing!

What were your hobbies as a kid?
Reading, singing, acting, playing the piano, climbing trees, riding my bike.

What are your hobbies now?
Reading, cheering on my kids, holding spontaneous dance parties in the kitchen.

Did you play sports as a kid?
Lots! Gymnastics, field hockey, basketball, softball, soccer.

What was your first job, and what was your "worst" job?
My first job was babysitting and my worst job, by far, was picking strawberries.

What book is on your nightstand now?
Carry On, Warrior by Glennon Doyle Melton.

How did you celebrate publishing your first book?
Ice cream and lots of dancing for joy.

Where do you write your books?
In my office overlooking the lake in my backyard.

What sparked your imagination for *The Other F-Word*?
I was inspired to write a story about teenagers searching for their sperm donor after watching *Generation Cryo*, an MTV reality series that explores this new generation of kids conceived via anonymous sperm donation and the issues they face.

What challenges do you face in the writing process?
Time! I have three kids, so there's never enough time in the day for anything.

What is your favorite word?
Mellifluous.

If you could live in any fictional place, what would it be?
Hogwarts.

Who is your favorite fictional character?
Pippi Longstocking.

What was your favorite book when you were a kid?
Are You There, God? It's Me, Margaret by Judy Blume.

Do you have a favorite book now?
My favorite book is always the one I'm currently writing.

If you could travel in time, where would you go and what would you do?
I would go back to age thirteen, knowing what I know now. I would stand up to all the people who made me feel small and worthless.

What's the best advice you have ever received about writing?
Show; don't tell.

What advice do you wish someone had given you when you were younger?
Be brave. Take risks.

Do you ever get writer's block?
I can't afford writer's block because my writing time is so limited, but when I do feel stuck, I read. Reading great books always inspires me.

What do you want readers to remember about your books?
Laughing and crying. Hopefully I can make my readers do both.

What would you do if you ever stopped writing?
I'd buy a summer camp in Maine and be a camp director until I was too old to paddle a canoe.

If you were a superhero, what would your superpower be?
Hosting talent shows.

Do you have any strange or funny habits?
I can speak a secret language called Oppy. Everyone in my family can.

Did you have any strange or funny habits when you were a kid?
I used to walk up and down the stairs on my hands.

What do you consider to be your greatest accomplishment?
My three children.

What would your readers be most surprised to learn about you?
I don't mind people thinking I'm weird. When I was younger, I wanted to be normal. The older I get, the more comfortable I am being different.

SQUARE FISH

DIAGNOSED WITH A CONDITION CALLED

alopecia, Quinn first loses all her hair—and then all her friends. But when she meets Jake, a football player who lost both of his legs in an accident, she doesn't feel so friendless after all. Can Quinn and Jake learn to believe in themselves with a little help from each other?

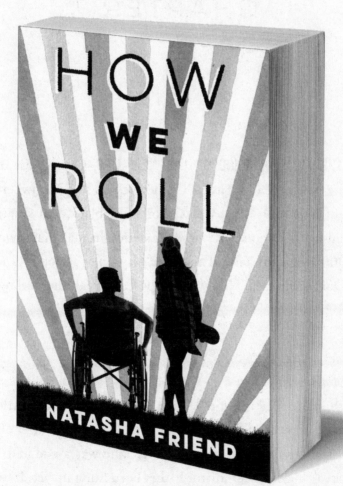

Keep reading for a sneak peek.

CHAPTER

1

ON THE FIRST MORNING OF HER NEW LIFE, Quinn was debating. Guinevere or Sasha? Guinevere was long, strawberry blond, and wavy. Sasha was short and black, glossy as a patent-leather shoe. They were Estetica human hair wigs, $2,000 a pop, no joke. They lived on two Styrofoam heads on Quinn's dresser. They were supposed to make her feel normal. Right.

G. I. Jane.

Hare Krishna.

Professor X.

Quinn looked at her reflection. Most of the time she tried not to, but today she looked. You would think that after 408 days she'd be used to it. She wasn't. She was a cue ball. A plucked chicken. Her mirror hadn't been hung up yet. It was propped on three cardboard boxes that she had yet to unpack.

ask what he was talking about, her brother had launched into one of his monologues. "Xie Qiuping from China has been growing her hair since nineteen seventy-three. She now holds the record for the longest female hair with a length of five-point-six-two-seven meters when last measured. That's nearly as long as the height of a giraffe. Susa Forster from Breitenfelde, Germany, has two thousand four hundred and seventy-three giraffe items that she has collected . . ."

Julius had droned on until Quinn tuned him out and continued practicing her back dive. But that night, when she was getting ready for bed, she'd looked in the mirror and seen what her brother had been talking about: a bald patch about the size of a quarter, right near her part. It was probably nothing, she thought. Maybe she'd been wearing her ponytail too tight. Then she showed her mom, and Mo found two more spots—one at the back of Quinn's head, the other above her left ear. Mo told her not to worry. Maybe Quinn had a vitamin deficiency. Maybe it was hormones. Still, Mo called Dr. Steiner first thing the next morning. Dr. Steiner sent them to another doctor, a dermatologist named Dr. Hersh, who stuck Quinn's head under a light and peered at her scalp through magnifying glasses. He took off his glasses and spoke: "Alopecia areata." The words sounded like some food Quinn had never tasted but already knew she would hate. Baba ghanoush. Ratatouille.

"It's an autoimmune disorder," he said. "Your white blood cells are attacking your hair follicles."

"Ah," Mo said.

Quinn didn't ask, as if not asking would defuse the situation.

"T and Cakes," her mom said anyway. "It's the bakery in Boulder. We used to stop on the way to his school."

"Tea and cakes, Mo. Tea and cakes."

"That's right, buddy. You miss those white-chocolate scones, don't you? They were part of our old Wednesday routine."

Quinn squeezed her basketball. She listened to her mom try to soothe Julius, but there was no soothing him. Now they were going to have to drive all over Gulls Head, Massachusetts, looking for white-chocolate scones. Quinn wished they didn't have to. She wished, just once, that a ride in the car could be just a ride and not an episode of *My Strange Addiction*. She wished so many things. She wished that her brother's brain could be rewired. She wished that their entire lives did not revolve around his food. She wished that her dad didn't have to get up at five a.m. to take the commuter rail to work instead of riding his bike the way he had in Boulder. She wished that she still had hair. Even though she had never been one of those girly girls like Paige and Tara, who worried about clothes and nail polish and bad hair days, now that it was gone she missed it. She really did.

It had started last summer, a week before Quinn's thirteenth birthday. They'd been in the pool in their backyard when Julius had said, "Hair, Q. Hair." Before Quinn could

"That skirt looks nice," her mom said.

It was denim with red stitching. Quinn felt stupid wearing it. She never wore skirts.

"Thanks," Quinn said. She should have worn shorts and her Colorado Rockies baseball cap. But no. *No.* That was the whole problem back in Boulder. Just thinking about eighth grade—her bald head, her mesh basketball shorts, long and loose around her knees—Quinn felt a small, sharp twinge of shame. *Mr. Clean. Vin Diesel.* "You're bringing this on yourself," Paige had said once. "Why don't you make an effort?"

Well, Quinn was making an effort now, wasn't she? The wig. The skirt. If she looked like all the other girls at Gulls Head High School, maybe she would blend in. She'd be one of those leaf-tailed geckos, mimicking the foliage of its habitat so no predators would eat it. This was Quinn's plan: avoid being eaten.

Snap, snap, snap.

She heard Julius start to snap his fingers. Slowly at first, then picking up speed. Her mom heard, too, and she glanced in the rearview mirror.

"Bud?" Mo said quietly. "You okay?" She always stayed calm, even when Quinn's brother began to lose it. They were like equal and opposite forces. The more he amped up, the mellower she became.

Julius mumbled something, still snapping away.

"What's that?" Mo said.

"Tea and cakes," Julius blurted out.

Shut up, Quinn sometimes wanted to whisper. But she never did.

. . . . .

"You don't have to drive me," Quinn said as she strapped herself into the front seat. "I can walk."

"I don't mind driving you," her mom said.

"I don't mind walking."

"It's your first day," Mo said. "I want to see you off."

Quinn shrugged, holding the basketball in her lap. It was a new one, barely scuffed. Her dad had bought it for her before they left Colorado. This basketball was her tabula rasa, her blank slate.

As the car backed out of the driveway, Julius began muttering to himself from the backseat, *Guinness World Records 2017* propped in his lap, bright yellow headphones clamped to his ears.

"So," Mo said, glancing over at Quinn. "Are you nervous?" They had the same eyes, hazel, that shifted from brown to gold to green depending on the light. Mood eyes, her mom called them.

"I'm okay," Quinn said. It wasn't exactly a lie. Even though her scalp itched and she worried that the five pieces of wig tape she'd used might not be enough. What if they didn't stick? What if Guinevere came flying off in the middle of PE?

"The most hardboiled eggs to be peeled and eaten in a minute is six." Quinn's brother said this without looking up. His hair was a mess. Spiky all over like a blond stegosaurus.

"Morning, Julius." Quinn pulled out a chair.

"Ashrita Furman of the USA." He added a fork to his utensil train. "At the offices of the Songs of the Soul, in New York, New York, USA, on twenty-three March two thousand and twelve. Each egg was weighed and was more than fifty-eight grams. All eggs were peeled and consumed within one minute."

That was another thing Julius did. He repeated things. Not just stuff he'd heard, like lines from commercials or TV shows or movies, but whole passages from books he'd read. He didn't care if you were interested or not. He'd say it anyway.

"All eggs were peeled and consumed within one minute."

"Wow," Quinn said, taking an egg from the bowl.

"*Wow* is a palindrome."

"Yes, it is."

"A palindrome reads the same forward and backward."

"Yes, it does." Quinn cracked the egg on the table.

"The longest known palindromic word is *saippuakivikaup-pias*, which is Finnish for a dealer in lye."

"Cool," she said.

"*Cool* is not a palindrome."

"I know."

"*Cool* does not read the same forward and backward."

downtown, but Gulls Head didn't have much of an art scene, so Quinn didn't know how it was going to work out for her mom here. Quinn didn't know how it was going to work out for any of them. Her dad had taken an adjunct professorship. They were only renting this house. Flying by the seat of their pants, that was what they were doing.

While Quinn was standing in the kitchen doorway thinking how crazy it was that her family had just picked up and moved two thousand miles for Julius to try a new school, her mom looked up from the box she was unpacking. "Morning, Q," she said. She was wearing an old flannel shirt of Quinn's dad's, ripped jeans, clogs. Her hair was in a messy bun, held in place with a pencil.

"Morning," Quinn said.

Her mom's eyes hovered on Guinevere. Quinn waited for her to comment, but she didn't. Even though this was the first time Mo had seen Quinn in a wig since she'd tried on about fifty of them at Belle's Wig Botik in Denver. Even though Quinn had been wearing the same ratty Colorado Rockies baseball cap every day for a year. Mo smiled, and her eyes crinkled at the corners. "Hungry?" she said.

Quinn's poor mom. She was trying so hard to act normal, like her daughter wasn't wearing a costume.

"A little," Quinn said.

"Hardboiled egg?" Mo gestured to a bowl on the table.

"Okay."

and filled out the paperwork, the Cove was internationally renowned. It called itself a therapeutic day school for exceptional children, which was Julius, no doubt. Exceptional.

You could tell just by looking at his breakfast, which he was eating right now at the kitchen table. Wonder bread and cream cheese. Yogurt. Hardboiled egg, no yolk. Because today was Wednesday, and Julius ate only white foods on Wednesdays. Mondays he ate only meat. Fridays he ate only foods that were fried. This was the first thing you learned about Quinn's brother: he did things his own way. Throw off his system and you would witness destruction like you had never seen.

"White Wednesday," Julius said, lining up his utensils like train cars. "Right, Mo?" This was what he called their mom: Mo. Her real name was Maureen. That was another thing about Quinn's brother: he had his own way of speaking. For the first four years of his life, he hadn't spoken at all. Everyone was afraid he never would. Then one day, out of nowhere, he opened his mouth, and *bam!* Their dad was "Phil," Quinn was "Q," and Mom was "Mo." Once Julius started talking, he was a faucet you couldn't turn off. Sometimes it was long streams of words, sometimes it was short spurts.

"Right, Mo? White Wednesday. Right, Mo? Right?"

"That's right, buddy," Mo said, placing a glass of white milk on the table. There was brown under her fingernails. Clay. Quinn's mom was a sculptor. Heads and busts, mostly. When they'd lived in Boulder her pieces had sold in galleries

Maybe she would do it later, put her new room together. Or maybe she would live out of cardboard boxes like a nomad until her parents came to their senses—until they realized that loading all their earthly possessions into a U-Haul and driving two thousand miles wasn't going to change anything. What was that expression? *Wherever you go, there you are?*

It had been a week, and so far they were still here. Gulls Head, Massachusetts, which was a weird name for a town. Even weirder was the accent everyone seemed to have. The real estate agent, the cashier at 7-Eleven, the secretary from Gulls Head High School who'd given Quinn a tour. Everyone in this town talked like the letter *R* didn't exist. *Far* was "fah." *Locker* was "lockah." *How are you?* sounded like "hawa-hya?" Quinn felt like she'd landed on another planet.

Her family hadn't moved to Gulls Head, Massachusetts, for her, although the suckfest that was eighth grade would have been reason enough. They'd moved because of Quinn's nine-year-old brother, Julius. Because the Boulder public schools hadn't been "equipped" to meet his "special needs." (This was code for Julius had a lot of tantrums, banged his face against a few walls, bit the lunch lady.) Sometimes Quinn's brother did things and you had no idea why. Were the lights too bright in the cafeteria? Were the kids too loud? Did the lunch lady say something that made him want to bite her?

Julius's new school, the Cove, was supposed to be different. According to Quinn's mom, who had done all the research

ALSO BY NATASHA FRIEND

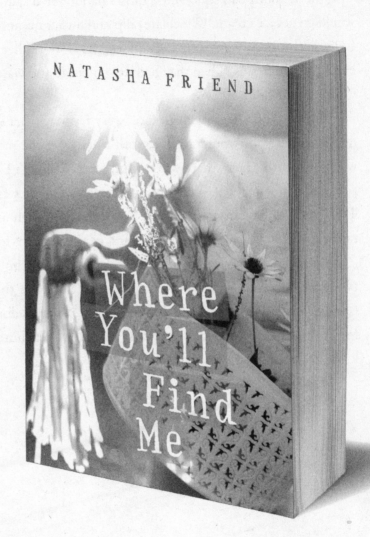

"The hair could grow back," he said, "or it could fall out completely. We'll just have to wait and see."

Quinn's mom had squeezed Quinn's hand. She'd said they would go get ice cream. Chocolate chip and butter pecan. Hot fudge. Whipped cream. Nuts, sprinkles, the works. They had eaten like goddesses. Then they had driven home and watched Quinn's hair fall out.

Paige and Tara had watched, too. Every few days that summer, another spot would appear, until finally, by the second week of eighth grade, there was nothing left. Paige and Tara pretended not to care. They knew it wasn't Quinn's fault. They knew she wasn't contagious. But still, Quinn felt a distance growing between them. She felt a gaping hole of loss.

Wasn't it weird to miss something you'd never thought twice about? And here was another weird but true thing: Quinn was glad her family had moved, even if they'd done it for Julius. Because no one in Gulls Head, Massachusetts, knew that Guinevere wasn't her real hair.